That Special Bond
By
Graham Avery

**Copyright © Graham Avery and Graham Penrose 2023
All Rights reserved**

The characters and events portrayed in this book are fictitious. Any similarities to any real persons, living or dead, is coincidental and not intended by the author.

No part of this book may be reproduced, or stored in a retrieval system, or transmitted in any form or by any means, electronic, mechanical, photocopying, recording, or otherwise, without express written permission of the publisher.

ISBN: 9798852050090

*To a dear Mum and Auntie
Twins born within minutes of each other
and died within a couple weeks of each other*

*Also to Jude, Becca and Ian. My wonderful family
and fiercest critics.*

PREFACE

From the road the house looked like any other. It could not have been built that long ago; perhaps the late eighteen-seventies. You could clearly see the slate roof and the gleaming white walls. The red brick chimney breast stood out a mile. The house, or I should say cottage, was protected from the road by wild garlic intermingled with wild grasses. A small laurel hedge was growing so that, one day, it would conceal a wood panelled fence which could have originally been the border before the hedgerow was planted for wildlife. Someone must have had a sense of humour because there was a line of approximately fifteen garden gnomes. Not the tall ones, but the smaller and medium sized ones in various poses.

This was the house that was visible. It was the façade that the owners wanted you to see. Even the interior was welcoming. the main room was being used as a reception room. The owners lived in accommodation on the grounds but away from this main property. No one knew, only the people who owned and managed the place, how the upstairs was arranged or what was kept up there.

But what you could not see from the road was the large building that was hidden in the woodland at the rear of the property. It was a one storey building that looked like something that would have held Prisoners of War. It even had a barbed wire fence surrounding it. A padlocked gate could only be opened by a key which was only carried by the owners and senior members of staff. It was a long rectangular building made of blocks with, mainly, only arrow slot windows. It had a corrugated iron roof. Only those who worked, or were staying there, knew it was there.

If she had known that giving birth was as painful as this, then she would never have gotten pregnant in the first place. The contraction pains were immense. God, she wished that she had not let him have sex with her. He knew that she was underage, but she thought that he loved her. It was obvious to her now that he had only told her that he loved her to get inside her knickers. Well! Look what happened after that. When she told him that she was pregnant, he looked shocked and needed to get some air. She had not seen him since. But boy, she would love to trade places with him now.

Another contraction began to erupt inside her. A soft moan started in the back of her throat which became louder and louder as the contraction became more powerful. It was a good job she was restrained, or she would have fallen off this bed by now.
    'Now, who is behaving like a big baby?' said a nun who had just entered the room.
'Have you ever tried to push an elephant out of

your vagina?' the young girl groaned before realising who she was talking to. 'Probably not,' she muttered under her breath. Her voice was difficult to understand. It sounded like she had a speech impediment or had severe learning difficulties.

'I've delivered hundreds of young lives, quite a few of them in this very room, but I have never had a screamer like you,' said the nun.

'It hurts,' said the girl.

'Well, you should have thought of the consequences before you committed such a vile sin,' said the nun.

'I didn't know this was going to happen,' the girl cried.

'Well, good catholic girls would never get into this situation,' said the nun harshly. 'Or make false accusations about how you got into this condition. Now let me see how far along you are.' The nun carried out her assessment of the young girl and was not surprised to see that she was close to given birth. 'I am just going to leave and get gowned up. You are close to making a childless couple incredibly happy.'

'Please don't leave me,' the youngster screamed as another contraction took hold of her body.

'Don't be such a baby,' said the nun sternly. 'I won't be long.'

'Please, Sister,' she begged but the midwife had already left the room.

She did not know how many rooms were in this

building, but she could hear the screams and groans of pain of the others who were, probably, around the same age as her and, obviously, in the same position.

Her mum and dad had booked her in here even before they had learnt that she was pregnant. They had been fuming when she told them she was in the family way, especially her father. At only fourteen, but nearly fifteen, how could she have been so irresponsible as to

ruin her life? It wasn't just her; she had informed them and got a slap across her face for her troubles. She hated her father then. Hated him with all her heart. But teenagers just do not see that most parents will do anything to protect their loved ones. She fought with all she had but she was still in this God forsaken place. And she knew that they were going to take her baby away from her. This life that had been growing inside of her for eight and a half months was going to be snatched away from her and there was nothing she could do about it.

Another contraction hit her suddenly. 'I wanna push,' the young girl bellowed. But no one was coming to aid her. 'I really wanna push now,' she screamed again.

'I tell you when you're ready to push, young lady,' said the nun sternly as she re-entered the room. She

was followed by a younger looking nun.
'Is that the head, Sister Ida?' the younger nun exclaimed.

'I told you she was close, Sister Abigail,' Sister Ida replied.
The two nuns helped the young girl into the correct birthing position. Sister Abigail soothed and wiped the young girl's brow. She coaxed her through the very traumatic experience. Sister Ida stayed down the business end and was barking her orders as to when to push and when not to. Only trouble being was that the young girl felt like she wanted to push all the time and was arguing with the nun, shouting and swearing. But the nun had heard it all before. All she wanted to do was deliver a healthy baby. After another five or ten minutes of this performance, although, to the girl it seemed like hours, she finally felt all the pain and agony slipping away as her baby gushed through her small opening. She could feel the midwife doing what had to be done and she finally heard her baby cry. She tried to sit up and see her child, but Sister Abigail was restraining her. Another midwife entered and took the baby from the older nun.
'I want to see my baby,' cried the young girl.
'Remember, this is not your baby,' Sister Ida replied. 'It is Mr and Mrs Culver's, as was agreed with your parents.'

'But it is my baby,' the young girl sobbed. 'I've just given birth to it.' The midwife carrying the baby made sure that Sister Ida was concentrating on her work before quickly showing the teenage girl a glimpse of the child. Its eyes were wide open looking at the young girl before the midwife covered the baby up and left the room.

'You have more pressing things first, my girl,' said Sister Ida. 'I've got to deliver the placenta. It should come away quickly.'

But it did not come away quickly, and the midwife noticed a small flow of blood coming from the vaginal passage. Although this was not unusual the nun was becoming a bit concerned.

'It's hurting again,' said the girl.

'What is?' soothed Sister Abigail.

'I feel like I want to push,' the girl murmured.

'Do not talk such nonsense, dear,' Sister Ida said condescendingly. 'You have already given birth. We just need to patch you up.'

And then it all went berserk. The young girl started screaming in pain and yelling that she wanted to push. Sister Ida noticed that the flow of blood was getting thicker and thicker. She shouted at Sister Abigail to go and get help. The nun did not need to be asked a second time and quickly left the room. Sister Ida waited for help to return and offered up a prayer for the young girl. She could tell that the teenager was in a lot of pain, but something was not right. The baby had been born healthy, there was no doubt about that. But the placenta was not giving an inch despite her gently coaxing it.

She noticed something that she had not expected to see at all. But her attention was drawn back to the face of the young patient as she had become quiet now. She had gone a deathly white and her breathing was becoming quite laboured. She had never lost a mother in childbirth before, and she was not going to lose one now. She had lost babies, but they were stillborn.

The door banged opened, and a young doctor and Sister Abigail came running in. One look and the doctor could see what was happening despite Sister Ida yelling at him that the girl was losing a lot of blood. But he could also see that the teenage girl was in difficulty. Perhaps, even, life threatening.

To Sister Abigail everything seemed to move in slow motion. She did not know whether to assist her midwife partner or help the doctor with the teenager.

The blood was now pouring from the patient. She went to soothe the young girl. She heard the girl murmuring. 'Promise me you'll look after the baby. Promise me...' Sister Abigail started stroking her face. It felt like an eternity. Sister Abigail looked at her colleague and then to the doctor. Both were frantic at their respective ends, but the doctor suddenly looked at her and shook his head. Then she noticed that the girl had stopped murmuring.

She suddenly sat bolt upright. Where was she? It was dark and she could not see much. She felt afraid. She felt very afraid. She thought she heard something. 'Is anyone there?'
'Yes,' a voice replied. 'I am here.'
'Are you one of the nuns?' the girl asked.
'I could be if you want me to be,' came the curious response.
'What do you mean by that?'
'Let us just say that I have to make sure you don't do anything stupid.'
'Is this real? Or am I dreaming?'

'Well, even if you are dreaming, why shouldn't it be real?'
'You are not making any sense,' said the girl confused. 'Did they take my baby?'
'Fortunately, your baby never made it with you,' said the voice.
'Where is my baby?' the girl demanded.
'Somewhere safe.'
The young girl jumped off the bed and started searching for her bag that held her clothes. 'I've got to go and find her. I want to go back. I want my baby.'

'I'm sorry honey,' said the voice. 'You might think you can check out any time you like but, unfortunately, you can never leave.'

Outside the house, Sister Ida and a young novice walked through the open door and down a couple of steps. Sister Ida was carrying a blanket. They looked sombre. The young nun certainly looked as though she had been crying. They reached the row of gnomes. They both looked around to make sure that no one was

watching, and the novice moved to hide what Sister Ida was doing. But the older nun bent down and placed something next to the last gnome. She stood up and said a prayer.
Sister Ida looked at the Noviciate. 'You stand before God and He does not want you to repeat anything that you witnessed just now. Do you understand?' The Noviciate nodded. 'Good. Because she will be well looked after now.' They both went back into the house.

CHAPTER ONE

The little girl was bored. Her car seat was also uncomfortable; it felt like one of the springs had broken. She knew that she was on her way home because her mum and dad had told her so. She just did not know how much longer she had to endure. Mind you, she had enjoyed the family holiday. It was the first one she could remember. She had loved making sandcastles and paddling in the sea. She found it fascinating eating egg sandwiches that her mother had taken from a wicker basket. She had particularly liked the ice cream that her father had brought for her, and she even had a chocolate flake in it.
It had felt strange to her sleeping in a different bed, but most days she was tired out because of all the things they had done during the day. She had never spent any amount of time away from her home and had been excited by this new experience. Her excitement made the journey up go very quickly, although she did sleep for much of it.
But on the way back she had so many memories of the last few days that sleep was not beckoning her.

She looked towards her mother and father in the front of the car. Her dad was driving. He was concentrating hard and very rarely spoke. She could hear her mum undoing a sweet and popping it into her mouth. She knew that her mother would not offer her one as they would "rot her teeth". So, what were they doing to her mother's teeth?
'That funny looking house will be coming up soon,' said her dad. 'You know, the one with all those gnomes lined up.'
This piqued the little girl's interest. She liked gnomes. But the look her mother gave her father was one of admonishment. She turned her head to look out of the window. She could just make out the house coming up in the distance. Unfortunately for her, she could only see the top half of it. Her attention was drawn to the main window. She could just make out a person; a very large person. No. Not a very large person but perhaps two figures who from this angle had merged into one. As they got closer, she could clearly define two separate outlines. There was a young girl in

front who looked to be in her mid to late teens. The light appeared to be obstructing the four-year old's view of the other, taller person. But she was sure that she saw this figure place a hand on the teenager's shoulder. She took a long hard look and concentrated on what she was seeing as if trying to commit this house to memory. But she felt like there was some sort of connection between her and this house. How? She had no idea. She could not remember ever being here before. She was, though, only four.

'That was her, wasn't it?' the teenager cried.

'You say that about every child you see,' said the guardian.

'But she saw me,' the girl persisted.

'Hush now,' said the other person.

'I have to go after her,' the girl persisted.

'And how are you going to do that?' the voice of reason asked. 'She was travelling in a car and, like you are kept being told, you can never leave here.'

'We'll see about that,' said the teenager and she stormed across the room, but try as she might, she could not open the door. 'You have no reason to keep me here.'

'Oh, but I do,' smiled the guardian. 'You see it is for your own protection. It is not safe for you out there. Until you realise, I need to stay close by.'

'Until I realise what?' said the girl. 'That my baby was taken from me? God, you people are not midwives or nuns. You are criminals.'

'You people?' the guardian scoffed. 'You think I work here? I can assure you, dear girl, that I am neither a midwife nor a nun.'

'Then who are you?' asked the teenager. 'My jailer?'
'I've already answered that,' came the reply. 'I can be whoever you want me to be.'
'That's not an answer,' sulked the girl. She stared out of the window at the now fast receding view of the car. 'Will I see her again?'
'I guess that depends on her,' said the guardian. 'She may want to come looking for you. Or, perhaps, she may not.
'Please come looking for me, my baby,' the young girl whispered. 'Please come and find me.

The little girl kept her gaze upon the house until it disappeared. For some strange reason she felt a tingling. It felt like this house had some kind of special force and was connected to her in some way.
'Did you see all the gnomes, Laura?' asked the little girl's mum. Laura shook her head. 'Oh, that is a shame.'
'What is that house?' little Laura asked.
'It's just a house, sweetheart,' said mum, but little Laura saw the nervous glance sideways that her mother gave her father.
'How much further do we have to go?' Laura asked.
'We will stop in half an hour so that you can have something to eat,' her father answered. 'How does that sound, Sweetpea?'
Laura appeared to think about this seriously. 'That

sounds very good, daddy.' She settled back into her seat even though she knew that she would never get comfortable. She watched the scenery fly by her window, and also caught the sight of her reflection, and her eyes got heavy. 'What is that place?'
'I have visions about that house, too,' a young girl's voice entered her thoughts.

Laura's eyes flew open. She looked frantically around the car but all she saw was her mother and father in their front seats. She concluded that she must have, briefly, fallen asleep and that voice must have been part of a dream. But the voice sounded very friendly, though. It also sounded like the other person knew her somehow, but Laura did not know how. She had no friends around her age.
'I have no friends either,' the voice responded. It was like someone was reading her mind. 'I know. Will you be my friend?'
She did not need much time to think about this. 'Okay,' she replied.
'Okay, what, love?' her mum asked turning her head to look at her daughter.
Laura shook her head and shrugged. Again, she watched as her mother glanced nervously towards her father. How on earth could she communicate back? Obviously not out loud. She tried to think of a way, but her eyes got heavier and heavier and soon she was asleep.

CHAPTER TWO

Laura hated school. She liked the English and the arts side; nature studies were okay, but she detested maths, science and physical education. At eight years old she still had no friends. Even that voice had stayed away since that day in the car nearly four years previously. She had thought about that voice many times over that time. It had reassured her. It had not, though, helped her with her schoolwork. She was stuck on a question involving division. Who cared what three hundred and seventy-eight divided by fifty-four was?
'It's seven,' a voice whispered to her.
She looked around but none of her classmates were near to her or, for that matter, even looking at her. The teacher, Mrs Miller, was helping Danielle, who Laura knew to be a year younger than her, on the opposite side of the classroom.
'Seven?' she questioned in her mind.
'Seven,' the other voice confirmed.

Laura wrote seven in her answer book. 'Who are you?' she asked out loud.

'Who is who, weirdo?' asked a boy who was sat on the next table.

'Nothing,' Laura muttered, and returned into her shell. She had just communicated with her new friend, but how had she done it. She remembered back to the car journey. When she had responded out loud there had not been a reply. And just a few minutes ago her "friend" had not spoken back when Laura had spoken. But she had when Laura just thought her response. And, so, she thought her question instead. 'Who are you?'

She waited a couple of seconds before that affable voice returned. 'My name is Cora. You've finally worked out how to talk then?'

'Not all of us are as clever as you,' Laura replied defensively.

'No offence,' Cora replied apologetically.

'So, what is one hundred and forty-seven divided by seven?' Laura asked.

'Twenty-one,' Cora replied instantly.

'You're good at maths,' said Laura scribbling the answer in her book.

'My maths is brilliant,' Cora replied boastfully. 'My English, on the other hand, is not very good. I don't know what a compound sentence is.'

'It's where two basic phrases are joined by a word, usually and but or for, and a comma or semi colon,' Laura answered. 'For example, the pirate lost the

map, but still managed to find the treasure.'
Laura waited for a reply. 'How on earth do you know that at eight years old? I'll keep to the maths thanks,' Cora finally replied which made Laura laugh.
'Wotcha laughing at, weirdo?' asked the boy who had spoken earlier.
'Nothing,' Laura spat. 'And mind your own business.'
'Laura! Billy!' an adult voice said from behind. They had not realised that the teacher was so close. 'Please get on with your work. If you need help, then please raise your hand.'
Yes, Mrs Miller,' they both sighed in unison.

Mrs Miller looked over Laura's shoulder to examine her work. She knew that the young girl was struggling with mathematics and with making friends. Initially, she had sat the young girl next to Amelia who appeared to make friends easily, but Laura was not having any of it. She would speak when she was asked something, but the young girl did not go out of her way to be sociable. She even ate her packed lunch by herself. And that was why Mrs Miller was surprised by this sudden outburst in class. She was more surprised to find that all her answers were correct. Although, she also noted that there was not much working out.
'That's very good work, Laura,' Mrs Miller said. 'How did you work out those answers?'

'My friend in my head helped me,' Laura smiled. Mrs Miller looked at Laura to judge if she was joking. She certainly appeared to be being truthful. 'You friend is very clever.'

'She's good at maths, but not very good at English,' Laura said getting on with her work. 'I mean, she doesn't even know what a compound sentence is.'

'And you do, Laura?' Mrs Miller asked surprised. Laura nodded. 'It's where two basic phrases are joined by a word, usually but and for or, and a comma or semi colon.'

Mrs Miller was taken aback. This young girl who did not participate in class discussions was clearly very bright. 'That's right. But can you tell me what an imperative sentence is?'

'It is a sentence that gives advice or instructions,' Laura easily replied.

'Very good, but can you give me an example?' Mrs Miller asked.

'Please be quiet,' Laura responded. 'Not you, Mrs Miller. I was just giving you an example.'

Mrs Miller laughed. 'I fully get that, Laura. When did you learn about English grammar?'

'I enjoy English, Mrs Miller,' Laura replied. 'Sorry because I know you prefer teaching mathematics. You should teach my friend, Cora. I'm sure that she'd like you as a teacher.'

'And where is Cora?' Mrs Miller asked.

Laura shrugged. 'She's just in my head,' Laura

replied.
'Oh, so like an imaginary friend?'

'No. Cora is real,' Laura simply replied.

After the lesson, Mrs Miller scooped up her paperwork and headed into the staff room. From the window she could see the children leaving with their mothers or guardians. She looked for little Laura and saw her seated beneath the protected large oak tree in the grounds. She saw that the young girl had her nose in a book.
'Penny for them.' A voice distracted her.
'What is your opinion of Laura Hadley, Mr Davidson?'
'You know that I like to use Christian names, Carly. Laura? I don't get her for a few years, Carly. You know that,' Geoff replied.
'But I know you've had dealings with her, Geoff,' Carly said remembering to use his name.
'She is a shy little girl who does not make friends easily,' answered Geoff. 'Why are you asking?'
'She is a bright young girl,' Carly Miller explained. 'She knows what a compound and imperative sentences mean, and she can give examples.'
'Impressive for an eight-year-old,' Geoff admitted.

'I know a lot of adults, and some teachers, too, who would not have a clue what you are talking about. But that's not what is troubling you, is it?'

'She claims that she has a friend who speaks to her, in her mind,' Carly responded.

'Many, many young children have imaginary friends, Carly,' Geoff smiled. 'I know I did.' Carly looked at him dubiously. 'What do you want to do about it?'

Carly sighed. 'No, you're probably right. I even suggested the same thing when I was with her in class. It was that she reacted so calmly by saying that the person was real.'

'She is only eight, Carly,' Geoff countered. 'Imaginary friends will seem real to them at that age. And, since you're asking my opinion, she does come across as being a young eight even though she's, what, third eldest in the class?'

'Second,' Carly confirmed. 'I do want to focus on her strengths, though.'

'That is what education is all about,' Geoff smiled. 'With your help, I'm bound to have the youngest university protégé ever when she comes into my year.'

Carly, playfully, punched him on the arm before turning her attention back to the young girl. She had expected her to look forlorn, but, instead, she seemed to be engrossed in her book. Most of the children had gone now, but the girl was still sat their waiting. She watched for another five minutes before she saw a woman approach Laura. The little girl dutifully put her book in her bag before standing up, pick up her bag, hold onto her mum's hand and leave the school. She then thought nothing more about the girl until the following week.

The class was working on a history project. It was about the heritage of the Royal Family. They were exploring the reign of Queen Victoria. They had cut out reports from newspapers and magazines. Some of the children had been allowed to bring in books that belonged to their parents, grandparents and even great-grandparents. Mrs Miller and some of the children were gluing some items onto a large piece of card. The children had really been enjoying themselves and, hopefully, they were learning something about the history of the monarchy.

'So, who came before Queen Victoria, Mrs Miller?' Billy asked.
'That's a very good question, Billy, and I wonder if anyone knows the answer,' Carly asked looking around her class. As she thought, no one put their hand up or, for that matter, shouted out. She was just about to reveal the answer when, out of the corner of her eye, she noticed that Laura had raised her hand. 'Yes, Laura.'
'William the fourth,' Laura virtually whispered.

'That's correct, Laura,' said Mrs Miller. 'And he reigned from?'

'Twenty sixth June eighteen thirty until the twentieth June eighteen thirty-seven,' Laura easily replied.

Carly Miller picked up her reference book on the British Monarchy and thumbed the pages until she found the part she was looking for. She was surprised to find the young girl was spot on. 'And before William?'

'George the Fourth,' Laura replied virtually straight away. 'And he was on the throne from the twenty ninth of January eighteen twenty until the twenty sixth June eighteen thirty. Prior to that was George the third who reigned for fifty-nine years and ninety-seven days. Before that was George the second who was King for thirty-three years and one hundred and twenty-six days. How far would you like me to go back, Mrs Miller?'

Mrs Miller was shocked for two reasons. One: because Laura appeared to be a very gifted child, and two: she had never heard Laura say so much. Carly flicked through her book and settled on a page. 'Who was monarch after Edward the fourth?'

'Most people think it was Queen Mary but, in fact, it was Lady Jane Grey. She was only the Sovereign for nine days; from tenth of July to the nineteenth of July fifteen fifty-three.'

'Wow! You're really clever,' said Billy who was clearly impressed.

Mrs Miller noticed a slight blush creep over the little girl's face. 'How have you learnt all this, Laura?'

'You know that I told you I love to read? Well, a lot of my reading is about history, and I particularly enjoy finding out about Kings and Queens,' Laura replied cautiously. 'Lady Jane Grey is one of my favourites. Don't you feel sorry for her, Mrs Miller? I mean she was only seventeen when she was executed, and she did not really have a say about becoming Queen.'

'Yes,' Mrs Miller agreed unsure. 'Unfortunately, though, much of it went on in those times.'

'Was it gory, Miss?' Billy asked excitedly and Carly saw the change in the girl's face and knew that the moment had been lost.

Later that day, after school had finished, Mrs Miller had somewhere to be. She was walking to the large oak tree and noticed Laura, once again, sat the other side. Carly could tell that the young girl had her book open and was just about to make a comment when the Laura spoke.

'I know I haven't spoken in a long time to you, but I've only just learnt how to comminute with you. I have to say the words out loud and think them at the same time.' There was quite a long pause before Laura continued. 'Well, now that I've learnt this way, we should be able to talk to each other every day.' Another Pause. 'And I will enjoy being your friend, too, Cora.'

'Is everything alright, Laura?' Mrs Miller had found herself becoming embarrassed at eavesdropping even though she knew that Laura could only be speaking with herself.
The little girl jumped in fright. 'Yes, Mrs Miller,' she finally said when she had composed herself.
'Your mum not here yet then?' Carly asked.
'Not yet, Mrs Miller. She shouldn't be too much longer.'
'I'll see you tomorrow, then,' Carly smiled. 'It's going to be a fun lesson tomorrow.'
Laura smiled back and nodded her head.

At home later, Mrs Hadley was preparing dinner for the family. Her husband was not home from work yet and her daughter, unusually, was in her bedroom and not in the front room with her nose in a book. She needed the young girl to lay the table. Mrs Hadley walked to the bottom of the stairs. 'Laura,' she shouted. Her daughter did not respond. 'Laura,' she called again but nothing. She cautiously crept up the stairs.

She went to knock on the door, but something made her hold back. She put her ear close to the wood so that she could listen more clearly. She could hear Laura talking to someone or something and she felt goosebumps on her arms as it appeared to get colder around her.

'Where do you live again?' Laura was saying. Whoever she was speaking to must have responded because she heard her daughter ask another question. 'Did you say Hogwell?... Oh! No H. That sounds a weird place to live' Another pause, a bit longer this time. 'Of course, we can be friends.' Pause. 'No. I haven't heard that other voice.' Silence. 'So, how can you talk to her, and I cannot?' A longer silence. 'Maybe you're right. Seeing as I've only just got used to speaking with you, I haven't been able to let her in yet.' Mrs Hadley leaned in a bit further. 'What do you mean she's told you there's someone listening at my door?' Mrs Hadley gasped and jumped back in shock as Laura's bedroom door flew open and the little girl was looking up at her as though questioning her. 'Would you please lay the table for dinner, dear?'

'Certainly, mother,' Laura smiled and skipped along the hallway before walking down the stairs. Mrs Hadley watched as her daughter, cheerfully, went downstairs. She was confused at what she had just witnessed. She, casually, pushed her daughter's bedroom door open and looked in. As she knew, there was no one else there. So, who on earth was her daughter just talking to?

CHAPTER THREE

Mrs Hadley had not spoken to her husband about the incident she had "overheard" a few days before. She put it down to it being one of things that many eight-year-olds go through. She was sure that she could remember reading somewhere about it being normal for young children to create an imaginary friend so had dismissed it from her mind.
It was at breakfast that she received the first part of bad news. Mr Hadley had just finished reading his

newspaper; he was a Telegraph man. It was Laura's job to collect the post and put it on the table next to her father. After folding his newspaper, he passed it to Laura who thoroughly enjoyed catching up on the latest news. She loved how the paper was laid out: the long pages which she knew by heart measured twenty-two and a half inches. But that did not bother her. She loved the smell of the paper; the bold headlines with its columns beneath. The relevant pictures accompanying the story and all of it told in black and white.

There had been five letters that morning. That was sort of average for a Friday. There were a couple of brown envelopes which Laura knew to be bills. Mrs Hadley had just tidied the dishes away and was now boiling the kettle for a drink. Three spoonsful of loose tea for each recipient of a cup and one for the pot. Three China cups and saucers had been placed on a wooden tray which had carry handles to the side. A matching milk jug was also placed on it.

Mr Hadley picked up a white envelope. It had the name of Laura's school embossed on the back of it.

'What have you been up to, Sweetpea?'

'Nothing, daddy,' Laura answered curiously.

'Why do you say that, George?' Mrs Hadley asked nervously.

'It's a letter from the school, Gail,' George said waving the envelope.

There was a clatter from behind him as Gail Hadley

had picked up the tray but became startled at her husband's words. 'T-the s-s-school,' she stammered. 'What do they want?'
'It's addressed to both of us,' her husband noted. 'Would you like to open it, dear?'
'You're the head of the household, George,' she said haughtily. 'It is your responsibility.'

Laura watched as her mother poured the boiling water into the teapot. She noticed that her mum was shaking considering and wondered to herself what had brought this on. Mrs Hadley placed the lid on the teapot and placed a tea-cosy over it to keep it warm. Gail picked up the tray, carried it to the table and put it down. She went back for the teapot. When she returned to the table, she put it on a brown, cork, round placemat.
Mr Hadley had opened the letter and was engrossed in its contents. Laura again watched Mrs Hadley as she poured the tea through a metal tea strainer into the first cup, knowing her mother would have already poured the milk in first. The shaking had become more pronounced, and Laura started to wonder if this had anything to do with her mother listening at her door the other day.
'The school want to meet with us,' Mr Hadley read. 'They want to discuss Laura.'
'What have you done, Laura?' Mrs Hadley snapped sounding worried and slammed the teapot back on the placemat.

'Nothing, mother,' Laura replied defensively.

'Do they think you're going crazy? Is that it?' her mother asked.
'Whoa! Whoa! Whoa! Gail,' said George holding up his hand. 'Why the hell would you say something like that?'
'Because I heard her talking to herself when she was up in her bedroom the other day,' Gail shouted back.
George handed the letter to his wife for her to read.
'They want to meet with us, dear, because they believe that Laura is well above average for her age, and want to discuss options with us,' he said. 'That does not sound to me like she's crazy, does it?'
Gail read the letter. Then reread it. And read it again for a third time just in case she had missed something important. 'No. It does not sound like she is crazy. They want us to arrange a time to meet with them at our convenience,' Gail said proudly. 'Did you know they were going to do this?'
Laura shook her head and looked wistfully at the teapot as if trying to command it to pour a drink for her itself.
'Have they been setting tests for you, Sweetpea?' George asked.

'Not really, daddy,' Laura replied thoughtfully. 'We did do a project about the Kings and Queens of Britain recently and Mrs Miller was a bit surprised that I was able to name them in order.'

George looked at his wife who looked as surprised as he was. 'Wow! Laura. That is clever. How did you learn that?' he asked.

'I set myself little projects,' Laura replied, but still eyeing the teapot. 'You know I like to read? Well, I read something the other day, in your newspaper, that our current King George the Sixth was not meant to become King. It was his brother initially, Edward the Eighth, but he abdicated so that he could marry his mistress, Wallis Simpson. Well, that just made me want to find out about the line of monarchs that had ruled Britain.'

Her mother and father were speechless for a while. Mrs Hadley picked up the teapot again and finished pouring the drinks. She passed one to her husband and the other one to Laura who mumbled thanks.

'Have they asked you anything else?' her father asked. 'Especially in sums or, perhaps, science?'

Laura chuckled. 'You know I'm useless at maths and science, daddy,' she smiled. 'But Mrs Miller and the Headmaster were asking me questions about adverbs, collective nouns, definite articles and quite a few other English grammar phrases.'

'And you could answer them?' Mrs Hadley asked.

'Of course,' Laura replied matter-of-factly. 'Between you and me, the questions were quite easy. I could have answered them two or three years ago.' Laura

reached for her tea and took a sip. It was still hot, so she blew on it, but it did not make it any cooler. George looked at his wife who was already staring at him with her mouth agape. 'I think that we should arrange to go to this meeting together,' he said. His wife nodded in agreement.
They took a drink of their cup of tea in unison.
'Oh, and by the way, mother. I was not talking to myself the other day,' Laura said casually. 'I was talking to my new best friend, Cora. She's very good at maths and even helps me sometimes. Although, I must help her with English in return. She's terrible at English'

In slow motion, Mr and Mrs Hadley stopped looking at each other and turned their attention to their little girl. 'You must never say that out loud to anyone, Laura,' said Gail. 'Do you understand me?'
Laura nodded and finished her tea. 'May I go and get ready for school, please?' she asked, a little bewildered as to why her mum was making such a fuss about her new friend. She gently pushed her chair away with her Popliteal Fossa. She was just about to run upstairs when her mother gently coughed. She came back and pushed her chair under the table. Her mother dismissed her with a nod. She had almost made it to the stairs when she heard her parents strike up a conversation.
'It could be an imaginary friend she has made up,' Mr Hadley suggested.

'I thought that myself, George,' Gail replied. 'I have read about children create their own friends when they find it difficult to make friends at school.'
'That must be it,' George agreed.
It went quiet and Laura thought that must have been it. She put her hand on the banister rail and was just about to lift her foot on to the bottom, carpeted, step when she heard her mother's voice again.

'You don't think that it has anything to do with when she born, do you?'
'She is our daughter, Gail, let us not forget that,' her father responded strongly.
'I know she is, and I love her dearly,' Gail said trying to pluck up the courage to say what she wanted to say next. 'But you know what happened that night...'
'She is our daughter, Gail,' her father repeated more strongly this time. 'That is all we need to know.'
"Perhaps we should not drive by that house anymore,' Gail said. 'On the way to our holiday home.'
'We all love our holiday home, Gail,' said her father. 'Now, let's just forget about it. If Laura wants an imaginary friend, then let her have one. What harm will it do her?'
Laura heard her father's chair scape across the floor. She bounded up the stairs and fled into her bedroom. She got her school clothes out of her wardrobe. It was a calf length navy dress with a white frilly pinafore over the top. As she took off her pyjamas, she started to think of the conversation between her

parents. What had happened the night she was born? and why didn't her mother want to drive past that house anymore? She assumed her mother had meant the one with the gnomes. What was so special about it. She made a mental note to ask Cora.

'Ask me what?' Cora's voice entered her head.

Laura yelped in surprise. She had forgotten that her new friend could hear her thoughts. 'My parents have just said something about the night I was born and that house with all the gnomes,' Laura replied in a whisper.

'Do you think you were born in that house?' asked Cora.

'I don't think so,' Laura said confidently. 'I mean we've driven by it so many times and they've never said that I was born there before. Have you worked out anything about the house?'

'No,' Cora replied admitting defeat. 'I know that house is important, but I cannot figure out why.'

'I'm sure that we'll figure it out,' said Laura. 'Perhaps we could meet there one day.'

'I don't even know where it is,' Cora said.

'When we are older, I'll tell you where it is,' Laura said happily. 'I may be even able to send you a picture of a map by then.'

'You're a good friend, Laura,' Cora responded

honestly.

'So are you, Cora,' Laura agreed earnestly. 'It's like there is something special between us.'

'You can feel it too, huh?' said Cora. 'But I don't know how. We've never met each other. I live in Devon, and you live...Where do you live, Laura?'

'Cornwall,' Laura replied.

'That's like a million miles away,' Cora sighed. 'But I just know we're going to meet up one day, and I cannot wait for that day.'

'Me either,' said Laura. 'I really must try to learn not to speak out loud when I'm talking to you. People are already starting to look at me as though I'm weird.'

'Get used to that, Laura,' Cora joked. 'I get people looking at me as though I'm weird all the time.'

'Are you nearly ready, Sweetpea?' her dad's voice came from the holiday.

'Yes, daddy,' she replied to her father. And then whispered to her best friend, 'got to go. Speak to you later, Cora.'

CHAPTER FOUR

Carly was getting excited. Although she had had talented children before, she had never had a pupil like Laura before. She was pleased that her parents had agreed to come and meet with her. Carly had been setting her a few tests to make sure that it had not been a fluke. She had written a sentence that had a few grammatical errors in it. Laura had spotted them all and even one that had been unintentional. The only one the young girl had struggled on was explaining long words Carly had set her, and to be fair the girl managed to get six of them correct which had surprised the headmaster. He had taken them home for his fourteen-year-old son to look at and he only got two right. However, when Carly had asked Laura to spell the words, she had got them all right.
Carly was also surprised to see that her maths had improved. She had tried to coax out of the girl the reasoning behind this, but the girl just went quiet. Perhaps her mother and father would have a better idea. She wondered if they even knew that they had a super-talented daughter. This was something to

take their minds away from what was happening in Europe.

Carly also understood that many school masters and mistresses frowned upon her style of teaching. Usually, the teachers were strict, but Carly liked to coax their intelligence out of them. Luckily for her Geoff, the headmaster, was not a disciplinarian. It was true that he had used the cane many times but only as a last resort. Miss Cummings certainly did not approve of her methods. She was of the opinion that children should be seen but not heard, unless they were spoken to. She would write a sentence on the blackboard, say it out loud and get the children to repeat it. She would also get them to recite the times tables by heart. She would also carry a stick with her and was not afraid to use it if she thought a child was misbehaving. She was, as Carly called her behind her back, Dickensian in her ways. But that was the morals she was raised on and they had worked for her. And although Miss Cummings did not approve of the way Mr Davidson applied his discipline, she tended to keep it to herself; except for the occasional tut when he said or did something she did not agree with.
But Carly considered herself fortunate to be in employment. It had been a testing few years for England. Ever since the end of the war it had slowly been sinking into depression. The school, which had

been built just over fifty years ago, needed renovations. Budget restrictions had meant that this would not be possible. The teaching staff had been cut from five to just the three of them which meant larger classes. And probably one of the reasons why Carly still had a job was because she had agreed to a pay cut.

But it was because of the children that Carly enjoyed teaching so much. Each child was different and had different abilities. That was one of the reasons that Laura had stood out from the crowd. Yes, she knew that the girl was shy; although she had never known anyone this shy before, but she was clearly intelligent. The girl deserved a chance. She just did not know how Laura's parents would react.

She was also not sure if she should broach the subject of the young girl talking to herself with her parents. It was happening very often now. She had listened to her one afternoon, when she knew Laura would be waited for her mother to collect her. It had not sounded like a discussion between a girl and an imaginary friend. It sounded, to her, to be like a conversation between two actual people. Carly had heard Laura ask what Ogwell was like. When she got home, she had taken out her atlas of the Southwest and looked for Ogwell. She discovered that it was in the district of Newton Abbot and was near Torquay and in between Exeter and Plymouth which she had heard of. Why would an eight-year-old girl randomly select a village called Ogwell for an imaginary friend to live?

Carly went over the options in her head again. First one was to do nothing and carry on as they were. The second one was to give Laura extra tuition which would build her knowledge. Next would be to send her to a boarding school. Finally, would be to get her assessed to see if there was a higher education she could attend.

She looked at the clock; quarter past four. Mr and Mrs Hadley would be here in fifteen minutes. Laura was sat on an old wooden chair outside the office. Carly had let her choose a book to read whilst she was waiting for her parents. She was surprised that the girl picked one about the war. She thought it wise just to go and check on her, so she went and opened the door.

'How are you finding the book?' Carly asked.

'it's very informative,' Laura replied. 'It's going to be different next time, Mrs Miller.'

'Next time?' Mrs Miller quizzed.

'It's not going to be the assassination of one man

and his wife that will start the next world war,' Laura replied. 'I think Germany is going to invade Poland even though everyone keeps on denying it.'

'You really think that will happen?' Mrs Miller asked.

'The evidence is in the reporting, Mrs Miller,' said Laura. 'You need to read between the lines sometimes but, if I was you, I would not make plans to go on holiday next year.'

'Right,' Carly said, although she was completely unsure of what to say. This girl was bright, extremely bright, but she certainly scared her sometimes. 'Your parents should be here soon. Would you like a drink or anything?'

'No, thank you, Mrs Miller,' Laura politely replied and went back to reading her book.

Carly felt very concerned at the remarks the girl had just made and looked at her worryingly. She closed the door and went and sat at her desk. She picked up the newspaper that was folded neatly on the desk and

opened it. The headline was about Neville Chamberlain, Adolf Hitler, Benito Mussolini and Édouard Daladier signing the Munich Agreement. Much of the article had proclaimed it as an appeasement that had stopped a war. Reading the article again she noted that much had been given to Germany and little to any other country and Czechoslovakia seemed to be being ripped apart.

She now understood what young Laura meant. You concede that much to one person, and they'll just want more.

She heard voices outside and knew that Mr and Mrs Hadley had arrived. She stood back up and went over to open the door.

'Mr and Mrs Hadley,' she greeted them pleasantly. 'It's lovely to meet you both. Please come in.' She noted that Mrs Hadley, in particular, appeared to be extremely nervous. 'Come and join us, Laura.' Two wooden chairs had been arranged in front of the desk and one to the side. This was the one that Carly guided the young girl to. 'Please sit down.' Carly gestured to the two remaining chairs for Mr and Mrs Hadley to sit upon.

'Thank you,' said Mr Hadley as he took off his hat and sat down. He crossed his right leg over his left and held his hat, so it was resting on his knee. Mrs Hadley sat on the edge of the chair and grasped her black handbag for dear life, as though it was about to be stolen.

'Thank you both for agreeing to meet with me, today,' Carly began. 'Can I begin by saying what an exceptional child Laura is. You must be very proud of her.'

'That is kind of you to say, Mrs Miller,' Mr Hadley replied. 'We are both very proud of our daughter.' Mrs Hadly just nodded and smiled briefly.

Undeterred, Carly ploughed on. 'I know my letter

probably made you nervous and you may have thought that Laura was in trouble of some kind?'
'Initially, we did think Laura had done something naughty,' Mr Hadley smiled. 'But then we read it again and saw that you wrote that you considered our daughter to be above average, Mrs Miller.'
'Well above average, Mr Hadley,' said Mrs Miller. 'She is very gifted in English. Laura, what is a palindrome?'

'It is something that reads the same forwards and backwards,' Laura responded completely uninterested.
'Did you know that at her age?' Carly asked Laura's parents.
'I don't think I even knew that now,' Mr Hadley joked which made them laugh except for his wife who still sat bolt upright and stony faced.
'You must forgive my manners, would either of you like a drink?' Carly asked.
Mr Hadley looked as though he was about to accept one, but Mrs Hadley got there first. 'We do not have much time, Mrs Miller. We have a routine that we like to adhere to so please continue about our daughter.'
'Of course,' Carly said taken aback. She cannot remember meeting anyone like Mrs Hadley before.
'As I was saying, Laura is a very gifted child. I would like to pursue her ability, with your permission. There are four options, but the first one is to do nothing and carry on as we are. The second

is that Laura receives extra tuition so she can expand upon her gift. Not only does she excel at English, but she is also well above average in History and Geography.'

'She was explaining to us about the Kings and Queens of England and Britain,' Mr Hadley explained. 'She can recall them in order which to me seems strange for an eight-year-old to do.'
'I memorised them all when I was six, daddy,' giggled Laura.
All three adults gazed her way. Mrs Miller cleared her throat and continued. 'Option three would be to send her to a specialised boarding school so that she could get expert tuition. Lastly, I think Laura would benefit from being assessed to see if she could be accepted into the highest education establishment that this country has.'
'You think she's that clever?' Mr Hadley asked.
'I do, Mr Hadley,' Carly replied honestly. 'I really do.'
'Will that not be expensive, Mrs Miller?' Mrs Hadley asked.
'The last two possibly will be,' Mrs Miller conceded. 'But I see that you are surgeon, Mr Hadley and you were formerly a...'
'...A housewife, Mrs Miller,' Mrs Hadley interrupted. 'Just a housewife.'

'And I am sure that we all would like what's best for Laura,' Carly smiled.

Mrs Hadley returned it with a false smile of her own. 'What good will become of it?' Mr Hadley asked.

'With the right guidance and education,' Carly answered, 'Laura could rise to the top of any profession she desired.'

'In case you have not noticed, Mrs Miller,' Mrs Hadley scoffed, 'but Laura is a female and is destined to become a housewife and mother.'

'It is not impossible for her to go onto better things if she wanted to, Mrs Hadley,' Carly persisted. 'You are probably aware that in Plymouth, Nancy Astor is the sitting Member of Parliament as was the first female to sit in the House of Commons.'

'But she was not the first woman elected as MP,' Laura whispered.

'I'm sorry, Laura?' said Mrs Miller.

'Constance Markievicz was the first female elected,' Laura explained. 'It was twenty years ago, in nineteen eighteen, but she did not take her seat because she was a member of Sinn Fein.'

'You see what I mean about her being intelligent?' Carly said. 'And that should not be wasted.'

'I'm guessing that to get into boarding school or

this assessment would require her to have all round knowledge? Including Mathematics and Science?' Mr Hadley asked.

'Normally it would,' Mrs Miller conceded. 'You're probably going to say that her maths is not strong.'

'It's not,' said Mrs Hadley.

'I would probably agree with you,' Carly admitted. 'However, it does appear to be getting better.'

'And what do you mean by that?' asked Mrs Hadley.

'I'm sure she is working hard to improve her maths by herself,' said Carly. She had become unsure of Mrs Hadley's tone and even noticed her husband looking at his wife with that "here we go again". She tried to lighten the conversation. 'She tells me that an imaginary friend is helping her.'

The faked smile was replaced by a stony glare. 'Would you go and wait in the hallway, please, Laura?'

'Yes, mother,' Laura said getting off the chair and left the room. Carly noted that Laura had said "mother" and not 'mummy" even though she had heard the young girl call her father "daddy".

Laura sat back on the chair she had used before her parents had arrived and opened the book about the war, she had been reading. She could just about hear her mother ask the question she knew was going to come when she had been sent out of the room.

'Do you think my daughter is mad? Is that what this is all about?' Mrs Hadley asked scathingly.
'Gail,' her father warned.
'I do not think anything of the sort, Mrs Hadley,' said Carly, keeping her voice completely level. 'As you are aware, I believe your daughter to be completely gifted.'
'Well, thank you for that, Mrs Miller,' said Mars Hadley hotly. 'I think that we may have troubled you enough.'
Laura heard the sound of the chairs being scrapped on the floor and the footsteps as her parents crossed the room. She listened as her teacher tried to get them to get back. The door flew open.
'Come on, Laura. We're going,' she said as she stormed by her.
Her dad came out next and he turned to look apologetically at Mrs Miller as she followed them out, still trying to get them to change their minds. Her father reached out to take her hand after she had stood up. She held out the book to Mrs Miller.
'Thank you for letting me start this wonderful book, Mrs Miller,' she said.
'Why don't you take it home and finish it, Laura?' Carly replied. The girl smiled her thanks. 'Oh, and Laura? I'm so sorry I've ruined everything. I wanted everything to turn out well.'
'I know you did, Mrs Miller,' said Laura and then whispered to her teacher. 'You may have to leave

the next bit to me.' Laura smiled as she turned and walked with her father.

The argument between her mother and father reverberated around the house for most of the evening. Her father accused her mother of being conceited and just thinking of herself. Her mother retorted that her father was soft and did not have the family's interest at heart. It was like a tennis match going backwards and forwards.
Dinner was eaten in frosty silence. Laura helped her mother with the dishes but did not say a word. She knew better than to try and have a conversation with her mum whilst she was in this kind of mood.
The row escalated later but Laura went upstairs to her room and closed the door. She tried to contact Cora, but, initially, was unsuccessful. She tried again.
'What's wrong?' Cora asked concerned.
'My parents are having a blazing row,' Laura replied.
'What about?' said Cora.
'Me. I think,' said Laura. 'They were called into school by my teacher, Mrs Miller. She thinks I'm a gifted child and wants the best for me. She believes that with the right education I could go far.'

'And your mum and dad don't want this for you?' Cora asked incredulously.
'It was when Mrs Miller mentioned my imaginary friend that it started to go downhill,' Laura explained.
'I'm guessing it would have done,' Cora agreed sympathetically.
'I believe they both want what's best for me, but they just cannot get it into their heads about me speaking with you.'
'What do you want?' Cora asked.
'What do you mean?' Laura asked back.
'From your education, what do you want to get out of it?' Cora asked again. Laura gave it some thought. She took a little while thinking about all the options. 'Are you still there?'
'I'm thinking,' Laura responded. 'I would like to see how far I can go. Mrs Miller believes I have the ability and I would like to repay her faith in me.'
'Then, somehow, you have to convince your mum and dad,' Cora replied matter-of-factly.

'That's easier said than done,' Laura laughed.
'I didn't say it was going to be easy,' Cora laughed along. 'If it makes you feel any better, I do not

believe that my mum and dad are my real parents.'
'Really?' Laura asked in shock.
'Really,' Cora confirmed. 'I'm eight years old and I should be resembling at least one of them, if not both. But I don't look like either of them.'
'Hmmm,' Laura said thoughtfully. 'Now that you mention it, I don't think I look like mine either.'
Laura heard the door slam and knew that her father had stormed out. It wouldn't be too long before she came upstairs carrying a glass of sherry. Although they hardly ever argued, when they did, this is what she always found solace in.
'Are you still there, Laura?' Cora's voice interrupted her thoughts.
'I'm still here, Cora,' Laura replied at once. 'I'm going to need your help, Cora. I can tell you now that my mother will write to the school probably requesting that I change class.'

'Okay,' Cora responded excitedly. 'Are you afraid of pain?'
'WHAT?' Laura replied startled.
'Are you afraid of pain?' said Cora. 'Because I'm coming up with an idea, but it will mean you being hit with the stick.'
'Perhaps it was not a good idea to ask you for help,' said Laura sounding very unsure.
'Do you want my help or not?' Cora was very confident, and Laura decided that she would go

along with it.

CHAPTER FIVE

Mr Miller knew something was wrong as soon as he arrived home from work that evening. Saucepans and dishes were being slammed down in the kitchen. He stood in the hallway and took off his coat, hanging it on the free hook. Next, he took off his boots and placed them tidily in the corner. He replaced them with his slippers. He took his old cardigan from off the peg and put it on. He picked up his pipe and tobacco from the table before plucking up the courage to enter the kitchen. He tucked his baccy in his pocket and went in.
'Hello, Love,' he said and went over and kissed her on the cheek. He was fifteen years older than his wife and was the local bobby on the beat. He tended to change into his uniform at the station and only wore it home when it needed a wash and press. His beard was neatly trimmed, and his hair was Bryl

creamed flat.
'Hello, darling,' said Carly. 'How was your day?'
'Obviously better than yours,' he said. 'Would you like a drink?'

'The kettle is on,' Carly said pointing towards the gas stove.
'Coffee? Or tea?' Mr Miller asked.
'Yes, please,' Carly replied, obviously not listening.
'Okay. I'll make you both in one cup, then,' said her husband.
'What?' Carly asked confused. 'Oh! Tea please, darling.'
'What went wrong with your day?' Mr Miller asked.
'You know that I've told you about that gifted young girl in my class, Sam?' Carly replied.
'Little Laura? I seem to remember you saying quite a few things about her,' Sam responded. 'She does seem a very intellectual pupil.'
'She's more than intelligent,' gushed Carly. 'I've had intelligent students before, but I've never known anyone like her before.'
'So? What went wrong?' Sam asked.

'I had her parents in today,' Carly explained. 'I was

hoping to convince them to get Laura into a specialised education establishment.'

The kettle started whistling its tune to say that it was ready. Sam grabbed a tea-towel to lift it from the hob. He switched off the gas ring first. He poured the boiling water into the two cups that his wife had placed near the hob before he had arrived home. He placed the kettle back on the ring. He put the tea-towel on the kitchen unit and went over to the icebox which housed the milk. He poured it into the two cups of coffee before returning it to the box. He picked up the jar of sugar enroute to the drinks as well as grabbing a teaspoon from the kitchen unit drawer. He put three heaped teaspoons into one of the coffees and stirred it vigorously.

'And they didn't want to have anything to do with it?' he finally asked.

'I didn't really get the chance to find out,' Carly replied. 'I made some remark about Laura being helped in her sums by an imaginary friend, and Mrs Hadley completely took it the wrong way.'

'How?' Mr Miller asked feigning interest.

'She accused me of saying that her daughter is mad,' Carly fumed, waving a knife she was holding, to cut a pie, in the air 'I never said anything of the sort. I don't think she's mad. I do think she is a genius. I therefore must question whether the mother thinks her daughter is insane. And another

thing, she calls her father "daddy" and her mum she calls "mother". What does that imply to you?'
'That she has a better relationship with her father?' Sam replied. 'And can you put that knife down before you take my head off with it?'
'Sorry,' Carly apologised. 'But you are correct, she obviously has a better relationship with her father, even though she spends more time with Mrs Hadley.'
'Do you think she is crazy?' Sam asked.
Carly briefly hesitated. 'Uh - no,' Carly replied.
'You hesitated, Carly,' Sam said. 'You sound like you don't quite believe yourself.'
'I don't think she's crazy, Sam. I have heard her talking to herself but, like I said, she told me she had an imaginary friend.'

'That's not usually a good sign, is it?' Sam asked.
'Many children have imaginary friends,' Carly said. 'Especially ones who find it difficult to make ordinary friends.'
'So, what are you going to do?' Sam said bringing the two cups over to the table and putting one close to his wife while continuing to hold the other one.
'I'll have to invite them back in,' Carly said. She had been thinking about this since the end of the meeting. 'I'll have to apologise to them. But hopefully, we both want the same thing. And that's the best thing for Laura.'

'Maybe a few days breathing space will do both sides a lot of good, and it will all calm down,' suggested Sam.

But a few days later, it was clear that one party had not calmed down. Mr Davidson, the headmaster of the school, was waiting for Carly. She could tell by the

look on his face that he had some news for her, and it did not look good. She approached him slowly. Some of the children ran past her but the look the headmaster gave them made them stop and walk instead.
'Before you start, Mrs Miller, I would like to see you in my office,' said Mr Davidson.
Not a good sign. Now was not the time to call him Geoff either. 'Yes, Mr Davidson,' she responded. He turned and headed that way, and she had no choice than to follow on behind. He let her enter the room before closing the door. She waited for Geoff to sit at his desk before she did.
He picked up a piece of paper which was obviously a letter as the opened envelope was still on the desk. She noted the precision and neatness of the writing.
'I have received a letter, Mrs Miller,' Geoff confirmed. He did not use her Christian name; yep, definitely not a good sign. 'It is from Mr & Mrs Hadley.'
'Laura's mother and father,' Carly said for no

reason at all.

''They have made a decision regarding Laura's education,' he read. 'For the rest of this year they would like you to carry out one-to-one further education lessons for two hours a week if that is convenient for you.'

Well, that was certainly unexpected. 'Of course, it is,' she smiled.

'On one condition,' Geoff continued. Uh-oh, here it comes. 'Laura must be transferred to Miss Cummings class.'

'What? But she's doing so well in my class,' Carly almost shouted. 'She will not progress in Miss Cummings class.'

'We never speak ill of another teacher, Mrs Miller. NEVER,' he bellowed making Carly jump.

'Sorry, Mr Davidson,' Carly said.

'Just because her methods are not your methods, does not make her style of teaching wrong,' Geoff said, and Carly could tell that he was still fuming. 'Miss Cummings has taught many hundreds of children and has the respect of this community. People she taught still come back and thank her. Not once have I had a letter from a parent of a child in her class to be transferred to another. Do you understand?'

'Yes, Mr Davidson,' Carly said feeling admonished. 'You are quite correct. I am not in any position to question Miss Cummings teaching. I just feel ashamed that Mr & Mrs Hadley feel the need to transfer Laura from my class.'

'I know the meeting did not go as you wished, Carly,' said Geoff. Good, he was calming down because he called her by her first name. 'But this letter proves that the parents want what is best for Laura.' He waved the letter towards her. 'They want you to have one-to-one tuition with her. They are going on holiday and will look at the other two options after the summer holidays. They have asked that you research specialists that you were talking to them about. So, that's good. Your letter of apology must have appeased them a little.'

She had to concede that he did have a point. At least she would still get to see Laura. She had noticed that the girl had gone a little into her shell but was still showing signs of her genius. Hopefully Miss Cummings would notice it too.

When Gail Hadley told Laura the news that she was surprised with how well her daughter took the news.

'If you think that it is for the best, mother, then who

am I to argue,' she had said.
Gail watched as the young girl skipped away to get ready for school. Although she knew that Mrs Miller had never actually said that her daughter was insane, in fact, as she now recalled, Mrs Miller only referred to an imaginary friend, she wondered if the teacher did think there was something wrong with her. Mrs Hadley certainly did.
She had been listening at Laura's door the other day and heard the young girl describing that house; the one with the gnomes. Her so-called friend had, apparently, just seen it. Gail knew, no, hoped that it was because of the memory of driving by it every year.
Why did her daughter think that house was so special? There was no way Laura could figure out her link to the place. She was worried, that was for sure. Her husband had eased her concerns. He assured her that when they go to the holiday cottage in a few weeks, their daughter will not think anything about it.

He promised that he would not draw her attention to it like he usually did.
She was fortunate that he supported her decision for Laura to change classes even if he did not agree with it. His only proviso was that Laura was to have one-to-one tuition with Mrs Miller. He made her realise that the teacher only wanted to make sure that their daughter got the best education for her

exceptional talent.

Perhaps they should not have done it. Perhaps they should sell their holiday home so that they do not pass that house so that Laura did not become obsessed with it. Yes. That was the answer. She decided that she would broach the subject with George later. Maybe they should get a pet for Laura. That would take her mind off it and, maybe, make her leave her imaginary friend behind.

She certainly hoped that she had done the best for her daughter. Correction, she thought she had done what was best to stop Mrs Miller from delving into Laura's mental state. She was sure that Laura would do well in Miss Cummings class.

But Laura was not settling into Miss Cummings class. She was too clever by half. She sighed when the subject was aimed at the younger members of the class. She finished the work set at the older members long before they ever did. She watched as the teacher wrote a sentence on the blackboard, "In the beginning there was light".

'What are you waiting for? Write it down in your books,' Miss Cummings ordered. 'I want you to write a short story using that sentence as the opening line.' She noticed Laura had put her hand up. 'Yes, Laura?'

'Do you want us to put the comma in it, Miss Cummings?' Laura asked.
'Don't be a silly girl,' said Miss Cummings. 'There is no need for a comma in that sentence.'
'Surely it should come before the main clause, Mrs Cummings?' Laura pointed out. The other children were looking at the young girl in awe.
'You think you know better than your teacher, Miss Hadley?' said Miss Cummings.
'No, Miss Cummings,' Laura said honestly. 'I just thought that you had made a mistake by leaving out the comma.'
'There is no comma, Miss Hadley,' said the teacher.
'But there should be,' Laura replied not backing down.
'Laura Hadley come out here, please,' Miss Cummings shouted. Laura stood up and walked towards the teacher. She gasped as Miss Cummings picked up the stick that was on her desk. 'Hold out your hand.' Laura tentatively put her hand out. She grimaced as the stick began to descend.
The stick hit skin with a loud whack. 'Ouch!' said Laura.
'Ouch,' said Cora.
'What are you saying ouch for? It's not you that's just been hit,' growled Laura.
'It felt like I did,' said Cora.
'What did you say?' Miss Cummings demanded looking very angry.

'Nothing, Miss Cummings,' said Laura.

'Go back to your seat and write one hundred times "I will not contradict Miss Cummings again,"' said the teacher.
'Yes, Miss Cummings,' replied Laura.
'Say "unless you've made a mistake" back to her,' Cora said in Laura's head
'Unless you made a mistake,' Laura said out loud.
'LAURA HADLEY COME BACK HERE,' Miss Cummings shouted.
'Are you enjoying this, Cora?' Laura whispered.
'It was all part of our plan,' Cora shot back.
'You're not the one being hit,' Laura retorted.
'WHO ARE YOU TALKING TO?' Miss Cummings demanded.
'Myself,' Laura responded quietly.
'Hold out your hand,' ordered Miss Cummings
Laura did as she was told. Whack! Whack! Went the stick against the palm of her hand. Laura tried to

pull it away after the first smack, but Miss Cummings forced it closer.
'Stop it,' Cora cried.
'STOP IT,' Laura yelled. 'You're making Cora cry.'

After school, it was Laura's first one-to-one tuition with Mrs Miller. The young girl had been looking forward to it, but after what had happened in Miss Cummings class she had crawled back into her shell. She walked into the classroom and noticed that the teacher had already laid out books and paper on her desk.

Carly watched Laura approach. She could see that something had made the young girl withdraw. She got up and walked over to the eight-year-old. She reached out and took Laura's hand. She felt the girl wince and yelp. She examined the Laura's hand and notice the red welts that were forming. She bent down to the young girl's level. 'What happened, Laura?'

'Miss Cummings made an error, so I corrected her,' Laura sniffed.

'In what way?' Carly coaxed the girl.

'She made us write the sentence "In the beginning, there was light," but she didn't put the comma in before the...' Laura replied.

'...Main clause,' Carly completed the sentence.

'Correct, Mrs Miller,' Laura said.

'Let us go to my desk, Laura and see what I've prepared for you,' Carly said kindly. They reached the desk. Laura saw a sheet of paper with twenty sentences written on it. 'As you can read, there are some sentences written here but I have clumsily forgotten to put in any punctuation and was hoping that you could help me out.'

'Okay, Mrs Miller,' Laura had cheered up a bit.

'While you do that, I just need to get something from the headmaster's office,' Carly explained.

'Okay, Mrs Miller,' Laura said as she sat down at the desk and picked up a pencil and beginning her project.

Carly casually left the classroom before storming up the corridor and barging into the headmaster's room without knocking.

'We've got a problem,' she ranted before acknowledging Miss Cummings's presence.

'We sure do, Mrs Miller,' Mr Davidson responded equally as robustly.

'What's she doing here?' Carly said pointing at the other teacher. 'Do you know what she's done? She has hit Laura so hard across the hand that there are welts appearing.'

'Perhaps if you did not mollycoddle these children and discipline them once in while then my strictness may not be needed,' Miss Cummings remarked.

'Your Dickensian methods you mean,' Carly was clearly not backing down. 'Even when a child is right, you embarrass them in front of the whole class by hitting them with a stick.'

'By showing them the difference between right and wrong, Mrs Miller,' Miss Cummings smiled. 'I am quite sure that Laura Hadley will not answer back in my class now.'

'I am quite sure that Laura Hadley will never speak in your class again, Miss Cummings,' Carly retorted vehemently.
'THAT'S ENOUGH,' Mr Davidson bellowed.
'From both of you. As I have said, both of you have your own methods and neither of you should judge if the other is incorrect. I will not have two teachers fighting in my school. Is that understood?'
'Yes, Mr Davidson,' Miss Cummings answered affronted. Carly merely nodded.
'Miss Cummings has raised another concern about Laura Hadley,' Geoff said. He sounded like he did not really want to broach the subject, but as Miss Cummings was in the room, he could not really avoid it. 'She is concerned about Laura's mental health as she has heard her talk about someone called Cora who seems to be a fictitious person in Laura's mind. Now, I know that we have had a conversation about this, and you raised those same concerns.'
'You knew about this and did not bother to inform me?' Miss Cummings enquired accusingly.
'We thought that she could have made herself an imaginary friend,' Carly admitted.

'This goes much deeper than an imaginary friend, Mrs Miller,' said Miss Cummings. 'She was shouting at me to stop because I was making someone called Cora cry in pain.'

'Perhaps you should have stopped,' Carly said instantly regretting it.

'And perhaps you should have reported this to the correct authorities like you are supposed to when you have suspicions,' Miss Cummings replied haughtily.

Carly looked aghast from Miss Cummings to Mr Davidson and back to Miss Cummings. 'You cannot be serious,' she said.

'We have a duty, Mrs Miller,' Geoff began, 'not only to protect ourselves, but also that of the child.'

'This will break that child and her family,' Mrs Miller replied.

'As she is no longer in your class, Mrs Miller, that is our concern not yours,' said Mr Davidson.

Carly knew that meant she was being dismissed. She turned to leave and, as she reached the door she turned around. 'She was right, by the way,' she said.

'There should have been a comma in the sentence you got them to write. "In the beginning, there was light" it comes before the main clause. Any good teacher would know that.' She slammed the door as she left.

CHAPTER SIX

Carly had been half right. It had broken Mr and Mrs Hadley when they were informed that Laura was to be referred to a specialist medical institution. It had hit Mrs Hadley particularly hard. She had shouted and screamed. She almost struck Miss Cummings when the teacher had remarked that it was no wonder why her daughter turned out like she did.

Laura, on the other hand, took the news in her stride. It was her father who had broken the news to her. He had managed to arrange a deal where Laura would be supervised at a hospital near to their holiday home. It had helped with him being in

the profession and was able to pull a couple of strings. To Laura it sounded like she was going away on holiday and was going to be out of Miss Cummings class for a little while. For that she would have agreed to anything.
It had also been agreed to transfer her back into Mrs Miller's class. This was mainly because Miss Cummings refused to have the "disruptive" child in her class. Carly was delighted about this. The girl seemed to flourish under her guidance once more, and Carly

treasured these days because she did not know how long it would be before she saw Laura again.
Before too long the agreed date had arrived. Laura was quite excited as she knew they would be driving by that house again. Both she and Cora had worked out that her parents were avoiding discussing the house with her now. She had asked them about the gnomes, but they changed the subject.
Laura could sense that they were avoiding it. Usually, her father mentioned it, telling her to keep an eye out. They had obviously made some kind of pact because they were trying to keep her mind occupied by playing games, which they had never done before, and asking her about things she would like to do on "holiday". Again, they never did this as she had to usually go along with whatever they wanted to do.
Laura kept an eye out for the house. She knew that

they must be getting closer as the conversation became more incessant. And then, suddenly, it came into view. She looked up at the top window and kept her gaze on that.

She looked out of the window and saw the car. She could feel something; a presence of some sort. She wasn't sure but knew that the vehicle was special.

'Is that you in the car?' she asked. She knew that she would not have to wait long for the reply.

'No,' the voice came back to her.

'Do you know who it is? Only I can feel something special about it,' said the girl.

'I don't know what car you are talking about it,' said the other voice. 'You never send me a picture of what you are seeing – Hang on a moment, someone else is trying to send me something.'

'What is it? Who is it?' the girl asked eagerly.

'Wait a moment,' the other voice snapped.

'You never were very good with patience, were you?' said the guardian.

'She is in the car,' said the other voice. 'She's sending me a picture of the house.'

'Who do you mean by "she"? Why can't I talk to her?' the young female asked.

'How do I know?' the other voice snapped. 'Can't that other person with you answer that question?'

'How does she know about me?' said the guardian. 'To her I should not exist.'

The car was drawing nearer and nearer. The young woman looked out the window and watched. She could not really see into the back of the car. But she saw the female in the front of the car look up and then recoil in horror as she noticed her. The young woman could not believe who she was looking at. She knew this person but from where? She searched in her memory but was nothing was coming forward. Perhaps the woman was why she felt the special connection with the car.

'She cannot hear you,' said the other voice. 'Why can't she hear you like I can?'

'I don't know,' the girl replied, and the tears began rolling down her cheeks. 'I don't know. Perhaps she does not want to.'

It went quiet for a long time. She watched as the car passed the house and there was nothing more she could do. She thought the other voice had left her.

'She wants to,' the other voice said suddenly. 'She really wants to but just doesn't know how.'

The young woman looked really sad. The car had driven past. She did not know if there was a child inside it, but that woman – on, where had she seen that woman before?

'I think you need to rest,' said the guardian.

'Will I ever get out of here?' the young woman sobbed.
'One day,' the guardian promised. But she had more pressing things on her mind now. She had to find where this voice was and put a stop to it. She could not have anything or anyone getting in the way.

Laura saw her mother flinch at something and knew it had something to do with the house. What? She did not have a clue. Did her mother and she share something with this house. Had they been here before? Laura could only remember them driving by it, but, perhaps, when she was younger, they stopped off here.
'Did you see the gnomes?' Laura asked excitedly. 'I could see them clearly this time. I'm sure that there were a few more.'

'What would you like to eat tonight, Sweetpea,' Mr Hadley asked. It was unusual for her father to change the subject. 'I was thinking fish and chips. What do you say to that?'
'Yes, please, daddy,' she smiled.

And that's what they had when they got to the holiday home. She savoured every bite. They tasted slighted different than the ones they have at their own village. To be honest, she preferred her home ones, but these were fine. She was interested in the newspaper article that the food came wrapped in. It certainly appeared that war was becoming inevitable. It was about the German Foreign Minister giving an ultimatum to Lithuania regarding the Klaipeda region. Some of it she could not read because of the grease smears. It was not looking good at all.

When she went to bed that night, she waited for her mother and father to kiss her goodnight. She usually read a book but this evening she feigned tiredness; claiming that the journey had made her sleepy.

She gave it a good quarter of an hour until she felt it was safe. 'Are you there, Cora?'
'I'm here,' came the response. 'I saw you near that house.'
'I'm sure I could see someone, an older girl, in the top floor room,' Laura whispered. 'I wonder if she is the same one who talks to you.'
'No idea,' replied Cora. 'I guess there's no way of finding out.'
'You could always ask her,' Laura pointed out.
'Oh, yes. Silly me,' Cora giggled. 'But no more about that, let's talk about you. Do you know what's going to happen tomorrow?'
'Not really,' Laura admitted. 'I'm guessing that the doctor will talk to me and get me to do some tests.'

'Okay,' said Cora. 'Do you fancy playing a game with everyone?'
'What do you mean?' Laura asked.
'I'm currently on a train with my mother. I've no idea where we're going, so I have had a long time to think this through,' Cora laughed. 'Here's what we're going to do,'

The hospital was a lot bigger than the one Mr Hadley worked at in Cornwall. There were so many windows. She held onto her daddy's hand as they walked along the corridor. Directions had been given to them by a lovely woman at reception.
As they walked, she saw a couple of nurses looking fantastic in their starched uniforms. Laura thought they looked lovely. If she could not become a teacher when she left school, then she definitely wanted to become a nurse. She then remembered that she was not too keen on blood or people being sick. Maybe a job in the health profession would not be such a good idea.
Mr Hadley had informed Laura that they would be meeting a Dr Turner. He wanted to talk to Laura. Laura had asked her father what about and he replied that it would probably be about a number of things. She tried to get him to be more specific, but he changed the subject. Her parents were doing that a lot lately.

They arrived where they were meant to be. At least Laura assumed that was the case as the name on the door read Dr Turner. Mr Hadley knocked on the door and it was soon opened by an elderly gentleman. He had sparse white hair that he grew long on one side of his head and combed it over is bald patch. His suit was loose fitting as though it was two sizes too big for him.
'Good morning, Mr Hadley,' greeted Dr Turner pumping the other man's hand in a warm shake. 'And how is the eminent surgeon from Cornwall?'
'Fine, Dr Turner,' Mr Hadley smiled. 'And how is the world treating the world's greatest psychiatrist?'
'Cannot complain. Cannot complain,' the older man smiled. 'And you must be Laura?'
'Yes, I am, Dr Turner,' said Laura. She held out her hand and the doctor happily shook it.
'Please come inside,' Dr Turner said as he stood aside to let them pass.
Laura was a little disappointed with the interior. It was very similar to her father's office. Even the décor

was similar. Perhaps all offices were painted this way. There was a wooden desk over by the window which had a large leather chair which was obviously where the doctor sat. There was a wooden chair this side of the desk and three others along the far wall. Doctor Turner led Laura to the chair next to the desk and he went and sat in the leather one opposite. Her father went and sat on one of the three chairs.

Laura sat through the preliminary questions which just seemed to confirm her details. Her father was needed for most of these. When that was completed, Doctor Turner closed the file and looked at the young girl.

'You and I are going to play a couple of games, Laura, would you like that?'

'Yes, please, Doctor Turner,' Laura replied eagerly. 'Can daddy join in?'

'These games are not for adults,' Doctor Turner explained. 'Your father would just get bored.'

'You're an adult, Doctor Turner,' Laura sounded confused, 'won't you get bored?'

'No, because I'm a child at heart you see,' Doctor Turner replied. 'Your father is going to leave us, but he will come back later. Is that alright?'

'I guess so,' Laura said.

Her father got up, shook hands with the doctor, kissed his daughter on the forehead and left.

'Now the first game, Laura, is all about friends,' said

'This shouldn't take too long, Doctor Turner,'

Laura smiled. 'I don't have any.'
'None at all, Laura,' Doctor Turner said taken aback. 'I find that difficult to believe.'
'Well, I did make this one friend in my mind,' Laura admitted, and she noticed that the doctor was writing notes. 'She was called Cora and she was good at maths. You see, I'm no good at maths, but she was extremely good.'
'I notice that you said she was good at maths, Laura,' Doctor Turner said. 'Is she no longer good at maths?'
'Er, doctor, she wasn't real,' Laura pointed out. 'I just imagined her. I find it hard to make friends. I much prefer to read and look at history.'
'Do you count your mummy as a friend, Laura?' Doctor Turner asked.

'My mother? She's not really a friend, is she? She's just my mother,' Laura smiled. 'By the way, may I borrow a piece of paper and a pencil, please?'
'Certainly,' Doctor Thorne replied confused but passed her the items anyway. He watched as she started writing ace of clubs, two of diamonds, queen of clubs and so it continued. He sat watching amazed.

George Hadley had managed to find the canteen. As a surgeon he was allowed to eat and drink there even if he did not work at the hospital. He had the Telegraph opened. A cup of coffee was on the table next to him. The news was not good. He did not like the sound of the German Chancellor, Adolf Hitler. He had had his reservations about him when Hitler was appointed in nineteen thirty-three. There were murmurings in his line of work that surgeons would be called up to the services if war was declared. He hoped that it would not come to that but, if it did, then he would do his duty for his King and country. He really needed to discuss this with his wife.

He turned the page of the paper and then reached for his coffee and took a sip. He heard some people enter the canteen. It was two nurses. They were laughing at something, probably something a doctor had just said them. They went to the counter and ordered two teas. He watched them as they finally got their drinks and went to sit by the corner table. He heard someone else come in and his attention was drawn back to them. They were not in nurses' uniforms. What they were wearing made his heart freeze. She was in a nun's habit. Memories came flooding back to him, but he went back to his newspaper to try and suppress them. He knew that some nuns made excellent nurses and midwives. He started reading an interesting report about Winston Churchill.

He reached for his coffee and, as he did so, his eyes locked on a young girl standing in the doorway. It was Laura. He almost spat his drink out. He looked back towards the doorway, but the girl had gone. He quickly finished his drink, stood up, folded his paper and tucked it under his arm before leaving the canteen.

He stood in the corridor and looked left and right. He was sure that the girl was headed right so he set off at a brisk pace. He looked in on wards as he passed them. Maybe she was being taken there. Perhaps Doctor Turner had decided to intern her for further investigations. He could not see her anywhere.

'Can I help you, Sir?' a passing nurse asked. George felt flummoxed for a second before composing himself. 'I was looking for Doctor Turner's office and I must have taken a wrong turning.'

The nurse smiled at him as he turned and walked back the way he had come. He went to Doctor Turner's room and listened at the door. He could just about hear Laura talking. Which meant that it could not have been Laura he had seen. Perhaps he had just imagined it.

The door opened abruptly, and Doctor Turner almost walked into Mr Hadley.

'Ah, Mr Hadley,' said the doctor. 'I was not expecting you back so quickly. I just had...I just had to go somewhere.'

'Is Laura in there?' George asked.

'Yes, she is. She's doing a test for me. Why do you ask?'
'It was just that I thought I saw her a moment ago,' George replied. 'It must have been someone who looked a lot like her.'

'Perhaps I should be doing the tests on you, George,' Doctor Turner joked.
'Maybe you are right, Bernard,' laughed George.
'I suggest you go for a bite to eat. 'It's going to be a little while yet. I'll send my assistant to find you when it's over.'
'Is it too early to say that you'll be admitting her?'
'George! From what I've seen and heard so far, Laura is doing very well,' Bernard replied. 'These next tests will find out if she's been deceiving me. Now go and get something to eat. Like I said, it's going to be a while yet.'

And it must have been a good couple of hours later before the assistant came to find him. He had finished the crossword and read and reread the newspaper, becoming more and more alarmed if the situation developing in Europe. He kept an eye out for the girl he saw. She may have been a patient here. He felt embarrassed that he had initially thought it had been Laura. He knew his own daughter and could have only imagined that the girl had looked like her. He must have been thinking about Laura at the time. Yes; that was it. Thinking about her had made is brain trick him into thinking that the girl looked like Laura. In reality he was sure, now, that she did not look anything like his daughter.

The assistant took George back to Doctor Turner's office. It was clear that the specialist had something to say but not in front of the young girl. It was agreed that the assistant take her to the canteen for a drink.

Laura held the assistant's hand and felt more comfortable than she did with her own mother. She wondered why that was the case. She was amazed with how large the canteen was. It was as big as a house. The assistant ordered her a juice and treated Laura to an éclair cake.

Laura gathered that the dinner break must be over as dishes were left on tables and the kitchen staff were clearing them. They found a clean table and sat down. The assistant placed the cake in front of Laura and the girl looked at her. The assistant realised that she was waiting for permission. The assistant smiled and the girl took her first bite

Laura closed her eyes as she savoured the choux pastry mixed with the custard filling. She chewed and chewed until it felt like it had dissolved in her mouth. When she opened her eyes, she was looking at a girl who looked very familiar. She was immediately drawn to this child. The other girl showed no recognition and seemed to be staring through her. She could not have been there long when a woman, possibly the girl's mother, came and took her hand. For a moment the woman looked towards Laura and Laura saw the look of realisation and fear. She took the other girl's hand and left quickly.

'Did I know her?' Laura whispered.

'Pardon, Laura. I could not hear you,' said the assistant.

'Lovely,' Laura said. 'I said that this is lovely'.

'I'm glad you are enjoying it,' the assistant smiled.

Later that day, when they arrived back at the holiday home, Mrs Hadley was waiting for them on the

doorstep. She had a look of concern on her face, but

when she saw Laura in the car some of that worry appeared to ebb away. She had not expected her daughter to come home with her husband. After listening to her daughter, both teachers, the headmaster and others, Gail was of the opinion that Laura was mad. She blamed the past. She knew that one day it would catch up with them. They should never have agreed with it, but, at the time, it seemed like a good idea.

As they got out of the car, she noticed that George was reaching across to the passenger seat for something. She soon got to see that it was a bottle of champagne. Her daughter came skipping across the gravelled driveway. She gave her a mother a hug, which startled Gail. Her daughter had never shown so much emotion to her before.

'May I go to my room, mother?' Laura asked.

'How was your day?' Gail asked.

'Fine,' Laura responded quickly. 'May I, mother?'

'Of course, you may,' Gail smiled tentatively. 'It will give me time to speak with your father'.

She did not watch as her daughter ran inside. Usually, she would have chastised the child for running, but her attention was firmly on her husband. He was smiling like a Cheshire cat. What 'on earth was going on?

'Go get the glasses ready, Gail,' George shouted from by the car.

'What's happened?' Gail asked suspiciously.

'I'll tell you all about it in a moment,' George laughed. 'Now go and get those glasses, woman'.

Gail went inside and went to find the champagne glasses. George followed her in. When he reached the kitchen, Gail had just found the glasses in the wall cupboard. She was just taking them down as George popped the cork. It made her jump. She put the glasses on the table and George filled them up. The froth spilling over the top and cascaded down the side damping the tablecloth as it reached its destination.

'George!' Gail scolded. 'I'll have to clean that now'.

George placed a bottle on the table and picked up the two glasses, handing one to Gail. 'A toast to our wonderful daughter'.

'A toast?' Gail questioned. 'George? What is going on? Is Laura mad?'

'Far from it, Gail,' George laughed. 'Doctor Turner

could not find anything that would have made him alarmed and would recommend her admittance to the mental institution. In fact, he thinks Laura is intelligent – no – correction, highly intelligent. He was setting her tests and she was passing them all, even correcting him when he made a mistake. He thinks that is why she made her own imaginary friend. It was someone she created who would match her own intelligence'.

'So, that's all it was? An imaginary friend?' asked Gail she took a sip of drink. The bubbles tickled her mouth.

'That's all it was,' George confirmed. 'He has had many cases where this happens. He is more concerned with children – and adults – who tend to have conversations with themselves; like asking a question and answering it. Laura showed no signs of that'.

'Mrs Miller was right, then,' Gail said.

'Pardon?' George had not been listening. He was still concentrating on the news about Laura. He had felt so elated when Doctor Turner was telling him his findings.

'That teacher was right,' Gail repeated. 'She only mentioned an imaginary friend. Mrs Miller was more focussed on her intelligence. It was me who thought she was mad. I had already had a word with Miss Cummings to get her opinion. I wanted to get her to confirm what I had already decided. I had thought Laura was mad. I heard her talking to herself and some of the things she was saying. I linked it to the past; about where she came from.'

'She did not come from anywhere, Gail,' George said trying to keep his calm. 'She is our daughter.'

'What if we're being punished for what we did, George?' Gail said. 'What if God is looking down on us and has not liked what we have done?'

'We have given life to a wonderful child, Gail,' said George. 'Do not forget that. I think it's time to tell you what else the doctor said.'

'Ah ha,' said Gail. 'I knew you were hiding something.'

'Doctor Turner is concerned about the relationship between Laura and… us,' George said, obviously trying to choose his words carefully.

'By us, you mean me,' Gail clarified.

'She calls me daddy and you…'

'Mother,' Gail completed her husband's sentence. 'She always has, George, and you know that I have always installed that in the child.'

"'In the child," Gail? Not in our child?' George said.

'The child. Our child. They are just the same thing, George,' said Gail taking another drink. 'We both know that you were always her favourite. She never took to me.'

'Oh, come off it, Gail,' George said completely sidetracked by how this conversation was going. The day had been a rollercoaster. It had started off with a concern through to an emotion of absolute joy to now. 'You have never shown any emotion towards her. And when she tried to show you some, you completely ignore her. Even just a moment ago, when she gave you that hug, you looked startled and tense.'

'You knew from the off, George, that I had no maternal instincts,' said Gail. And then the penny dropped. 'I'm the reason for her creating her imaginary friend and not making any real friends of her own.' George looked sheepishly away. 'Oh, my God! I see it now. I will have to try to be different. I know that I don't show it, but I do love

'I love you, too, mother,' said Laura.

The two parents had not noticed their daughter sneak into the room. 'How long have you been standing there?' demanded Gail.

'And it's not your fault, mother,' said Laura. 'I'm just like this. This is who I am. Mind you, I have noticed that I have been looking at us all and I do not appear to resemble either of you'.

Gail looked at her husband and George returned the look. 'Sometimes, Sweetpea, it takes a bit longer for family resemblances to come through'.

'Okay, daddy,' Laura seemed to accept the explanation. 'I came down for a drink of water'.

'I know what, Laura,' said Gail smiling. 'Why don't we pour you a small glass of champagne?'

'Am I allowed it, Mother?' Laura questioned.

'If we permit it, Laura,' said Gail. 'It will only be a small one and we won't tell anyone, will we, George?'

'No, we won't,' George agreed.

'Go and get her a small glass, George,' Gail ordered.

George retuned with a small sherry glass and poured some bubbly in it. He handed it to Laura. The two parents watched as Laura tentatively took a sip. She giggled as the bubbles fizzed up her nose and in her mouth.

'What do you think, Sweetpea?' asked George.

'The bubbles make me laugh,' Laura replied. 'It's very nice.' She drank the remaining in one go.

'Whoa! Whoa! Whoa!' Gail said laughing. 'You're meant to sip it, honey'.

'Oh! Sorry, mummy,' Laura replied. Mummy! Her daughter had called her mummy. It made her feel quite warm inside and she did not think it was the champagne mellowing her. 'May I have another one?'

'Not tonight, Sweetpea,' George said. 'I'll pour you a juice and you can take it upstairs whilst we prepare dinner'.

'Okay, daddy'.

Laura waited whilst her father did her the drink. She looked towards her mother. The woman had transformed. A smile certainly made her mother look a completely different person. She shone. If only she would do it more often. Her father handed her the drink. Her mother said that she would call her when the food was ready.

Laura went upstairs and went to her bedroom. She put her glass down on a coaster that was on her bedside cabinet. Her mother did not like rings being left that were difficult to clean. She knew this mainly meant tea or coffee marks, but she had gotten into this routine and did not want to break it.

Her head was feeling a little fuzzy from the alcohol, and she felt giggly.

'What on earth is wrong with you?' Cora asked.

'Me? There's nothing wrong with me,' Laura replied merrily.

'Why does my head feel so lightheaded?' Cora said.

'I've been given some champagne,' Laura admitted. 'I think I may have drunk it a bit too quickly.'

'Are you drunk?' Cora reprimanded.

'Drunk? What's that?' Laura asked.

'My dad gets like it when he's had too much

alcohol,' said Cora. 'That's when the arguments start, and he hits my mum. Sometimes he even hits me.'

'Did he hit you three or four days ago?' Laura asked. 'Quite late at night?'

'Yes, he did,' Cora confirmed.

'I woke up when I felt a pain across my cheek,' said Laura. 'It stung for a bit afterwards, too.'

'Tell me about it,' mumbled Cora.

'How is it you can feel my pain and I can feel yours?' Laura asked.

'We have a unique bond,' Cora responded, and Laura noted the excitement returning to her voice.

'But I don't know you and you don't know me, so, how come we can communicate with each other?'

'That I cannot answer,' Cora replied. 'How did it go at the hospital?'

Laura had decided against saying anything about the girl she had seen there. It was not like Cora was going to know the girl anyway. 'As well as you said it would,' Laura answered. 'I did not like saying that I no longer have an imaginary friend, though.'

'We've been through this, Laura,' Cora replied sternly. 'We are not imaginary; we are real people.

As I said a moment ago, I don't know how or why we can communicate, but we are definitely real. I was at a hospital earlier. We were visiting my father. He had injured himself during one of his drunk states.'

The way she said it made Laura think that Cora was not telling the truth but she decided to let it slide. 'I don't think I'm ever going to drink again,' said Laura as she picked up her juice and took a sip. 'And one more thing, Cora?'

'Yes?'

'Be careful over the next few months,' Laura said. 'I do not like how things are progressing in Europe. I'm sure that we are heading for war.'

'Whatever,' said Cora. 'I'm not interested in it.'

'You should be,' Laura rebuked. 'If it doesn't go well, then we could all be speaking German soon.'

CHAPTER SEVEN

And as Laura predicted, war broke out on the third of September nineteen-thirty-nine. Mr and Mrs Hadley and Laura sat around the kitchen table and were listening to the broadcast made by Prime Minister Chamberlain just after eleven o'clock in the morning, on their wireless.

"This morning the British ambassador in Berlin handed the German government a final note stating that unless we heard from them by eleven o'clock that they were prepared at once to withdraw their troops from Poland, a state of war would exist between us. I have to tell you now that no such undertaking has been received, and that consequently this country is at war with Germany."

'What does that mean, George?' Gail asked as George switched off the wireless.

"It means, Gail, that all hell is going break loose," George replied.

'You won't be called up will you, George?'

'With my skillset, darling, the likelihood is that I will get called up,' said George. 'No doubt we will be having a meeting at work sometime soon. A high percentage of doctors served in the military during the first World War. I can see no reason why it should not be the same for this war. There are going to be thousands upon thousands of injuries and casualties; perhaps even millions.'

'With RAF Portreath just up the road, daddy, do you think that we'll get bombed?' Laura asked.

George looked towards Gail who also looked like she was waiting for his reply. 'I don't think Adolf Hitler and his cronies will worry too much about little old Portreath. I'm sure he'll have a lot more on his plate when we start bombing Germany. It will all be over before Christmas'.

'Something similar was said about the last war, daddy, and that went on for four years,' Laura pointed out.

'Ah, but our technology has come on in leaps and bounds since then, Laura,' her dad replied. 'I mean aircraft were mainly used for reconnaissance purposes back then. Nowadays they are used in combat. Our Navy is the envy of the world'.

'I will still be able to go to school won't I, mummy?' Laura asked.

'There has not been any notification that school is being closed,' Gail replied honestly. 'Would you still like to go? Or would you feel safer here?'

'I would still like to go, mummy, if you don't mind?' said Laura. 'Now that I'm back in Mrs Miller's class,

'I'm learning ever so much.'

"Then, of course you can still go to school, darling," Gail smiled.

George had noted how much the relationship between Gail and Laura had changed since the visit to the hospital. They had been getting on like a normal mother and daughter. Laura had been calling Gail mummy a lot more which his wife seemed to enjoy. They were doing more things together and Gail was even helping her daughter with her maths. He could pinpoint the moment it changed when Gail realised that she was to blame for Laura almost being committed to the asylum. Since then, they had not heard Laura talking to, or about, any imaginary friend.

And the reason why they did not hear it was because Laura had finally worked out how to communicate with Cora by only using her mind. It was great fun. Laura still had to be careful not to laugh out loud when anyone was near, but Cora made her giggle quite often. She had never asked Cora if she had been at the hospital that day. There was no reason for her to be there so Laura had just assumed that, since it was a very quick glance, she had only imagined that the girl was the spitting image of her. But there was something in the mother's reaction that she could not shake. The woman had looked alarmed, fearful even.

Mrs Miller had also noticed a change. She was delighted to have Laura back in her class. Miss Cummings, on the other hand, was delighted that the mischievous child was not her responsibility anymore. As far as she was concerned, she had done her duty and was disappointed that Laura was not considered to be insane. She still thought the child was mad and every time she caught the young girl looking at her, she thought the girl was the devil-child.

Mrs Miller rarely spoke to Miss Cummings which, admittedly, made things difficult in school. Mr Davidson tried to reconcile the two, but neither were willing to submit. He was relieved when Miss Cummings decided to take early retirement and was to leave at the Christmas holidays.

If anything, Laura got more intellectual in class. She had started to talk to the other children and even Billy was asking her for help. Carly had also seen a vast improvement in the relationship between mother and daughter. Mrs Hadley had even apologised to the teacher and the two had become close friends. Mrs Hadley had realised that they both wanted what was best for Laura. They had met with each other to work out next steps. And then war broke out and changed everything.

One breaktime, when it was raining outside, the children were in the classroom colouring or just playing. Laura, as was usually the case, had her nose in a book. Carly walked around the children, making sure that there were no disturbances. When she got close to Laura, she noticed that the girl had put her book down.

'Mrs Miller? May I ask you a question?' Laura whispered.

'Certainly, Laura,' Carly said, and she crouched down to be on the girl's level.

'Is it possible to have a sibling that you know nothing about?' Laura asked.

'What do you mean, Laura?' Carly asked confused.

'Well, I'm reading Oliver Twist,' Laura began to explain and held up the book for the teacher to see,

'and Oliver is an orphan. And I was just thinking would he know if he had a real brother or sister?'

'He did have a brother...' Carly was about to answer.

'Half-brother,' Laura corrected. 'Edward Leeford was his half-brother because of the relationship between his mother and "Monks" father. But what about his actual mother and father? What if they had had another child and Oliver did not know about them? How would he find out?'

'Well, Laura, that is quite a difficult one to answer,' Carly admitted. 'They do try to keep siblings together when they are orphaned. There have been cases where they have been parted. I would guess that unless Oliver knew that he had a brother or sister, there would be no way he would know. Why do you ask?'

'Just curious,' Laura smiled. 'I thought there might have been some sort of psychic connection between the two'.

'Well, that is certainly a wonderful theory, Laura, but I do not think that humans can do that'.

Mrs Miller smiled at the young girl before standing up and moving on to the next child.

'I believe there is a connection, Laura,' said Billy.

'Really,' said Laura who knew that she was not going to be impressed with what Billy Penhale was about to say.

'My mummy has a twin sister,' Billy explained. 'Last month my mum started to have tummy pains. The doctors could not understand what was wrong with her and then, suddenly, the pains stopped. We learnt later that Aunty Elsie had given birth to my cousin Jeremy. So, it was like mummy could feel the pain that aunty was going through'.

Laura looked at Billy amazed. 'Is that the only time something strange has happened between the two?'

'It's the only one I have heard about,' Billy confessed. 'Would you like me ask if there have been others?'

'Would you do that for me, Billy,' Laura asked.

'Of course, I would,' said Billy.

They looked at each other, neither one quite sure about what was happening. 'Would you like to come over and play on Friday?' Laura asked completely unsure of what words had just escaped from her mouth.

'As long as it's not dollies,' Billy said pulling a face.

'I hate having to play that when we visit my cousin Dot.'

'I'm more a teddy person,' Laura replied. 'I don't have many dolls, so we won't be playing that. I'll make sure that it's okay with my mummy and daddy and you should get permission from your parents.'

If Mr and Mrs Hadley were surprised by Laura seeking permission for Billy to come and play on the Friday after school, then they hid it very well. In fact, they were very pleased that Laura was actually making friends. It had come with some other good news; George had been put on a reserve list to be called up. Some of his colleagues had already volunteered for the services but his bosses still needed skilled surgeons to remain because they knew that there would be casualties here.

However, both knew that, if the war was not over quickly, George would soon be sent to the frontline.

It was agreed by Mrs Hadley and Mrs Penhale that Billy could come over for dinner on the Friday, and that Mr Hadley would walk Billy home just after they had eaten.

Mrs Miller was amazed to see the two sat together when she entered the classroom. They were talking together but stopped when the teacher walked in. She also caught Laura helping the young boy with his English and Billy, in return, was trying to help her with mathematics. She shook her head in wonder. Then

she realised that something must have changed within Laura. The change had been sudden and dramatic. She wracked her brain as to when she had noticed the change. It must have been when she was transferred to Miss Cummings class. Now, Carly knew that Laura had been considered sane, but she was starting to see a pattern; talking to an imaginary friend, asking about how Oliver Twist would know if he had a sibling. Something was behind this.

Mrs Hadley picked the two children up from school on the Friday. They walked home. The Hadley's did not live too far away and only took a few minutes to get to the large house which was situated on what the locals called the tram. It overlooked the small village of Bridge and down to Portreath. You could see the Methodist Church and the local inn.

Billy was overawed by the size of the house and its grounds. It was a vast difference from the property that he lived in. Laura's bedroom was larger than his lounge. He decided that he loved this place.

They started off by playing cards. Snap was the favourite and Billy showed his prowess at playing. Laura was usually very good, and she had to up her game, so it wasn't a whitewash. But they had a great laugh. They next played pick-up-sticks. Billy kept on making Laura laugh when it was her turn, and she nudged the sticks. She tried to get her revenge on her new friend, but his concentration was amazing.

After they had finished playing Billy looked at her. 'I thought you would have asked me by now,' he said.

'Asked you about what?' Laura replied a little puzzled.

"About the connection between my mum and aunty," Billy reminded her.

'Oh, yes,' Laura said excitedly. 'We've been having so much fun, I almost forgot. I also didn't think you would find out so quickly. What did they say?

'They did agree that they believe they know what the other one is thinking,' said Billy. 'They have felt *poorly when the other one feels ill.'*

'Could they communicate with each other in their minds?' Laura asked holding her breath.

'No,' Billy replied, and Laura felt deflated. 'They could not speak to each other. They could sense certain things but, no, they could not talk to each other secretly.'

'Well, thank you for asking them, Billy,' said Laura. Billy looked like he wanted to ask something but was too scared to. 'What is it, Billy?'

'I've heard you talking to someone when no one else is around,' Billy began hesitantly. 'Can you talk to someone else with just your thoughts?'

Laura looked hard at him. 'Are you making fun of me, Billy Penhale?' she snapped.

'No. No. No,' Billy replied visibly shaken. 'I-I-I just wanted to say, I believe you.'

Billy hung his head in embarrassment. All of a sudden, he felt Laura's arms around him pulling him into a hug. 'Thank you, Billy,' Laura whispered in his ear.

CHAPTER EIGHT

Laura and Billy became best friends after that. Mrs Miller was noticed that Billy was a good influence on the young girl. Billy had included her in the group of his other friends and Laura particularly started playing and talking to Danielle.

The war had been going on for nine months. It was not going as planned. Although there had been conflicting reports, Laura could tell, from what she had heard, that there had been many, many casualties already. It had also been hindered by "friendly fire." Laura recalled listening to a report where a British submarine had torpedoed another Bristish submarine mistaken it for a German U-Boat.

Cornwall had mainly escaped large bombings and everyday life looked as though it had never changed. Behind closed doors though, things were quite different. Families worrying about loved ones who were on the front line; not knowing if they were injured or worse.

Mr Hadley kept on listening to the reports. Although he was on a reserved list, he knew that it was unlikely he would be called any time soon because of his profession and he was guilty about not being able to do his duty for King and Country. Gail kept on telling her husband that he should not be feeling that way; that he was doing his duty by patching up the ill and injured, even though not many soldiers had been transported to Truro hospital. They both wanted to do more for the war effort so decided to turn their holiday home over to the government.

They arranged some time to get away so that they could clear the house and hand the keys over. Mr Hadley had organised to drive a van up whilst his wife would take the car. Gail was not looking forward to driving so far. She had not taken her test because they had been suspended because of the war. George had taught her how to drive which had resulted in her once stopping the car in the middle of the road before getting out and walking the rest of the way home. There was an angry toot as the driver behind waited for George to move the car.

Laura loved the van, in particular the colour. It was sky blue and had a large spare black tyre secured on the side very near to the front passenger wheel arch.

She wanted to go up with her father to their holiday home in it, but her parents would not allow it.

The day got closer when they were going, and Laura was getting very excited. She knew someone who would be as equally excited as well, when she heard that Laura would be going past the house again.

'Hi, Cora, it's me,' she said trying to contact her friend. Nothing. She waited a little longer but there was no response. 'Cora? Can you hear me?' Laura waited and waited but did not receive anything back. Something was wrong. Why couldn't she contact her friend? Then she thought she would try a different tact. 'Are you annoyed with me for some reason?'

'Oh, you finally want to talk to me now, do you?' Cora replied scathingly. 'I've been trying to speak with you for a long time and have not been able to. Don't you realise that there is a war going on? I thought something had happened to you'.

Laura felt ashamed. 'You're right,' she responded guiltily. 'I'm so sorry, Cora. Please forgive me'.

'What have you been doing to ignore me like that?' Laura could tell by the tone that her friend had not quite forgiven her yet.

'I've been following our plan,' Laura replied. 'I'm back in Mrs Miller's class and I've been making friends just like you suggested. It was a good idea of yours, Cora. I now play with Billy and Danielle'.

'Danielle? Is she French or something?' Cora asked, and the bitterness was still very clear in her voice.

'I think she was born in Cambourne,' Laura replied, not quite understanding what Cora was going on about.

'Is that near Paris?'

'Redruth,' Laura said and then caught on. 'Oh, you mean her name sounds French. She told me that her mother named her after the French actress Danielle Darrieux'.

'You'll have to run that by me again,' said Cora.

'Danielle Darrieux,' Laura repeated.

'Nope. Am never going to get that in a month of Sundays,' said Cora. 'My plan never included you totally forgetting about me'.

'I'm so sorry, Cora,' Laura felt chastised. 'You're absolutely correct'.

'Okay, you've already said that,' said Cora. 'So, why are you getting in touch with me now?'

'I'm going to be going by that house again, in a couple of days,' said Laura.

'Why are you going up?' asked Cora.

'My parents are letting the government use at as a base for the duration of the war,' Laurea explained.

'That's good of them,' said Cora. 'At least they are doing something for the war effort. My parents are not doing anything. I think my father wants Hitler to win. He said that the Jews are taking over everywhere'.

'He sounds like a bigot,' said Laura.

'He doesn't sound like one, he is one,' said Cora. 'You'll have to visit that house'.

'How on earth can I visit the house?' asked Laura.

'Can't you pretend to want to go to the toilet or something?' Cora responded.

'Hmmm,' Laura thought. 'I'm pretty sure that I can do that'.

'You'll have to let me know how you get on,' said Cora.

'I will,' said Laura.

A couple of days later the family set off. Mr Hadley left in the van first whilst Laura and her mother followed on behind. Mrs Hadley sat bolt upright behind the steering wheel of their car. It was black in colour with a long bonnet. It had white rim tyres. Laura loved the car, especially the interior. It had this lovely grey fabric, and the seats were quite comfy. The dashboard was completely foreign to her. All the dials and knobs just did not make any sense. Obviously, they were completely foreign to her mother as well because she had hardly looked at them. Sometimes when her mother moved the big stick it made a very weird sound, like two metal objects scrunching against one another. All she heard her mother say when this happened was that she had to remember the clutch – whatever that was.

They stopped a couple of times so that they could both have a drink. Gail had made a small picnic and a couple flasks of tea. It usually took her father between five to six hours to reach the holiday home. It was going to take Gail a couple of hours longer.

They played eye-spy and sang a couple of songs. Laura actually found herself enjoying this time with her mother. She looked out the window to watch the scenery go by.

She suddenly felt strange. Not in an ill way but in the Deja-vu sort of way. She closed her eyes.

'Yahehiouoooooo' a voice screamed in her head.

'What was that?' she gasped.

'What was what, honey?' Gail asked. 'What's wrong, Laura. You've gone as white as a sheet'.

Laura caught a glimpse of the house coming up in the distance. 'I'm not feeling well, mummy,' she said. 'I think I'm going to be sick'.

'There's nowhere to stop, Laura,' Gail replied in a panic.

'There's a house up ahead, mummy,' said Laura. 'We're going to have to stop there'.

It was Mrs Hadley's turn to go white. She did not want to go in that house. She did not want to see someone. Someone who she had not seen in years. She turned to look at her daughter. She was definitely not looking well. She could see beads of perspiration developing on her forehead. She was going to have to stop. There was no way around this. Laura was certainly looking poorly. She turned to pull into the large driveway of the house. Gail got out of the car and went around to the passenger door and opened it for her daughter to climb out.

She took hold of Laura's hand as they walked across the gravel. Gail walked up the three, white, concrete steps to the front door. She rang the bell which Laura likened to the school bell put was connected to some sort of pulley system. They did not have to wait long for the door to open. Laura saw a woman dressed in a strange garment with a funny looking hat on her head which fell like a veil at the back of her head. Laura thought she was quite wrinkly and looked old.

'Yes?' the nun enquired.

'It's my daughter,' Gail said indicating at Laura. 'She's not feeling very well. Can she borrow your toilet?'

The nun looked towards the young girl and saw that she was looking very pale. 'You'd better come in,' the nun said, standing aside.

The room they entered was a bit of a disappointment

for Laura. It certainly was nothing like she imagined. A large wooden crucifix hung on the left side wall. The furniture was sparse; a couple of school-like chairs were placed either side of the cross, a table and a further chair which Laura assumed was for the receptionist. The ceiling was plain, and Laura noted the bare floorboards. The layout was, as she had heard her mother say many a time, simplistic to say the least. Her eyes fixed upon a solitary book on the desk. It was not a reading book as she was used to, but quite large. It was opened so Laura could see that it was a register of some kind.

'Please follow me,' the nun said. 'I will make you a drink to calm your stomach'.

Laura had immediately felt better when she had entered the house. She followed the nun because she did feel the need to go to the loo. The hallway was not long but was wide and had three doors. There was a stairway to the right-hand side. The nun opened the door next to the stairs. There was a toilet and a wash-hand basin. Although her house had an inside toilet, she knew that many did not. Billy's house had an outside one as did Danielle's. She was not sure if Mrs Miller had one. She began to realise that there was a gulf between people, mainly related to their jobs. Her father, apparently, was in a good profession. She wondered what Cora's house was like but realised that Cora had said that her father was a drunk, so the likelihood would be an outside toilet.

Her mother moved to go in with her but saw that there was not much room. 'Shout if you need me, Laura,' she said concerned.

'Come on, Abigail,' said the nun. 'Come and help me prepare that drink. I'm sure the girl will call if she needs you'.

Laura had never seen her mother look so worried as she was led away by the nun. She did decide to go to the toilet because they still had some way to go. Laura could not reach the flush chain for the hi-level cistern and made a mental note to tell the old woman. She washed her hands when she had finished and wiped them in the towel that was hanging on a hook.

She walked out of the bathroom and was going to follow the others but decided to go back to the reception room. She went straight over to the book she

saw on the desk. She made sure no one was watching her as she opened the book. She read that it was like a patient guide that her father kept in his office. It had a name, address date, and further names in the last column. Laura really did not have any idea on what she was looking for. She had another quick glance around before flicking the pages of the book to find the date she wanted. She got to nineteen-thirty. She thought she heard a noise and, quickly, tore out the two pages before closing the book again. She tucked the pages into her undergarments.

She skipped back towards where her mother had been led. She could hear talking so she put her ear closer to the door. She could barely make out what was being said but she could just catch snippets.

'How long has it been? Six – seven years?' the older voice said.

'She's eight. Nine this year,' said her mother.

'You just disappeared,' said the nun. 'You and Doc...' Laura could not hear the rest.

She thought she heard the noise she had heard just a moment ago. It was like someone sighing. It was coming from upstairs. She turned and looked up them. She bravely stood on the first wooden step. She took a deep breath and climbed up the rest.

She counted twelve in total. At the top it opened into a vast expanse with four doors. She looked back down the stairs, but no one was coming. She went to the door on the left and tried to turn the door handle, but it did not open. She tried to one of the handles on the door in front of the stairs and got the same response and of the door next to it. She heard the sigh for a third time. It seemed to be coming from the room behind the door to the right. She walked slowly over to it. Everything had gone cold, or, perhaps, she was feeling poorly again. Her fingers, tentatively, reached for the handle.

'Yahehiouooooooo,' the voice she had previously heard in the car screamed out loud.

'And what are you doing up here, young lady?' asked the old woman.

Laura jumped. She had not heard anyone come upstairs. 'I couldn't find my mummy,' Laura said starting to cry.

'There, there, my dear. No need for tears,' said the nun trying to sound caring but Laura could tell she had never had children herself. Her actual tone was like that of how her mother's used to be. 'She's only downstairs. Let me take you to her. I've made that drink to soothe your stomach. How are you feeling?' She took the young girl by the hand and led her down the stairs, but Laura kept her eye on the door until she

could see it no longer. There was something or someone behind that door. She could feel their presence.

Inside the room the young lady was frantic. She was trying to open the door, but it was not budging. She was desperate, so desperate.

'She's there,' she sobbed. 'She's there. I can feel her. Why are you keeping me locked up here?'

'You will be allowed out when you're ready,' said the guardian.

'What do you mean by that?' the young woman cried. 'When will I be ready?'

'You will know when you're ready,' soothed the other.

'Why can't I see her? Why won't you let me see her?'

'For your own good,' said the guardian. 'And for her own good.'

The woman rested her head against the door in frustration. 'I speak with her, you know,' she said.

'No, you don't,' said the other.

'Yes, I do,' she insisted.

'No, you don't,' the other replied sternly. 'You certainly talk to one of them, but you do not communicate with the one who is here at the moment.'

'But I can feel her. Why can I feel her?'

'You'll work it out one day,' said the guardian.

'Can't you just tell me?' the woman responded.

'Unfortunately, not,' the guardian sighed. 'I have told you this so many times. You have been making progress lately, but we always hit this stumbling block. But I'm not concerned. You'll get it in the end.'

'Oh, I hate you,' the female responded vehemently. 'I really hate you.'

The guardian just smiled.

Laura kept her gaze upon the nun until she and the house were out of view before turning back to look out of the windscreen.

'How are you feeling?' Mrs Hadley asked.

'Fine,' Laura replied. 'I don't know what that lady

put in that drink, but it has certainly calmed my insides. Mind you, having that poo may have helped shift it as well'.

'Laura!' her mother admonished. 'A young woman does not speak that way'.

'Sorry, Mother,' Laura apologised.

'If you need me to, I will pull over so that you can get out,' said Gail.

'Thank you, mummy,' Laura responded. 'But I should be fine'.

They carried on their journey. Laura could sense her mother taking a couple of sneak glances at her as they continued. She was fussing, as well; kept on asking her if she was still feeling okay.

'I think we're only about ten minutes away, now, Laura,' said Gail. 'Mind you, you father has always done the driving so I'm only guessing'.

'How do you know that we're ten minutes away, then?' Laura asked.

'It's from noticing things and remembering them from previous journeys,' Gail explained. 'Like that farm over there. I always remember it being close to

'our home.'

'What's the farm called?' Laura wondered out loud.

'How on earth should I know, Laura?' laughed Gail.

'You must have driven by it quite a few times, I thought you may have known,' said Laura.

'Just because we've driven past it quite a few times, doesn't mean that I will know what it's called,' Gail said still laughing.

'True,' Laura agreed. 'It's just that the old woman we just met has never seen us before, but she seemed to know your name.'

Her mother had gone white again. As white as a ghost. Laura wondered if she had pushed her mother too far.

'I knew her,' Gail admitted. 'I worked with her about eight or nine years ago. We were midwives.'

'You helped deliver babies?' Laura's eyes opened in astonishment. She had never known this about her mother. 'Wow! That must have been brilliant and so rewarding.'

'Mostly it was,' Gail confirmed. 'It was a pleasure placing new-born babies with their mothers and *watching them bond. Sometimes, though, the mothers could not look after their babies, and we had to place them with parents who could not have children for whatever reason'.*

Laura was surprised that her mother was opening up with so much information about her past. Gail had rarely said anything about her history except that she was born in nineteen hundred and five, and that her father had been a major in the army and her mother had been a nurse. That was roughly all she knew about her mother. She didn't even know how her mother met her father. Now that she had gleaned this bit of information, she assumed that they must have worked together in the medical profession.

'But to see life being born, you cannot get anything more wonderous than that,' Laura said in awe.

'It didn't always go to plan,' Gail said eventually, looking very serious. 'I did, occasionally, see things that I wouldn't wish upon my worst enemy'.

'Is that why you gave it up?' Laura asked.

There was a slight hesitation; only slight, but Laura noticed it at once. 'Yes,' her mother replied.

Why would her mother be lying about this? She did

not want to press her any further. She was shocked that her mother had said so much already. But she was definitely holding something back. She sat back in the car seat and wondered what on earth it could be.

CHAPTER NINE

The twentieth of August nineteen-forty began like any normal day. The children were looking forward to the school holidays on the twenty-fifth. The class size had grown as the young evacuees from the cities had been sent to the countryside during the blitz, particularly that of London. Portreath school was very close to not being able to cope. Mr Davidson, the Headmaster, was now teaching as his budget would not permit recruiting a teacher to replace Miss

Cummings.

Mrs Miller was finding it particularly difficult. There was no time for her style of teaching. Instead, she found herself standing in front of the class and getting them to repeat, parrot fashion, what she was saying or writing on the blackboard. It was very much like how Miss Cummings would teach and many of her predecessors. She had really started to hate her job. But then she looked at the evacuees and some of their faces were filled with terror and her heart went out to them.

At only nine and a half years of age, she would not be ten until December, Laura was helping Mrs Miller. Carly felt for the young girl. War had really thwarted the young girl's future. Laura, though, was really enjoying herself. She loved helping the younger pupils but secretly enjoyed it when the older ones came and asked for her assistance. Many of the evacuees wanted to be her friend. Carly had never seen Laura so popular. The girl had certainly come out of her shell.

Billy and Danielle came round to play after school. Mrs Hadley was preparing a fish pie. Billy was showing particular interest in what she was doing. He kept on asking her questions about certain ingredients. But, like most boys, he got bored pretty quickly. The three friends went outside to play. Billy wanted to play football, but the girls were not so keen.

Gail was surprised when her husband arrived home a couple of hours before his shift was supposed to end. As per their normal routine, she offered her cheek so that he could kiss it.

'You're home early, George,' she noted.

George picked up the kettle, gave it a swish and decided that there was not enough water in it so went to fill it up. 'Hmm?' he said absently

'I was just saying that I wasn't expecting you home until about half past seven, when your shift finished'.

'Would you like a cup of tea?' he asked.

Gail nodded and watched as he returned to kettle to the gas ring on the stove. For some reason she got an uneasy feeling in her stomach. Some bad news was about to come from her husband.

'I'm making a fish pie for dinner,' she said.

'Nice,' George replied distractedly. He stood by the stove waiting for the kettle to boil.

'A watched kettle never boils,' said Gail.

'Hmm?' George grunted.

'What is it, George?' asked Gail. 'Although you are standing there, you don't seem to be with us.'

George appeared to ponder how he was going to break his news to his wife. 'Although we have suffered some bombing here in Cornwall – especially the ones dropped just up the road in Camborne, a few days ago – but it's been a lot worse in the cities, in particular London.' Gail stood there waiting for the punchline to come. 'There's been a lot of casualties coming back from the frontline, Gail, and they are in a terrible state. They are near to death. London hospitals are calling out for skilled surgeons to transfer to them to assist with the cases. I believe that every available surgeon should be called upon to do their duty and I have agreed to transfer to London. I'm so sorry that I did not discuss this with you, darling, but the decision had to be confirmed today.'

'Of course, you must go, George,' said Gail, although her face was probably saying something completely different. 'You are the best surgeon in the country. If anyone can fix up our brave boys, then you will. Just promise me one thing, George'.

'Name it,' said George.

'Promise me that you will stay safe,' ordered Gail.

'I promise, sweetheart,' George replied. 'I promise.'

George dropped Billy and Danielle to their homes. When he came back, they sat Laura down at the table and explained her dad's decision to transfer to London. Although she could understand the reason behind it, she did not want her father to leave them. She ran around to his side of the table and flung her arms around his neck.

'I don't want you to go, daddy,' she cried.

'Look, Sweetpea,' said George. 'This war will be over soon, and I'll be back, and you'll hardly notice I've been gone.'

'But I've been speaking to some of the evacuees at school, and they've been telling me how bad the bombing was in London,' Laura sniffed. 'I don't want them to drop bombs on you.'

'London is a very big city, Sweetpea,' said George, looking at his wife for help.

'I'm sure that Hitler thinks that he has destroyed

London with all those bombs we've been hearing about in the reports,' said Gail. 'I don't think he'll be returning anytime soon. I'm sure that your father is right and that this war will soon be over'.

'But what if it isn't?' Laura said tearfully. 'What if it goes on and on and Hitler does send his planes back on bombing raids'.

'Do you really think our brave lads will let Germany do that?' George said. 'Our boys are going to defeat those German no-hopers and send them back with their tails between their legs. That's if they don't kill them first'.

'George!' Gail said reproachfully.

'Just saying that our guys are going to show those Nazi bast...' George felt his wife look at him, '...beasts a thing or two and we will defeat them. I know that we will defeat them. But I need to go to London, Sweetpea, and patch up our soldiers and thank them for what they are doing for us'.

Laura was now sat upon her dad's knee. 'I understand that, daddy, and you're right. You've got to do all you can to help them. I'm immensely proud of you, daddy. And I'm very proud of you, too, mummy. Like me, you probably wanted daddy not to go, but then realised that if these poor men have any chance at all, then daddy is the man to help them.'

Both Mr and Mrs Hadley were choked with emotion at what their daughter had just said. George cuddled his daughter. Gail pulled herself together.

'I'd better get dinner ready,' she said standing up. 'Can you set the table, please, honey?'

'Yes, mummy,' Laura replied. She got down from her father's knee and walked over to the kitchen drawer that housed the cutlery. She looked up at the kitchen clock and saw that it was well after six o'clock.

Suddenly a loud bang reverberated around her head followed by a piercing scream, and Laura fell to the floor.

CHAPTER TEN

The first memory Cora had about her early life was being struck by her father when she was three years old. She thought it was because she had spilled a little water on the floor. She remembered going back to her bedroom, lying on the bed and crying herself to sleep.

The dream she had then seemed very real. It was about this house that had these funny ornaments outside; like extraordinarily little men with this grotesque smile on their faces, and an overwhelming colour of red and blue. Although the looked hideous, Cora found them funny and decided that she liked them.

What was special about the house, Cora had no idea. She could not remember seeing the house before. It did not belong to any family member as far as she was aware.

'Hello,' said a voice in her head said. Cora's eyes sprung open, and she looked around her bedroom.

'Can you hear me?' There was no one there.

'I hear you,' Cora thought back. She did not speak out loud. As the speaker was in her head, she just assumed that communication would be that way to. 'Who are you?'

'Where are you?' the voice asked ignoring the little girl's question.

'I live in Newton Abbot with my mummy and daddy,' Cora replied.

'Newton Abbot? Where on earth is that?'

'In Devon, I think,' Cora responded.

'Never heard of it,' the voice said. 'How old are you?'

'I'm three,' Cora answered. 'But will be four a couple of weeks before Christmas'.

'My baby was born a couple of weeks before Christmas,' said the voice. 'She would have been three, the same as you'.

'Where is she now?' Cora asked.

'No idea,' sobbed the other. 'She was taken from me just after she was born'.

'That is so sad,' said Cora.

'I know,' cried the voice. 'And now they keep me locked up here like I'm crazy or something.'

'I don't understand,' said Cora.

A loud bang from downstairs made Cora jump and the link with the other voice was broken. She opened her door and listened. She could hear her mother crying downstairs. Cora, tentatively, crept down the stairs.

She found her mother sat against one of the kitchen cupboards. She was in tears and was nursing a bloodied lip. Cora reached up to take the towel from the back of the kitchen chair and walked over to her mum. She passed her the towel.

Her mother pulled her into an embrace. 'I'm so sorry that I agreed to let him bring you into this environment. You don't deserve it, baby,' she sobbed. 'Your mummy should have kept you.'

Now this did not make any sense to the young girl. 'But you're my mummy,' she said.

'I know, dear. I know.'

Cora did not give it any more thought. She learnt quickly to avoid her father, especially when he was *drunk, which was most nights. She became very close to her mother. She loved it when they went for a walk, especially to the park. There were quite a few around Newton Abbot. Her favourite was Forde Park. It was because of the large houses that surrounded it. They were so much bigger and grander than the one she lived in. She kept on imagining herself living in one like a princess. She also played games with her mother; she would ask Cora to count the flowers and add that number to the amount of trees in the park.*

Cora and her mother were in the park about a year after she first saw that house and had the conversation with that strange lady, when a picture of the house flooded back into her mind. She could also see a car. 'What is this place?' said a young girl's voice. Cora had no idea what it was about, but she thought she would try to reach out to whoever was sending this picture.

'I have visions about that house, too,' she sent from her head. She got something mumbled back and then something about not having any friends. **'I have no friends either,' she responded.** 'I know. Will you be my friend?'

'Okay,' came the very clear reply and then it went silent.

CHAPTER ELEVEN

Cora loved school. She liked all the subjects, although she struggled a lot with English, she was very clever when it came to math. She got the answers to sums way before the older children in the class and, sometimes, before the teacher could work it out. Her teacher, Mr Pearson, was very impressed by her. He tested her on long division and complicated multiplication, and she always got the answer very quickly and with relatively little working out. He asked her once how she did it and she replied that she could just see the answer.

It was her English that was letting her down. Her spelling was atrocious, and her grammar was less than desired, but she showed willing and could form a sentence.

She was a popular girl who made friend easy. Even the older children wanted to play with her at breaktime. She was chatty, very chatty, which did get her into trouble in class a few times. And some of those who were the same age as her thought that she was bossy. To be fair to the young girl she did not suffer fools gladly. She felt that they should be doing what they were told and if Mr Pearson was unable to control them then she had to.

Cora loved the school and its draughty old walls and wooden roof. She knew that it was built about sixty years ago and needed repair. It became a junior school in nineteen twenty-nine. Cora found it wonderous in winter when the rain was dripping through the roof. Buckets were placed beneath the drips to collect the water. The desks were laid out in straight lines and the younger children sat in the front while the older ones were at the back.

She knew why she enjoyed school so much; it was because she was away from her father. He currently worked at the railway station in Newton. They could not afford a car, but he would walk the two miles to work. It was different on the way home from work, as he would visit a couple of pubs before arriving at the house blind drunk, normally incoherent, and beating his wife because his meal was a little cold.

Cora was sat in class one day; she was trying to write a story about what she would do if she had a lot of money. Mr Pearson had asked them to write a short story. She wracked her brains but couldn't come up with much except to buy a house where her mum and she could live, and her violent father could never find them. Suddenly the other girl's voice returned inside her head.

'Three hundred and seventy-eight divided by fifty-four?' the girl said. 'How on earth is anyone expected to know that? Why would anyone want to know that?'

'It's seven,' Cora whispered back.
She looked around but none of her classmates were looking at her, so she knew that she had said it with her mind and not out loud.
'Seven?' the girl queried.
'Seven,' Cora confirmed confidently. She waited for her new "friend" to get back in touch.
'Who are you?'
'My name is Cora. You've finally worked out how to talk then?'
'Not all of us are as clever as you,' the girl replied defensively.
'No offence,' Cora replied apologetically.

'So, what is one hundred and forty-seven divided by seven?' the voice asked.
'Twenty-one,' Cora replied instantly.
'You're good at maths,' said the girl who was obviously writing the answer down because Cora could see a picture of it.
'My maths is brilliant,' Cora replied boastfully. 'My English, on the other hand, is not very good. I don't know what a compound sentence is.'
'It's where two basic phrases are joined by a word, usually and but or for, and a comma or semi colon,' the voice answered. 'For example, the pirate lost the map, but still managed to find the treasure.'
The girl was obviously waiting for a response. 'How on earth do you know that at eight years old? I'll

keep to the maths thanks,' Cora finally replied, and she heard the other person laugh. Then it went quiet. Her friend must have gone. Then she realised that she didn't even get the other girl's name.
The conversation had actually helped her with her story as she came up with an idea that, if she had

the money, she would help other children who would be less well off than she and her mother were.

A few days later when she was up in her room playing, the young girl came back into her head.
'Hello? Are you there?' it asked.
'Yes, I'm here,' Cora replied.
'Thank you for telling me how to communicate with you properly,' she said. 'It's a lot easier now than visualising and speaking the words out loud.'
'I bet you're getting less looks and comments from people now?' Cora laughed.
'You can say that again, Cora,' the girl replied joining in with the laughter. 'I only talk out loud, now, when I'm in my bedroom by myself.'
'You know something else that's funny? I don't even know your name,' Cora said.
'It's Laura,' the girl replied.
'That's a pretty name,' said Cora. 'Where do you live?'

'Cornwall,' replied Laura. 'A pretty village called Bridge. It's near Portreath.'
'Never heard of it,' said Cora.
'What? Cornwall?' Laura asked.
'No. I've heard of Cornwall, just not the other part of what you said,' Cora explained.
'Where do you live again?' Laura asked.
'Ogwell. The nearest town is Newton Abbot,' Cora answered.
'Are you saying Hogwell?' Laura said sounding confused.
'No. Ogwell,' Cora smiled.
'That's what I said,' came the response. 'Hogwell."
'Drop the "H",' laughed Cora.
'Oh! Drop the "H". Ogwell. That sounds a weird place to live.'
'Nearly as weird as Portreath,' Cora shot back.

Out of the blue another voice came into her head. It was another one she recognised from before, belonging to the older girl or young woman.
'Who are you talking to?' she asked.
'Laura,' Cora replied.
'And who is Laura?' the other girl asked.
'She's my friend,' Cora replied. She directed the next part of the conversation to Laura. 'We can be

friends can't we, Laura?'
'Of course, we can be friends,' replied Laura.
'Why can't I hear her?' the other voice asked.
'I don't know,' said Cora. 'I wonder if she can hear you?'
'I think I've located her,' said the other.
'Can you hear another voice, Laura?' Cora asked.
'It's like a teenage girl's voice.'
'No,' replied Laura. 'I haven't heard that other voice. So, how can you talk to her, and I cannot?'
'I guess it's because she hasn't found you yet,' Cora explained. She just told me that she has found

you. Perhaps it is because you are so new to this that you do not know how to let her in to your mind.'
 'Maybe you're right,' Laura sighed. 'Seeing as I've only just got used to speaking with you, I haven't been able to let her in yet.'
'If it is the same child, then I can see someone listening outside her door,' said the other voice.
'She's just told me that someone is listening outside your door,' Cora repeated to Laura
 'What do you mean she's told you there's someone listening at my door?' said Laura angrily. It went quiet.
'Well, she's a stroppy kid,' said the other voice.
'Bit like someone else I know when they do not get their own way,' said Cora.
'Are you suggesting that I'm stroppy?' asked the

voice.

'Well, you do get in a huff when the conversation does not go your way,' Cora pointed out.

'You can't begrudge me that after what I've been through,' the other protested.

'What have you been through? I've asked you so many times before, but you never tell me,' Cora persisted.

'And now is not the right time,' the girl replied. 'I have to go. My jailer is back to give me orders.'

'Your jailer?' Cora asked but the other voice had gone.

CHAPTER TWELVE

Cora was very attentive one day at school. It was a lesson she was thoroughly enjoying. It was about deciphering codes. There was a row of numbers that spelt out a word. So, 1, 16, 16, 12, 5 became apple. She was crazy about this lesson. She was soon setting codes for her friends to crack. She even got Mr Pearson to set codes that were a bit different. He wrote 2,3,5,7 what is the next number? Cora looked at it and wrote 11 next to it.
'Why eleven, Cora?' Mr Pearson asked.
'Because they are prime numbers,' Cora replied.
'That's very good,' Mr Pearson praised. 'How about this one?' He took his pen and wrote the following; 1, 8, 15, 22, 29, 36...
Cora took the pen from her teacher and wrote 43. Mr Pearson nodded and asked her to explain her reasons for selecting that number.
'Because you are adding seven to the last number to make the next,' Cora explained.

'Very good, Cora,' said Mr Pearson. 'Let me make it a bit more difficult.' He wrote 1, 1, 2, 3, 5, 8, 13, 21. 'What are the next 3 numbers?'
Cora looked at the sequence of numbers for a good couple of seconds. 'Thirty-four, fifty-five and eighty-nine. You are adding the last two numbers together to get the next one.'

'Wow! You're good at this, Cora,' said Mr Pearson. 'I don't think I've ever known anyone get these so quickly. How do you do it?'
'I can just see a pattern,' replied Cora. 'It just jumps out at me.'
Mr Pearson wondered for a moment. He looked at Cora and looked at the blackboard. He stood up and picked up a piece of chalk. He started writing numbers on the board. Cora watched as he wrote 7, 13, 25, 45 and 75. He sat back down again. 'Now this one had me wracking my brains for quite a while. Now, I'm not expecting you to get this at once, Cora but give it a go,' he said to the young girl and held out the piece of chalk.
Cora took the chalk and went over to the board. She looked at the numbers; and looked. She could feel the stares of all her classmates but dismissed the pressure immediately to concentrate on the task. Mr Pearson sat in his chair looking at the girl. Was he pushing her too hard? He knew that she was very clever and very proficient with numbers, but this was advanced mathematics. Perhaps he was expecting too much from her.
A little under five minutes later Cora wrote one hundred and seventeen to complete the answer. She walked back to the teacher's desk and placed the chalk on the table. She went back to her seat.
Mr Pearson looked astonished. He looked from the

board to Cora and back again. He knew the answer was correct but could not comprehend how the young girl had worked I out so quickly.

Cora put her hand up and Mr Pearson acknowledged her. 'It's a multiplication puzzle sequence,' she said. 'It's the number added to by two multiplied by three, which is six so, seven add six is thirteen. Then you have to increase the multiplication to the next number so, three times four, which is twelve. Thirteen plus twelve is twenty-five. Then its four times five – twenty – twenty added to twenty-five is forty-five and so on and so on.'

'Perhaps, Cora, it should be you teaching the class and not me,' Mr Pearson joked.

'You're better at the sentences and history than I am, Sir,' Cora joked back.

Cora felt embarrassed as she felt the whole class still gazing at her in awe. Marion, a girl the same age as Cora, who had curly red hair and freckles, and sat next to Cora just stared and stared at her friend. 'Wow! Cora. You're very clever,' Marion said. 'Would you like to come to my house, after school, and we can play at breaking codes.' Normally Cora would have jumped at the chance as it meant not going home in case her father was there. She also wanted to share this new skill with her other friend, Laura. 'Unfortunately, Marion, I have something on later,' she said. 'How about I come over at the weekend and we can play longer at it?'

Marion's face lit up at the prospect of spending even longer with her friend. 'That's a very good idea,' she said. 'I'll tell my mummy later.'

When Cora arrived home, she was relieved to see that her father was not there. Her mother was in the kitchen preparing the meal for later; steak and kidney pie, her favourite. She did her chores which included folding up the washing that was on the airer and drying the dishes. She watched her mother preparing the food and noticed for the first time that she looked nothing like her. She knew that a child would never fully resemble their parents, but she didn't have any of her mother's structure in her; their eyes were different shapes and colour; the noses were different; hair colouring, bone structure and, now she came to think of it, she did look a little like her father, which made her angry. Why could she not have just have her mother's good looks.

'Cora? Are you there?' Laura's voice flooded her mind in tears. As she had completed her tasks, she asked for permission to go to her bedroom and play.

As she closed her door, Laura's crying erupted in her mind. 'Help me, Cora. Please help me.'

'What's wrong?' Cora asked concerned.

'My parents are having a blazing row,' Laura replied.

'What about?' said Cora.

'Me. I think,' said Laura. 'They were called into school by my teacher, Mrs Miller. She thinks I'm a gifted child and wants the best for me. She believes that with the right education I could go far.'

'And your mum and dad don't want this for you?' Cora asked incredulously.

'It was when Mrs Miller mentioned my imaginary friend that it started to go downhill,' Laura explained.

'I'm guessing it would have done,' Cora agreed sympathetically.

'I believe they both want what's best for me, but they just cannot get it into their heads about me speaking with you.'

'What do you want?' Cora asked.

'What do you mean?' Laura asked back.

'From your education, what do you want to get out of it?' Cora asked again. Laura gave it some thought. She took a little while thinking about all the options. 'Are you still there?'

'I'm thinking,' Laura responded. 'I would like to see how far I can go. Mrs Miller believes I have the ability and I would like to repay her faith in me.'

'Then, somehow, you have to convince your mum and dad,' Cora replied matter-of-factly.
'That's easier said than done,' Laura laughed.
'I didn't say it was going to be easy,' Cora laughed along. 'If it makes you feel any better, I do not believe that my mum and dad are my real parents. Well, certainly my mother.'
'Really?' Laura asked in shock.
'Really,' Cora confirmed. 'I'm eight years old and being a girl, I would have thought I would start to look like my mummy. My friend Marion has some of her mother's looks.'
'Hmmm,' Laura said thoughtfully. 'Now that you mention it, I don't think I look like mine either.'
They both appeared to take some time to digest this information. Cora started to wonder if she and Laura were related in some way, but she could not work out how. She lived in Ogwell with her parents, and Laura lived in that funny named place in Cornwall with her mum and dad. It just was not possible.

'Are you still there, Laura?' Cora knew her voice would interrupt Laura's thoughts.

'I'm still here, Cora,' Laura replied at once. 'I'm going to need your help, Cora. I can tell you now that my mother will write to the school probably requesting that I change class.'
'Okay,' Cora responded excitedly. 'Are you afraid of pain?'
'WHAT?' Laura replied startled.
'Are you afraid of pain?' said Cora. 'Because I'm coming up with an idea, but it will mean you being hit with the stick.'
'Perhaps it was not a good idea to ask you for help,' said Laura sounding very unsure.
'Do you want my help or not?' Cora was very confident, and she knew Laura would decide to go along with it.
'Okay?' Laura replied still sounding unsure. 'Is it going to hurt much?'
'Only for a few minutes. I promise,' said Cora.
So, the two girls' made the plan that would help Laura. Both of them knew that it was going to hurt one

of them, but Laura desperately wanted to get back into Mrs Miller's class. They went over and over the plan until it was perfect.
'Hey! If it makes you feel any better, my mummy and daddy argue all the time,' said Cora. 'My dad likes his drink. He likes a lot of it and then doesn't know what he is doing.'
'It doesn't make me feel any better, Cora,' said

Laura. 'My parents rarely argue but it concerns me that you are caught in a family like that. It makes me feel...I don't know...'
'Lucky?' Cora suggested.
'No. Upset for you,' said Laura.
'Don't worry for me, Laura,' said Cora. 'I can look out for myself.'
'With my help, Cora. With my help,' Laura came back with, and Cora smiled reassured that her new best friend would always be there for her. She heard her mother shouting to her that tea was ready, and she bounded downstairs.
'Pour me a whiskey,' her father growled.

She groaned inwardly. She should have known that her father would be home. She went and poured the drink. 'Here you are, father,' she said placing it down in front of him.
Her father looked at it in disgust. 'What is that?' he said sarcastically.
'It's your drink, daddy,' Cora replied confused.
'How much do I usually have in my glass, Cora?' he asked.
'About halfway,' Cora replied realising her mistake. Her father, drunkenly, got to his feet, and picked up us glass before crouching down to her height and thrusting the glass towards her face. 'Does this look like half-full to you?'
Cora shook her head. 'I just thought...'

'Thought what?' her father demanded. 'That I had had enough? I'll decide that, little madame.' He stood up and she thought that would be it, but suddenly he swung his arm so that his open palm connected with her cheek. Cora went flying to the floor.
'Ouch!' she heard Laura's voice say and wondered why her friend had said that.
'Go to your room,' her father bellowed. 'I'm sick of the sight of you.'
Cora went crying to her room. She knew that Laura was trying to contact her, but she had managed to block her. She could also feel that other person trying to invade her thoughts, but she was just about able to repel them. All she could hear was that the voice said 'I'm so sorry. I had no idea.'
Cora was still sobbing, and her stomach rumbling when her mother brought her up some food later. She knew that her mother had risked doing this.
'Don't worry, Cora,' her mother said as if reading her mind. 'He's fast asleep in his armchair. I know how much you like steak and kidney pie.'
'I love your steak and kidney pie, mummy,' said Cora as she cut into the crispy pastry and put that and piece of steak onto her fork before raising it to her mouth and popping it inside. The flavour was instant. Her mother put some sort of herb on the meat. She

thought it was thyme but would not want to swear on it. She savoured the taste as she masticated on the meat. 'This is fantastic, mummy.'

Her mother smiled down at her. 'He's not a bad man, Cora,' she said. 'He used to be kind and loving – on some of the better days he still is. It hurt him hard when we lost Danicl.'

Cora stopped chewing and looked agog at her mother. 'Daniel?' she asked in a whisper.

'Daniel,' her mother confirmed. Cora could see that she was still smiling but her eyes were definitely starting to water. 'He was so proud when our son was born. He had plans and dreams for him. He was allowed to hold him. And then Daniel was struck down with meningitis and died within the week of being born. We had him buried in the cemetery just down the road.'

Cora had been holding the fork with some food on it near to her mouth whilst her mother was telling this story. She did not notice the meat had fallen off and landed back on the plate. 'That is so sad,' she said. 'I didn't know that I had a brother.'

'Your father never recovered from his death,' said her mum. 'And then he was accused of something by someone he knew but they ended up in a mental asylum. That was when he turned the drink. He said it helped him to numb the pain.'

'But you suffered the loss, as well, mummy,' said Cora. 'You must have found it hard.'

'The dear Lord works in mysterious ways, Cora,' said her mother. 'He wanted Daniel to be with Him, and then he granted us you. Now that was a special day, Cora. I wore my special dress. Your father had wanted a boy but appeared to be happy with a girl. He even stopped drinking for a while.'

'So, it's my fault he started drinking again,' said Cora.

'Oh, no, honey,' said her mother. 'He lost his job. A job that he loved to do which made him return to the bottle. It had nothing to do with you.' Cora was not convinced but did not say anything. Instead, she went back to her plate of food. Her mother reached up and touched her faced. Cora winced. 'I'll put some foundation on that tomorrow to cover it up.' She got up and walked over to the door. 'Don't hate your father, Cora. I know that deep down he loves you.'

Her mother left the room, so Cora carried on eating. It was delicious. She finished every last morsal.

She quietly made her way downstairs. Listening to her dad's snoring coming from the front room, she probably could have made a lot of noise. A bomb would not have woken him from his drunken stupor.

Her mum was in the kitchen tidying up. She put her

plate on the draining board. She opened a drawer and pulled out a tea-towel and started drying the dishes for her mum. Her mother smiled down at her.
'Can I lay some flowers on my big brother's grave?' Cora asked.
Her mother picked up Cora's plate, knife and fork and put it in the bowl which held the soapy water. Although most of the suds had disappeared. 'Of course, we can, Sweetie,' Cora's mother said. 'I'm finishing early at the Manor House in a couple of days, I can meet you from school and we can walk down to the church, and I can point the grave out to you.'
'I'd like that very much, mummy,' said Cora.

Cora wanted school to finish quickly that day. Even sums could not hold her attention. She didn't know what it was, but she was quite excited about seeing where her brother was buried. She suddenly let out a small yelp and said "ouch" as she felt something strike the palm of her hand.

'Are you okay, Cora?' whispered Marion.
'I think that I've just been stung,' said Cora.
'What are you saying ouch for? It's not you that's just been hit,' growled Laura.
'It felt like I did,' said Cora.
'What did you say?' Miss Cummings demanded looking very angry and Cora was surprised that she

could hear the teacher
'Nothing, Miss Cummings,' said Laura.
'Go back to your seat and write one hundred times "I will not contradict Miss Cummings again,"' said the teacher.
'Yes, Miss Cummings,' replied Laura.
'Say "unless you've made a mistake" back to her,' Cora said in Laura's head
'Unless you made a mistake,' Laura said out loud.
'LAURA HADLEY COME BACK HERE,' Miss Cummings shouted.
'Are you enjoying this, Cora?' Laura whispered.
'It was all part of our plan,' Cora shot back.

'You're not the one being hit,' Laura retorted.
'WHO ARE YOU TALKING TO?' Miss Cummings demanded.
'Myself,' Laura responded quietly.
'Hold out your hand,' ordered Miss Cummings
Cora felt the sharp pain across her palm twice.
'Stop it,' Cora cried.
'STOP IT,' Laura yelled. 'You're making Cora cry.
Cora realised that it had gone quiet in the classroom. She groaned inwardly as she became aware that she must have screamed her last words out loud. Even Mr Pearson was looking at her with his mouth agape. Before she knew what was happening, the teacher was escorting her to the office. He sat her down on a chair.

'What was that about, Cora?'
'What, Sir?'
'It sounded like you were talking to someone who was not in the room,' said Mr Pearson.

Cora realised that she only had a few seconds to come up with a believable story. 'My daddy is an alcoholic and the rows and beatings he has with my mummy,' she began. 'Some nights I cannot sleep because of the fighting. I'm so sorry, Mr Pearson, but I must have fallen asleep in class.'
Mr Pearson looked at the young girl. He could tell that she was not telling the complete truth, but the story was probably factual. He could make out a bruise on her cheek which someone, her mother more than likely, had tried to cover up with make-up. He caught sight of her hand. There were red marks on her palm which were developing welts. He gently lifted her hand up to examine it. These marks could not have been caused by her father or mother as they were fresh. 'How did you get these marks, Cora?'
'My father strikes me with a stick when I'm naughty,' Cora replied.
'They look pretty fresh, Cora,' Mr Pearson pointed out.
'It was this morning, Sir,' Cora responded quickly.
Mr Pearson just nodded and let go of her hand. He was not going to get the truth out of the girl. He

knew that. He just had to hope that her mother would collect her from school.

For that he got his wish. Cora waited as the two adults were talking about her. She kept seeing them look over at her; sometimes individually and sometimes together. Her mother nodded occasionally. Cora could see the flowers, bright yellow daffodils, poking their heads out of her mother's bag. They must have been in conversation for a good fifteen minutes before they shook hands and her mother started to approach her.

They walked down the road together before turning right and heading up the lane towards the church. Her mother opened the gate for them to walk through. They followed the path to the right and her mother led the way to a small grave in the right-hand corner very near to the drystone wall. When they got there, her mum bent down and pulled some weeds that were growing near the headstone. 'Hello, Baby,' she said.

Cora crouched down so she was level with the grave and started to read the inscription. DANIEL CULVER BORN 14th OCTOBER 1927 DIED 20th OCTOBER 1927. BELOVED SON

It brought tears to her eyes. She asked her mummy if she could take the flowers from the bag and lay them on the grave. Mrs Culver nodded and smiled. Cora took them from the bag and arranged them into a neat bunch before laying them on the grave. Whilst she was doing this Mrs Culver had the opportunity to see her daughter's hand. The mark the teacher had mentioned was still there, but it was fading.

'Did you get the cane in school today, Cora?' Mrs Culver asked.

'No, mummy,' Cora replied.

She did not raise her voice and she kept herself calm. 'Mr Pearson told me about what happened in class earlier. He said that you started to shout, "stop it" and those marks appeared on your hand.'

'I fell asleep and had a bad dream, mummy, that's all,' said Cora, but it was obvious to her mother that the young girl did not want to discuss it.

'He said that you told him that your father hit you this morning,' said Mrs Culver quite casually. Her daughter did not respond. She decided to plough on. 'We both know that that was not true. Your father has never struck you with a stick.'

'No. Just his hand,' said the little girl.

That one did hit home, and the mother smiled sadly at the daughter. 'Okay, you got me there.'

They tended the grave some more making it tidy.

'You wouldn't believe me if I told you, anyway, mummy,' Cora said.

'Of course, I would believe you,' said Mrs Culver.

Mrs Culver waited. She knew that Cora would soon tell her. 'I have this friend,' Cora began after a while. 'I've never seen her, but I speak with her through my mind. You're going to think I'm crazy, aren't you? Well, my friend got smacked with the stick at school today, and I felt it.'

'But that's not possible, Cora,' said her mother.

'I'm just telling you what happened, mummy,' Cora simply replied.

'Can this friend feel your pain as well?' Mrs Culver asked.

Cora shrugged. 'I guess so.'

Cora did not look at her mother. If she had done so she would have seen the look of concern etched on it.

CHAPTER THIRTEEN

Cora was invited to Marion's birthday party. It was taking place on the Saturday. Cora was extremely excited. She could not wait to attend. Her mum had helped choose a present. Cora knew that Marion loved playing with dolls, so she had chosen a small tea set.

Mrs Culver had been thinking about nothing else than what her daughter had divulged at the graveside the other day. She had dared not raise it with her husband. There was no one else she could talk to. If she told Mr Pearson, then he would get the authorities involved. Likewise, if she went to her doctor to discuss, then he would also alert the institute.

The thing was, Mrs Culver did not believe that her daughter was mad. She could have fallen asleep like she said she had. However, that would not explain the marks that had appeared on her hand. And to be honest, they did like someone had hit her with a stick. She could not think of a logical explanation of why they would appear. Cora admitted that no one had struck her so how had those marks appear? Mrs Culver could not understand it. If you agree that no one had struck her daughter, then she had to admit that her daughter's explanation must be the only one. But how can someone that Cora had never met or, for that matter, knew transfer their pain to her daughter?

Overall, though, the day had no lasting effect on Cora. She had communicated with Laura that evening. Laura could not believe that Cora had felt her pain even though Cora was screaming in her head to try and get the teacher to stop. She found it interesting that marks had appeared on Cora's hand. And, for once, even Cora was flummoxed by this. They tried to come up with a reason on how this could happen, but each idea became more ludicrous than the one before. The last one involved Cora somehow managing to transport herself to Laura's classroom just in time to get hit with the stick before transporting herself back to her own classroom. The only thing Cora could say was that it was great fun coming up with these ideas. Laura certainly had a vivid imagination.

Fortunately, it was dry and bright when the party began. As soon as the doorbell rang, Marion rushed down and hugged her friend. Mrs Culver had agreed to stay and help. Cora handed Marion her present and she was allowed to open it. She loved the little tea set and pulled Cora into another hug.

'Let's go and play with it,' she yelled excitedly.
'Don't forget your other friends will be here soon,' Marion's mother called after to two disappearing girls.
'I won't,' Marion called back.
'You cannot blame her for being excited, Mrs Tucker,' laughed Mrs Culver.
'I'm glad it is only once a year, Mrs Culver,' Mrs Tucker said joining in with the laughter. 'Thank you so much for that tea set. I know that she's going to have many years of fun with that. She's been pestering me to buy her one for a couple of years now.'
'I used to have a tea set when I was her age,' Mrs Culver reminisced. 'I would play with it for hours and hours. Mind you, it taught me the correct etiquette.'
'If only some of the younger generation knew about etiquette today, Mrs Culver,' said Mrs Tucker.

'How right you are, Mrs Tucker. How right you are,' Mrs Culver agreed.
Marion had sat her dolls on chairs, in her bedroom. There were four of them seated around a small table. Marion and Cora were having so much fun.
'Would Miss Culver care for a cup of tea?' Marion

asked.

'That would be most kind, Miss Tucker,' Cora replied in a snobbish voice which made Marion crease up with laughter. 'I do believe, Miss Tucker, that you are spilling the tea.' This made Marion laugh even harder. Cora stood up from her kneeling position. She continued in her posh voice. 'Well! The service in this café is appalling.'

Marion rolled on the floor crying with laughter. Cora knelt on the floor quite heavily, joining her friend in laughing. She felt a pain and said "ouch!" but did not think much about it.

Unbeknown to Cora, Laura had been running in the garden at exactly the same time. Billy was with her, and they were playing tag. She was in a good mood because she was going to back in Mrs Miller's class. She

was also aware that her parents were arranging for her to an assessment. That was always going to be on the cards after what had happened in Miss Cumming's room.

Billy had just touched her on the arm. 'You're it,' he shouted.

'You just wait, Billy Penhale,' Laura responded gleefully. 'I'll get you.' She chased after him but tripped over a something, a rock protruding from grass she thought, and fell on the gravelled pathway. The pain was instant. Billy rushed over concerned and tried to help her up.

'Wow!' Billy exclaimed. 'Look at that blood. It's like a lake.'
To be fair Billy had exaggerated slighted. It was more like a very shallow puddle. They both looked at the deep gash just below the knee from where the blood was seeping.
'Go and fetch my mother, Billy,' Laura instructed.

Cora picked herself up. She laughed in embarrassment and thought that Marion would be about to joke about what had just happened. But then she caught sight of her friend's face. She looked horrified and was pointing at her Cora's leg. She looked down and saw the blood oozing out of a gash.
'Mummy!' Marion yelled. 'Mrs Culver.'
Mrs Tucker arrived first with Mrs Culver just a few paces behind. They both looked at Marion, and then towards where she was pointing. They saw the blood at the same time.
'I only knelt on the floor, mummy,' Cora said in her defence. 'And there was nothing around for me to kneel on.'
Marion nodded her agreement. 'What Cora said is true,' she sniffed. 'I was with her the whole time. She just dealt down and said "ouch" before standing up again and we saw the blood.'
'So, you did kneel on something then, Cora?' her mother questioned.

'No, mother,' Cora replied. 'I thought I had twisted my knee when I knelt down but there is nothing on the floor to kneel upon.'

'I'll go fetch a cloth,' said Mrs Tucker.
Mrs Culver bent down to examine the cut on her daughter's leg. She could see a graze from where she must have knelt, but the cut was slightly down from that, and the only logical explanation was a sharp object. However, like both children had said, she could not see anything in the near vicinity. Mrs Tucker returned holding a damp cloth. Mrs Culver took it from her and began to wipe Cora's leg. She felt Cora flinch as she dabbed at the wound. It looked much worse than it actually was. 'It doesn't look too bad, does it?' she soothed.
'I brought this,' Mrs Tucker said holding out another piece of cloth. 'It's the closest thing I have to a bandage.'
'That will do just fine, Mrs Tucker,' Mrs Culver said. She then heard two gasps and when she turned to look at the wound, it had healed itself and all that was left was a slight reddening. Mrs Culver looked incredulously at where the wound was. She switched her gaze to Mrs Tucker who was looking astonished. She quickly cast a glance towards Marion who jest looked dumbfounded.
'Can I go and play again, mummy?' Cora asked.

Her mother just nodded as she stood up. She followed Mrs Tucker back down to the kitchen.
'I don't think I've ever seen anything like that before,' Mrs Tucker said.
'Me either,' Mrs Culver replied. 'I sincerely hope that we can keep this between us, Mrs Tucker?'
'Of course, we can, Mrs Culver,' said Mrs Tucker. 'To be honest, Mrs Culver, I do not think many people would believe what we have just seen.'

But in a small village like Ogwell, news certainly gets around, and it was not long before everyone appeared to know. People would sneak looks at Cora. The younger children started spreading rumours that she was a witch. Marion became even closer to Cora. She had been there and witnessed it. She became very defensive of her friend, especially when the children wanted to look at Cora's leg. The only person who did not know was Mr Culver. Until one day he came home extremely late, and in a very drunk state. Cora had been asleep but was woken up by the noise. She could make out what her father was bellowing but not what her mother was

meekly replying. She could hear the blows landing on her poor mother.
'When were you going to bloody tell me, huh?' her

father shouted although it came across quite slurred. Her mother must have responded because Mr Culver continued. 'She is a freak, that one. I warned you; I did. I told you that no good would come out of taking her away from that home.'

This piqued Cora's interest. She quietly got out of bed and opened her door. She crept along the landing and started to descend the stairs.

'We've got no idea what her bloody mother was like,' Mr Culver was still in full flow. 'For all we know she could be a madwoman, and her daughter is starting to take after her.'

From the shadows, Cora could tell that her father was trying unsuccessfully to take off his boots. She almost laughed out loud when he fell over. He just lay on the floor. Another shadow joined the first and she knew instantly that her mother was helping him.

'The men at work are telling me that their children are saying that she's a witch,' Mr Culver continued. 'Perhaps she is. I'm going to get her examined, Gloria. If we don't then we could end up being the laughingstock of this community.'

'We already are because of you,' Cora muttered under her breath.

'She is just a child, Richard,' she heard her mother say.

'The child of the devil,' Mr Culver cursed.

'You've got that right,' whispered Cora vehemently, and she thought she heard her mother laugh.

'So, you think it's funny, you slut,' he said drunkenly. 'I'm gonna get her seen to before she gets worse and kills us both.'

'Well, one of you,' Cora said. She had heard enough and went back to bed.

CHAPTER FOURTEEN

And her father was good to his word. He arranged for the doctor to come and visit. She had not spoken with Laura about her problems as her best friend appeared to be having problems of her own. Namely, Miss Cummings had had her referred as being insane. It did not seem fair to burden Laura with her own trouble.

The doctor did all these tests and a couple of weeks later his report declared that he required a second opinion and was referring the case to a specialist in Exeter. This was arranged for two weeks before Christmas.

The one good thing to come out of it was that she hardly saw her father. And when she did, he made sure that he kept out of her way. However, this meant that the abuse her mother had to suffer increased. When Cora came down in the mornings, she could see her mother's split lip and bruises. When she went to bed at night, she could hear the shouting.

It did appear to calm down a bit before the festive season got into full swing. Mr Culver was flat out at work, and this led to him having less time in the pub. Mrs Culver kept on mentioning to him about money for Cora's Christmas present. They were going to get her a microscope despite Mr Culver's protestations about his daughter being insane.

He was working all hours to pay for the Christmas Fayre that he enjoyed with his family. He preferred the alcohol that was included. His wife usually bought this the week before the big day. However, one day his mind was more on his wife and daughter. It was the day of her assessment at Exeter Mental Institute. He was sure that his child was insane. There could be no other explanation. He had since learnt about the marks on her hand. What had he done to deserve this? He had lost his son and now he had a mad daughter. The only redeeming feature was that he knew that she was not his. Well, not biologically anyway.

He was with a team that was mending a piece of track near Kingskerswell. There was five of them. They mainly got on quite well and worked well together.

'It's Christmas bonus pay day at the end of the week,' the supervisor said. 'Anyone fancy joining in with a poker game that's happening?'

'I'm in,' said the first man.

'Me, too,' said the second.

'Count me out,' said the third. 'If I don't take my pay-packet home with me, then my wife won't speak to me.'

'Sounds like a good reason to join the game to me,' laughed the second man.

'Hey, you don't know my wife,' said the third.

'Culver? What about you?' asked the supervisor. Richard had been working and had not heard the conversation. 'What was that, boss?'

'Fancy a card game on Friday?' the supervisor repeated.

'Can't, boss,' Richard explained. 'My wife will need that money to buy the Christmas Fayre.'

'Don't be such a pussy, Culver,' said the supervisor taunting him. 'Who's the boss in your household? A few games of poker won't hurt.'

'And if you lose, your daughter can conjure up some more money with her witchcraft powers,' said the first man.

'What did you just say?' Richard said it quietly but

very forcefully.

'Hey, we all know, Culver, that your offspring is a looney,' said the first man.

Richard moved so quickly, that the first man had no chance to defend himself. Richard knocked him to the ground with his first punch and he then pummelled him with his fists. He kept on doing it until the others suddenly realised what was happening a sprang into action to pull Richard off his colleague.

The first man's face was not a pretty picture by the time they had grabbed Richard Culver from him.

'You're out of here, Culver,' the supervisor threatened.

'I want my union rep,' Culver countered. 'He provoked me.'

'You've half killed him, man,' the supervisor shouted.

'He called my daughter a witch,' Culver ranted.

It was decided by the end of the week that Richard Culver had been provoked but should not have used the force he did in retaliation. It was agreed to move him onto another team working on a different section on the railway.

On the Friday Richard Culver went in to collect his

wages. It was bulging brown packet. He saw his former supervisor walking towards him, and he turned to go.

'Culver,' the supervisor shouted. Culver hesitated before turning around. 'No hard feelings, Culver. As you know, we all gave our witness statements which corresponded with your version of events.' He held out his hand. Richard looked at it before deciding to accept it and they shook. 'Good man. Good man. Now why don't you come and join us for that card game? Management have proved crates of beer.'

The promise of drink made him agree and soon he was playing in the back room playing poker with seven other colleagues. After a couple of hours, and many drinks, Richard Culver had about broken even, perhaps slightly up.

'This is going to be my last hand, gentlemen,' he said. He picked up his five cards. Ace of diamonds and clubs, king of hearts, two and eight of spades. He put in his penny to show that he wanted to play. When it came to his turn, he requested two cards and threw away the eight and two. The dealer dealt him the two new ones. The first was the jack of hearts, but the second one made his heartbeat faster; it was the ace of hearts.

He waited as the man next to the dealer raised the pot by a sixpence which was too much for the chap next to him who threw in his hand. Robert matched the sixpence and raised it by a florin. The next person matched and raised it again by the same amount. The supervisor looked at his cards and then over at the two men. 'I think you're bluffing, gentlemen. I'm in for the florin and raise it a pound.'

This was too much for the person sat next to the supervisor and both he and the dealer chucked in their hands. The first person to raise was looking at his hand again. He matched the pound and raised it a pound. The sweat broke out on Culver's forehead. He looked at his cards; three of a kind. It was a very good hand. Better than any of the hands that had been played so far. He pushed his last two pounds forward to stay in

the game. The one next to him quit which left the supervisor to play.

The supervisor took a swig of beer and looked over at Culver. He had to admit that the drunk man had a good poker face. 'I'm out,' he said finally.

'Looks like it's you and me, Culver,' said the first gambler. 'What you got?'

Culver laid down his cards with a smile on. 'Three lovely aces, my friend,' he smiled.

There were loud cheers and the two sitting next to Richard slapped him on the back. He was just about to go and rake the money towards him when the first gambler spoke. 'Not so fast my friend. You

see I've got nine...' he put his cards down one at a time. '...ten, jack, queen and a king. I believe my straight beats your three of a kind.
Culver stood up abruptly. The table wobbled but did not tip. 'Well played, my friend. And so, gentlemen, I must leave. He picked up the remaining pittance of his wages and put it in his pocket. His thinking was that some money was better than none at all.

When he staggered indoors at home, he knew that by the look on her face, his wife was not going to see it the same way.
'Have you drunk all your wages?' she said accusingly.
'No,' he denied and then laughed. 'I lost most of it in a game of poker.'
'How much, Richard?' Mrs Culver asked.
Richard took out the five coins from his pocket. 'You see,' he said thrusting it towards her face. 'I've got this much left.'
'Oh, Richard,' Gloria sobbed. 'That's not even enough for the rent.'
She went and took her coat from the hook near the door. 'Where are you going?'
'Out,' she said. 'I won't be back for a couple of hours.'
'Going to go and lie on your back again?' said Richard and he hiccupped halfway through.

'One of us has to keep a roof over our heads, Richard,' she replied. 'And you certainly are not capable of doing that.'

She quickly went out the front door and slammed it shut behind her before Culver could reach her and give her yet another thrashing.

Upstairs, Cora had heard it all. It was going to be another great Christmas. She vowed that one day she would take her mum away from all this. Her father was only interested in the drink. He hadn't even asked how she had got on at Exeter. She was being referred to a special hospital in London.

'Merry Christmas,' she said to herself.

CHAPTER FIFTEEN

Cora was looking forward to a couple of days out in

London. She had already been assessed in Exeter and was referred to a psychiatric hospital in the Capital. Although her father worked on the railway, she had never been on a train. She had seen them. Of course, she had seen them, and she loved watching them. She could stand for hours admiring the beautiful steam engines and the freshly painted carriages; yellow and brown. Fortunately, her father had to work so was unable to go with them. They climbed up the steps to the carriage and found their seats. Cora loved the green upholstery and the ornate wooden seats. Her mother pulled the door close behind her. Cora climbed up on the seat and stared out the window. Mrs Culver sat down opposite her and placed her bag on her lap.

Cora had never seen her mother dress so smartly. She was wearing a new dress that she had made herself. It had a floral pattern but, at present, it was being covered by her green mac. She also had a thick green cardigan on as it was still a chilly March. Cora was also allowed to wear her best dress and red cardigan. She had gotten it for Christmas, and she knew

that her mother had made this one also. And that was why she loved it more than anything else. Christmas had been a tense affair. Both sets of grandparents had turned up, so it was agreed that she and her mother would do without any meat, on their Christmas meal, from the small capon that Mrs Culver had managed to acquire. Mr Culver got drunk again and had an argument with his own parents before falling asleep in his armchair. Both his parents and her parents hugged her mother and her tightly before leaving.

Cora never got the microscope she wanted but the dress more than made up for that. It was a lovely yellow with lace trim. Mrs Culver had managed to get from the Lady of the Manor House where she worked. She would have to pay for it out of her weekly wage.

Cora got excited as the whistle signalled that they were about to set off. She could hear the pressure of the steam building up and then the jolt as the train started to pull away from the station. She looked at the

scenery as it began to slowly go by. She turned and smiled at her mother. Mrs Culver smiled back. However, it was not too long before the novelty wore off and she settled back in the seat. Her mum had taken out a book to read; Agatha Christie's Murder at the Vicarage. Again, the Lady of Manor House lent it to her.

Cora had brought her homework that Mr Pearson had set. There were quite a few mathematical equations as well as some codes that she had to break. Cora also knew that her mother had prepared a light lunch, but she realised that it was way too early into the journey to ask for some food. She had spoken to Laura the night before. They had worked out a strategy for Laura's issue and that was to basically tell them that Cora was her imaginary friend. It wasn't a total lie as the two had never met. Laura had said that she felt uncomfortable doing this as she appeared to be betraying Cora in some way. Cora was quite touched by this, but she still kept it a secret that she was travelling up to London to be treated herself. She could sense that Laura was a worrier and telling her about it would only set the poor girl off. She still wasn't prepared for what Laura said next, though.

'I'm scared, Cora. So scared.'
'There's no need to be, Laura,' soothed Cora. 'You'll be fine. As long as you keep to the plan, then you'll be fine.'
'I wish I had your confidence,' said Laura. 'It sounds like nothing worries you.'
'There are many things that concern me, Laura,' Cora responded. 'Will my mummy survive the next drunken attack from my father? That's the main one. But I'm also of the opinion that if it's going to happen then there is nothing you can do about it, and if it doesn't happen, then what was the point about worrying about it in the first place.'
'True. But what if...' Laura said.

'What if the world is really flat?' Cora said. Why she said it she had no idea. It didn't make sense to her so it would certainly puzzle Laura.
'What you are saying makes sense,' said Laura. 'You think I'm putting barriers in the way to stop me doing something.'

'You wouldn't believe that we were only eight, would you?' said Cora. 'I know of some adults who don't talk this way; my father being one of them. But there is no point in saying what if. What if my father wasn't a drunkard? He is. What if I had pushed him down the stairs whilst he was drunk? I didn't. No point in dwelling on what might happen; it's either do or do not.'
'Like I said, Cora, you are so confident,' said Laura. 'I wish I were more like you.'
'Perhaps one day we will meet, and I can teach you how to be confident,' Cora replied.
'I'd like that very much, Cora,' said Laura.
'Cora? Cora?' the young girl felt someone shaking her. She hadn't realised that she had fallen asleep. She looked up and saw her mother standing over her. 'I wondered if you would like something to eat?'
'How long have I been asleep for?' Cora asked groggily.
'Just over two hours, I think,' Mrs Culver replied.

'I was having a dream about my...' Cora was going to say imaginary friend but managed to correct herself, '...friend, Marion. I must admit that I did not realise I had fallen asleep. But, yes please, I'll have some food. I'm famished.
Mrs Culver opened her bag and took out a package wrapped in brown paper and tied with a piece of string. 'Now, what is your favourite filling?'
'Cheese and pickle,' Cora replied excitedly.
'Oh,' Mrs Culver sounded desponded. 'I've done you ham and strawberry jam.'
'Ham and strawberry jam?' Cora said pulling a face. 'Yuck! Why on earth would you think I would like those flavours? Why would anyone want to eat those flavours?'
Mrs Culver had untied the string and was unwrapping the brown paper. 'Good job I've done cheese and pickle then,' she smiled.
'Thank you, mummy,' she said delightedly.
Mrs Culver offered a sandwich which her daughter took. She took one for herself. She bit into

and as she chewed, she looked out of the window at the passing scenery. 'Are you looking forward to seeing London, Cora?'
Cora pondered this question for a while. She even took another bite of her sandwich to mull over her

response. 'Not for the reason we are going up there, but I am looking forward to seeing London itself.' That was true. 'Do you think I'm insane, mummy?' Mrs Culver stopped mid-bite. 'Of course, I don't, darling. The reason for going is to hopefully find out why those marks appeared on your hands and the cut on your leg. Our doctor and the specialist in Exeter cannot explain it. They are hoping the expert in London can get to the bottom of it.'

'I must admit, I've been wondering that myself,' said Cora. She took another bite, chewed it quite a few times before swallowing. 'I can think of no logical explanation, mummy.'

'Did you feel pain before they appeared?' Mrs Culver asked.

'Yes, I did,' Cora responded honestly. 'It did not last very long. But the one on the hand felt like I was being hit with a stick.'

'And you said that your – friend – was getting hit at the same time,' Mrs Culver began. 'Does she feel your pain when something happens to you?'

Cora finished her sandwich but nodded at the same time. 'May I have another sandwich, please, mummy?'

'Of course, dear.'

CHAPTER SIXTEEN

The actual day in the hospital surprised Cora. It was not what she expected. She thought it would be a man in a white suit asking her loads of questions and trying to catch her out. It was nothing like that. She was amazed by the exterior of the building. She had never seen anything so big before.

Mrs Culver was equally as impressed. She knew that bigger did not necessarily mean better, but she had to admit that she quite liked the look of this building. She went to the reception desk where she spoke to an elderly lady whose grey hair was tied into a tight bun. She looked very stern but if Mrs Culver could stand the abuse from her husband, she could deal with a receptionist. However, she turned out to be very friendly. She showed them to a seating area and told them that someone would be out to fetch them soon. Mrs Culver had never been so pleased that Richard was her husband because they could claim for this from his railway medical insurance.

A man was sat in one of the comfortable armchairs. He was reading one of the broadsheets. Cora could not tell if it was the Times or the Telegraph, but the headline was about Germany invading Czechoslovakia. She had listened to Laura rabbiting on about some bloke called Hitler and how she thought that World War Two was on the way. Cora did not really have a clue what her friend was talking about, but all she kept on thinking was who on earth would want to attack Ogwell or Newton Abbot?

She turned towards her mother and noticed that she was reading the paper intently. She heard her tut as the man turned the page over. 'The world's going to be changing, Cora, said Mrs Culver. 'Mark my words, the world's going to be changing.'

'In what way, mummy?' Cora asked.

'I think we will be finding out pretty soon, Cora,' her mother smiled sadly.

They did not have to wait too long before a nurse came out to collect them. Cora started to get nervous, and she gripped her mother's hand tightly. The doctor, Doctor Paige, though made her feel at ease. He started off by pointing to something just below her chin, she looked down and he raised his finger up and flicked her nose which made Cora laugh. He asked her questions about her and what she enjoyed doing. They must have been talking for a good

half an hour when Doctor Paige asked her about her friends.
'Who would you say was your best friend, Cora?' he asked.
'Marion Tucker,' Cora replied without hesitating.
'Is she a very good friend?' he asked sincerely. Cora nodded. 'Good. Do you have any other friends?'
'Yes,' Cora replied. 'Do you want me to name them all? Only we'd be here for quite a long time.'
'No. That's fine, Cora,' laughed Doctor Paige. 'Now I've been told that you have a very special friend. Someone more important than you best friend, Marion Trucker?'
'Tucker,' Cora corrected smiling.
'Apologies. Tucker,' said the doctor. 'Is that true? Do you have a very special friend?'
Cora glanced over at her mother who nodded her support. 'I do have a special friend,' Cora confirmed. 'She's called Laura.'
'Laura? That's a pretty name,' said the doctor.

'Yes, isn't it?' giggled Cora. 'She is my very best friend and knows everything about me.'
'Really?' said the doctor making a note. 'That is

interesting. How does she know everything about you?'

'Because I invented her,' said Cora. 'She's a lot like me probably because she is me.'

'So - she's imaginary?' said Doctor Paige.

'Completely made up,' nodded Cora.

'That's not uncommon,' said Doctor Paige. 'That would explain the reaction when your friend was being caned. What it doesn't explain is the cut on your leg and also what you told your mummy. Do you have any sisters, Cora?

This question took Cora by surprise. 'Er...No,' she replied.

'None at all?' Doctor Paige repeated.

'That is correct, Doctor Paige,' said Mrs Culver. 'Cora is an only child.'

Doctor Paige started reading the file. 'It says here that Cora is adop...'

'She is an only child, Doctor Paige,' said Mrs Culver forcefully.

'Ah! I see,' said Doctor Paige. 'So how can you explain the cut on your leg, Cora?'

'I must have knelt on something,' said Cora.

'Your friend, Marion, said that there wasn't anything there for you to kneel on,' argued the doctor. 'And your imaginary friend getting the cane does not explain the marks that appeared on your hands that Marion, your mummy and Mr Pearson, your teacher, all saw. I take it you speak to this imaginary friend, Cora?' Cora just nods. This was not going the way she was expecting it to go. 'Do you see her in your mind when you speak to Laura, Cora?' Again, Cora just nodded. 'And who does she look like?'

'Me,' Cora admitted truthfully.

Now it was the doctor's turn to nod, and he spent a few minutes writing some notes. Cora waited anxiously and kept on looking for reassurance from her mother. Mrs Culver did smile at her, but Cora could see the concern in her eyes. That was not helping her.

'Now, Cora. How would you like to play a game?' Doctor Paige said suddenly.

Cora thought about it for a few seconds. 'I would like that very much, Doctor Paige,' she said.

The "game" consisted of an ordinary pack of playing cards. The doctor passed the top ten cards to Cora and asked her to try to memorise them. He gave her three minutes before asking for the cards back. He then talked randomly to her for about five minutes; about the weather and Easter and general rubbish. Then he turned to Cora and asked her to recall the ten playing cards in order. Cora did so, correctly, in ten seconds. As she recited each card, Doctor Paige revealed them from the top of the pack.

Her mother looked on, gobsmacked. She had never

seen her daughter do anything like that before. 'Wow!' was all she could say.

'Wow, indeed, Mrs Culver,' said Doctor Paige. 'A few people will recall up to six cards, but not many will remember all ten. Your teacher has informed us that you are good at seeing patterns in codes.'

'Yes,' Cora agreed. 'Although this is not the same thing. Here you must create your own code.'

'Are you ready for another game, Cora?' asked the doctor. Cora nodded. He shuffled the deck of cards and then passed it back to Cora. 'I want to see how many of these cards you can recollect in order. Do you think you can do that?'

Cora shrugged but Mrs Culver interrupted, 'But surely that is almost impossible?'

'It is a challenge that not many people will succeed at,' Doctor Paige replied. 'I'm sure that Cora will do her best, but I'm not expecting her to get them all correct.'

Cora just smiled. The doctor gave her twenty minutes to memorise the cards. He then told them to go for a little walk and to come back in about fifteen minutes.

Cora followed her mother out the door and held her hand as they walked down one of the many corridors. Cora was hoping that they were going for a drink or, even better, something to eat. And she was delighted when they headed for a reception room. They found two chairs and they sat down. From her bag, Mrs Culver produced a couple of pieces of flapjack which she had made before the journey. Cora loved the

taste of treacle and the oats combined. After eating the bars, they decided to explore a little bit more. They came to a room where the doors were closed and there was a sign stating NO ADMITTANCE STAFF ONLY. A nun opened the door just as they were passing, and Cora looked in. The only person she could really see was a gentleman sat at a table reading a newspaper. At that precise moment, the man put down his paper to reach for his coffee, and they locked eyes.
'Come on, Cora,' her mother whispered in her ear urgently. 'We need to get back.'
They walked away before some nurses came in their direction and they doubled back to follow them. Cora just managed to see the man emerging from the staff room and walking briskly in the other direction.
Mrs Culver had seen the man and recognised him instantly. There was no way she wanted to engage in conversation with this person as he would give the game away. He knew the secret she was keeping from Cora. She pulled her daughter quickly away.
'You're hurting me, mummy,' she said.

'Sorry, darling,' her mother apologised. 'But we really need to get back to Doctor Paige's office.'
It did not take them long to find it. Mrs Culver knocked, and his assistant opened the door and welcomed them back inside. They took the same chairs they had taken earlier. Doctor Paige noted that Mrs Culver looked a bit flushed and concerned but she was not his patient. Cora was.

'Okay, then, Cora,' he began. 'Let us see how many cards you can remember.' The cards were where he had left them when Cora had handed them back to him.'

'Would you like me to start now?' Cora asked.

'Yes, please, Cora.'

'Ace of clubs,' she started. He turned the top card over and there it was. 'Two of diamonds.' Another one correct. 'Queen of clubs.'

Mrs Culver watched in amazement as Cora reeled off card after card; five spades, ten of spades, king of diamonds. Each time the doctor turned the top card over she knew that her daughter was going to be correct.

'And finally, the king of spades,' Cora completed. There was no point in turning over the card as they all knew that this would be the remaining card, but he did it anyway out of courtesy. Sure enough, the bearded black king was looking up at them. Even Doctor Paige's assistant was sat there with her mouth agape. She had seen similar experiments to this carried out before, but not with someone so young and never had she seen it all completed correctly.

'Well, you certainly are a gifted child,' said Doctor Paige. 'Deidre? Would you just take Mrs Culver outside for a moment. I need to speak with Cora alone.'

'Yes, Doctor Paige,' Deidre replied as she stood up from her desk.

'But surely I need to stay in here with my daughter,' Mrs Culver said anxiously.

'My dear, Mrs Culver,' the doctor said somewhat patronisingly, 'Cora is my patient and I just need to have a one to one with her for a minute. I promise that I will not be long.'

Mrs Culver kept her gaze on her daughter until the door was closed and Deidre was showing her to the seating area. Mrs Culver perched on the edge of her chair whilst Deidre sat back in the one she chose. Mrs Culver kept her eye on the door.

'You both think she is insane, don't you?' said Mrs Culver in nothing more than a whisper.

'Far from it,' said Deidre. 'Your daughter is a remarkable child. It's true that mental people do have tendencies to be gifted in certain areas, but they certainly show signs of being mad. Doctor Paige is an expert in this field. He has been called on to diagnose insane people, even ones who hide their insanity so well. But you get to know the traits; perhaps a laugh or a mouth twitch. Doctor Paige can identify every detail of a mad person. At present, I cannot see anything of concern. But I'm not trained to recognise symptoms. I do get to watch, but I think Cora is way too young to pull the wool over Doctor Paige's eyes.'

Inside the office, Doctor Paige reclined back in his chair and looked at the young girl. Although he was staring at her, Cora felt quite relaxed in his company.

'Am I mad, Doctor Paige?' she asked.

'Do you think you are mad, Cora?' Doctor Paige countered. The young girl shook her head. 'I can honestly say that I do not think I have met anyone like you. No. You are not mad, but I do not think your special friend is imaginary. I think you can communicate with someone else just by using your mind. I have been doing tests regarding this and the only positive response has been coming from twins. I think you got Laura to help you memorise the cards, but that does not make you mad, Cora. It does make you clever. However, the thing I'm finding hard to digest is that your mother says that you are an only child.'

'I do not have any brothers or sisters, Doctor

Paige,' Cora confirmed.
'And do you know that you are their actual daughter? Have the told you that you may be adopted?' he quizzed.
'Adopted?' Cora asked puzzled.
'Yes. It means that they were allowed to take you away from your actual mummy and daddy,' Doctor Paige explained.

'Not that I'm aware of,' Cora replied. 'They've always said that I'm their special precious little girl.' Doctor Paige leant forward and scribbled some notes. 'They did have a son, but he died not long after being born. But that was a couple of years before I came along.'
Doctor Paige scribbled some more notes and then reread the file he had on Cora. 'Let us get your mother back in here, shall we, Cora?' Cora smiled and nodded.
Doctor Paige stood up and went to the door, he opened it and went out. It was not too long before Deidre came back into the office. 'Doctor Paige is just having a word with your mummy, Cora. They'll both be back in in a couple of minutes.'
'May I have a drink of water, please?' asked Cora.
'Certainly, my dear,' Deidre smiled. 'I'll go and fetch you one.'
She left the room again. Cora briefly glanced round

before getting off her chair and walked around to Doctor Paige's side of the desk. She looked once

more towards the door as she reached down to open the file on the table. She cast her eyes down and started to read.

It was mainly about her; her name, address, height and weight as well as a few other personal details. Her parents' names were there as next of kin but then she read that her birth mother was unknown and there was a mention of a Kneecap Cottage and that she was adopted. That word again. The same one that Doctor Paige had used moments earlier. She thought back to an earlier conversation where her mother interrupted Doctor Paige just as he was about to use that word. Why had her mother spoken over the doctor at that point? She closed the file and returned to her seat just as Deidre entered with her glass of water. She handed it to the young girl.

'Thank you,' said Cora as she received it, and she took a sip.

Doctor Paige had gone to sit next to Mrs Culver. He waited for Deidre to leave them. He could tell that Mrs Culver was nervous. 'Your daughter is not insane, Mrs Culver,' he said to relieve her anxiety. 'In fact, she is a very bright and intelligent child. She is a credit to you.'

'That's very kind of you to say so, Doctor Paige,' said Mrs Culver.
'I would like to do some further tests on her,' he said. Mrs Culver looked concerned, but he raised his hand as if to alleviate her fears. 'It really is to observe her intelligence. You must be aware that with Cora being adopted, there is a chance that there could be siblings?'
Deidre stepped back outside. 'I'm just going to get her a drink of water,' she said.
'There was no mention of her having any brothers or sisters when we adopted her,' said Mrs Culver. 'All we knew was that her mother was underage and that was the reason that her parents made her give the child up.'
Doctor Paige was flummoxed. He could tell that Mrs Culver had told him all she knew. He could not put his finger on it, but he believed that there was more to this little girl than meets the eye. There had to be a sibling, there just had to be. Nothing else could explain those marks on her hand or the cut on her leg. He had been doing a thesis on this special bond between siblings, but, at present, it only seemed apparent in twins. And it certainly did not appear that Cora had a twin.

'Well. At least you know she's not insane,' said

Doctor Paige. 'She is a remarkable and intelligent child. I just hope that you are agreeable to more tests.'
'I have no objections, Doctor Paige,' said Mrs Culver. 'I will need to discuss it with my husband, but if the tests are carried out locally to us, I do not think it will be too much of a problem.'

Doctor Paige was sat in his office a little later writing up the notes that he was going to pass on to Deidre to type up. His door was wide open, and he just happened to glance up as one of his colleagues, Doctor Turner, was escorting a man and a child from the premises. The doctor stopped and shook hands with the gentleman. It was at this point that the girl turned her head and looked in his direction. His insides turned as he recognised the girl instantly. For it was not that long ago that she was sat in this very room. He stood up, but by the time he had managed to get out of his office the man and the young girl had gone. He turned and saw Doctor Turner's retreating figure. He sprinted to catch up with him.

'Doctor Turner,' he said to get his colleague's attention. The other doctor stopped in his tracks. 'Doctor Paige,' he beamed. 'We don't see much of each other these days.'
'Not nearly enough,' Doctor Paige agreed. 'That

young girl you were just with. Do you mind me asking her name?'

'Miss Laura Hadley,' Doctor Turner confirmed.

Laura? Cora had called her best friend Laura.

'Does she have a sister by any chance?' asked Doctor Paige.

'There is nothing in her file,' Doctor Turner replied.

'I don't suppose you were seeing her because of an imaginary friend, were you?'

'As it happens, Doctor, I was,' said Doctor Turner who was now very surprised and intrigued. 'Why do you ask?'

'Her friend didn't happen to be called Cora, did she?'

Now Doctor Turner's eyes were opened very wide. 'It was,' he spluttered. 'But how on earth could you possibly know that?'

'I've had a patient in today called Cora who had an imaginary friend called Laura,' Doctor Paige explained. 'Did Laura by any chance write down some playing cards?'

'I suggest you follow me, Doctor Paige.'

They went to Doctor Turner's office. Doctor Turner went to the drawer in is mahogany desk. He pulled out a file. He handed it to his colleague. On top was a sheet of paper with what appeared to be an eight-year old's handwriting. He read Ace of Clubs, two of diamonds, Queen of clubs...Doctor Paige looked up.

'How did you know?' asked Doctor Turner. Doctor Paige explained the experiment he had carried out with the deck of cards. 'She was referred to me because the father thought she was a witch,' said Doctor Paige. 'She's not. She is just a normal child. As you are aware, Doctor Turner, I have been researching a special bond between siblings and their ability to communicate telepathically.' He noticed Doctor Turner trying to stifle a grin. 'I know many medical professionals scoff at this idea, and to be honest, there has only been limited success. It only seems apparent in twins.'

'And you think Cora and Laura are twin sisters?' Doctor Turner asked. Doctor Paige looked embarrassed but nodded. 'Even though it says in my file that Laura Hadley is an only child? What does it say in yours about Cora?'

'Her father is adamant that she was adopted from a facility called Kneecap Cottage,' said Doctor Paige. 'I've never heard of the place before. Her mother confirmed it today, but they are keeping it a secret from Cora.'

'I, also, have never heard of that facility which means that it does not follow the correct procedures. There is one person who would know,' said Doctor Turner. 'Although he probably would not admit to it.'

'Who?' Doctor Paige asked.

'Mister Richard Hadley,' Doctor Turner replied.
'The eminent surgeon? Why would he know?' Doctor Paige asked confused.
'Because he is Laura's father,' answered Doctor Turner. 'I believe you are right, Doctor Paige. There is more to this story than meets the eye.'

CHAPTER SEVENTEEN

Cora soon discovered, when they arrived back home, that her father was not impressed with the decision. He told them out loud that he thought they would have kept his daughter in. He could not believe that she was standing in front of him.
'They used to burn witches in the olden days,' he said.
'If you don't be careful, daddy, then I'll put a spell on you,' Cora responded nonchalantly. This earned her a slap across the face.
'Go to your room, Cora,' Mrs Culver ordered. 'I'll shout to you when dinner is ready.'
Cora did as she was told but gave her father a scathing look as she passed him. She did gain some satisfaction when she noticed Richard take a couple of steps backwards to get out of her way. He kept looking at her in disgust as she walked by him.
The next few days were exactly the same

possibly with one exception, her father being more drunk. She earned herself quite a few smacks and slaps. Mrs Culver tried to protect her which made Mr Culver respond with hitting her instead.

Cora spent a long time in her room. This did not make her unhappy. She set codes for Marion to try and break. Marion was allowed to come and play but had to leave before Mr Culver arrived home. Marion was finding them difficult to break. Cora could tell when her friend was getting bored, and she agreed to start playing dollies.

Laura contacted her quite a few times, especially just after her father had struck her. Laura told her that her cheek was going red. 'Why is it we feel each other's pain?' she asked Cora.

'I don't know,' Cora admitted. 'There must be some reason why we have this connection.'

'Out of all the people in the world, how did we manage to find each other?' Laura wondered.

'There has to be a reason,' said Cora. 'There just has to be. I think it all comes down to that house.'

'I think you're right,' said Laura. 'But why? I know that I'm drawn to that house every time we pass it, but I don't think I've ever been inside.'

'Me either,' said Cora. 'I mean I've never even passed the house but yet, when you see it, I see it

and it looks very familiar to me.'
'How is that possible?' asked Laura.
'I don't know,' Cora admitted.
'And what about that other woman you can communicate with?' said Laura. 'Have you spoken to her recently and is she connected to the house somehow?'
'I've spoken to her a few times, but she cannot have anything to do with the house as you cannot speak with her,' Cora pointed out. 'One of us has to get inside that house.'
'How are we going to do that?'
'Dunno,' said Cora. 'But I'm sure I will come up with something.'
'You'd better be quick because there's going to be a war soon,' said Laura.
'A war? Are you sure?' Cora replied.

'You must read the paper or listen to the wireless, don't you?' Laura said completely disbelieving that her friend was unaware of the impending threat emanating from Germany.
'I've heard that there's a man in Germany who is not very nice,' was all Cora could recall.
'Cora!' Laura rebuked. 'You really must take more of an interest in the news.'
'Why?' Cora countered. 'Sounds depressing to me. Anyway, my parents don't seem overly concerned about it'

'What I know about your father, that's not a surprise,' mumbled Laura.

'Are you forgetting that I can still hear you clearly?' said Cora.

'I'm just saying that I think you should take this threat seriously because it's going to happen whether we like it or not.'

'In that case, I'm going to have to rely on you to tell me all the news,' said Cora.

CHAPTER EIGHTEEN

"This morning the British ambassador in Berlin handed the German government a final note stating that unless we heard from them by eleven o'clock that they were prepared at once to withdraw their troops from Poland, a state of war would exist between us. I have to tell you now that no such undertaking has been received, and that consequently this country is at war with Germany".

Gloria and Cora were sat at the table listening. Her father, thankfully, was at work. He had been promoted at work, to supervisor, not that his family would know it. They did not see any more money. His drinking increased. On a positive he was usually too far gone to dish out any beatings and mainly fell asleep in his armchair.

'Well, that did not seem like good news,' said Mrs Culver.

'It wasn't, mummy,' Cora confirmed. 'Not good at all. Many, many, people will lose their lives'.

'But surly it cannot go on forever,' said Mrs Culver. 'It will be over by Christmas'.

'Better start learning German, then,' Cora responded. 'If it's over that quick, then Germany would have won'.

'Never,' said Gloria. 'Our brave boys will not allow it'.

Cora did not reply. She was concerned that she had not heard from Laura in a while. She had tried to contact her friend on numerous occasions but had met with a blank wall. She excused herself from the table to go up to her room and left her mother listening to the wireless.

In her room she lay on her bed and tried to contact Laura. Again, she was met with silence.

'I wonder why she is ignoring you?' the other woman's voice entered her head.

'I've no idea,' said Cora angrily.

'That touched a nerve,' said the woman happily. 'Perhaps you can talk to me a bit more often'.

'I don't even know who you are,' Cora retaliated. 'For all I know you could be a ghost, or a complete figment of my imagination'.

'But you are the one having the conversation with me,' said the woman. 'And we both know that you are not insane because of those tests you had at that hospital.'

'You were there?' Cora asked in disbelief.

'Of course, I was there,' said the voice. 'Not that you would let me in. You were doing to me like what's her name is doing to you now.'

'It's Laura. And you know it's Laura,' Cora screamed back.

'Okay. Okay. I apologise. It's like what Laura is doing to you now,' said the woman.

'What I don't get is why can you communicate with me but cannot speak with Laura?' said Cora.

'I've tried,' said the voice. 'God knows I've tried, but I have no image of her.'

'I have no image of her, yet I can still talk to her,' Cora replied.

'I cannot explain why that is,' the woman admitted.

'Hang on a minute. If you can invade my thoughts, then you must have seen me,' Cora said in realisation. 'Who are you?'

'Haven't you worked it out yet, little one?' said the woman. 'I listened to what you were hearing as the doctor explained about adoption. I must admit that I

thought you would have put two and two together then'.
'You're my mother. My birth mother,' Cora whispered.
'Finally got there,' said the voice.
'Then Laura is my sister,' Cora said in wonderment.
'Hold fire there,' said her mother. 'I only gave birth to one child'.
'Oh,' Cora said sounding disappointed. 'Are you sure?'
'I think I would know if I gave birth to two children,' said the voice. 'Mind you, I cannot remember much what happened after you came along'.
'How did you get to see me?'

'One of the kind-hearted midwives gave me a sneak peek,' the woman admitted. 'You were so beautiful'.
'Where was I born?' asked Cora. It went quiet. Cora thought the woman had left. 'Did you hear me?'
'It's hard to describe,' she finally replied. 'I was very young at the time. I just remember this house. Oh, this house was fantastic. It reminded me of a gingerbread house. But that was only the façade. I was taken to this metal building which was in the woods behind the house. It was there that I gave birth to you'.
'So, it's been you that sent me the mind pictures of the house?' Cora said.
'Perhaps,' said the voice. 'Although I'm pretty sure that you must see it every time you travel by'.

'I've never been by that house,' Cora said.
'You must have,' the voice replied.
'Never,' Cora replied vehemently. 'But Laura has. She goes by it quite regularly. There must be a link between all three of us and that house. Do you remember what it was called?'

'No,' came the reply. 'But I recall my fellow patients called it Kneecap House because the bend in the road looked like a kneecap'.
'Could you find it again?'
'Easy-peasy,' said the voice.
'You are sure of yourself'.
'Well, you see, I'm still here,' said the girl. 'I'm being held here. They keep the room locked'.
'Why would they do that?' Cora replied, not sure that the other was telling the complete truth.
'You don't believe me?' the voice sounded harsh.
'I didn't say that,' Cora answered.
'You've got to come and save me,' said the voice. 'You've got to get me out of here'.
'I'll do my best'.

Cora woke up with a start. She had fallen asleep. Had it all been just a dream? It had all felt so real. Perhaps her discussion with Doctor Paige had rooted into her brain. Laura had been telling her about psychology and reverse psychology. To be honest, Cora had lost interest because she did not really understand what her friend was going on about. She could not believe that Laura was just eight years old when she had the knowledge of someone much older. She decided that it had been a dream, but something was niggling at the back of her mind. She tried to contact Laura again but was met with a blank wall.

CHAPTER NINETEEN

'Hi, Cora, it's me.' Cora could hear her friend trying to contact her friend. She decided to give Laura a taste of her own medicine. *'Cora? Can you hear me?'* Cora could tell that Laura was becoming quite concerned but she still wasn't ready to let her off the

hook just yet. 'Are you annoyed with me for some reason?'

'Oh, you finally want to talk to me now, do you?' Cora replied scathingly. 'I've been trying to speak with you for a long time and have not been able to. Don't you realise that there is a war going on? I thought something had happened to you.'

'You're right,' Laura responded guiltily. 'I'm so sorry, Cora. Please forgive me.'

'What have you been doing to ignore me like that?' Cora hoped that Laura could tell by the tone of her voice that she had not quite forgiven her yet.

'I've been following our plan,' Laura replied. 'I'm back in Mrs Miller's class and I've been making friends just like you suggested. It was a good idea of yours, Cora. I now play with Billy and Danielle.'

'Danielle? Is she French or something?' Cora asked and the bitterness was still very clear in her voice.

'I think she was born in Cambourne,' Laura replied not quite understanding what Cora was going on about.

'Is that near Paris?'

'Redruth,' Laura said and then caught on. 'Oh, you mean her name sounds French. She told me that her mother named her after the French actress Danielle Darrieux.'

'You'll have to run that by me again,' said Cora.

'Danielle Darrieux,' Laura repeated.

'Nope. Am never going to get that in a month of Sundays,' said Cora. 'My plan never included you totally forgetting about me.'

'I'm so sorry, Cora,' Laura felt chastised. 'You're absolutely correct.'

'Okay, you've already said that,' said Cora. 'So, why are you getting in touch with me now?'

'I'm going to be going by that house again, in a couple of days,' said Laura.

'Why are you going up?' asked Cora.

'My parents are letting the government use it as a base for the duration of the war,' Laurea explained.

'That's good of them,' said Cora. 'At least they are doing something for the war effort. My parents are not doing anything. I think my father wants Hitler to win. He said that the Jews are taking over everywhere.'

'He sounds like a bigot,' said Laura.

'He doesn't sound like one, he is one,' said Cora. 'You'll have to visit that house.'

'How on earth can I visit the house?' asked Laura.

'Can't you pretend that you want to go to the toilet or something?' Cora responded.

'Hmmm,' Laura thought. 'I'm pretty sure that I can do that.'

'You'll have to let me know how you get on,' said Cora.

'I will,' said Laura. 'What am I looking for when I get there?'

'We need a name from around the time we were born,' Cora said. 'And we need to see if that other person, the voice I hear, is still being kept at that house.'

'You think she still is?' Laura asked.

'I don't know,' Cora admitted. 'I had a conversation with her a little while ago, I think it was more of a dream, but she told me that she was being kept there.'

'Okay. I'll see what I can do,' said Laura. 'I'll keep

'you posted. Oh, and Cora?'

'Yes?' Cora replied.

'I am really sorry that I neglected you,' said Laura. 'You're my best friend but I wasn't a friend to you. I wouldn't blame you if you stayed mad at me forever'.

'I could never stay mad at you, Laura,' Cora began. 'You're like a sister to me.'

And Laura was true to her word. Cora got a clear picture of them approaching the house. She thought her friend was a wonderous actress, feigning a stomach problem. Cora giggled as Laura's mother appeared to fall for it hook, line and sinker. She could see through Laura's eyes as they climbed up the steps to the front door. She waited with bated breath for Laura to update her. The vision she had had disappeared. This meant that Laura must be concentrating on something else.

'Help me get out of here,' she heard the other woman yell.

It went quiet. She knew that Laura had heard the voice because she could sense the uneasiness in her friend. She waited and waited. And then she heard it again, but it was louder this time. It was like Laura was right outside the door.

'HELP ME GET OUT OF HERE,' the voice screamed again.

It went quiet again. Cora wanted to ask the strange woman what was wrong but wondered if Laura would hear instead. She could tell that the young woman was tense, so she decided to throw caution to the wind and contact her.

'Are you okay?'

'You're here. You're here. I can feel you,' the young woman sobbed.

'I'm not there,' said Cora. 'I'm still at home.'

'Don't lie to me,' said the woman. 'I can feel your presence outside my door.'

'Honestly, I am at home, but Laura is there,' Cora explained.

'She can't hear me,' the girl cried. 'It should have been you here. It should have been you.'

'I'm sorry, but I still don't know where the house is,' said Cora. 'I will come and find you; I promise.'

There was no reply. Cora could tell that the young woman was upset but what could she do? There was no way to help her at present. And with the war taking hold, it was only going to become more difficult.

'I've got something,' Laura's voice invaded her thoughts, and she was sounding very excited.

'What?' asked Cora.

'I tore a page from a book,' Laura explained. 'It has names and things on it'.

'Well done, Laura,' said Cora. 'Keep it safe. There has to be a way that we can meet up. I'm sure that we will come up with something'.

Those words would echo in her mind a few months later.

CHAPTER TWENTY

August the twentieth nineteen forty started off like many others in the Culver household. Richard Culver awoke in a mood slumped in his armchair. His head was pounding, and he could not wait to get back to the pub after work.

Gloria Culver was in the kitchen preparing breakfast. She had been up since six o'clock making sure everything was ready in time. She groaned inwardly as her husband entered. He scraped the chair across the stone floor before sitting heavily upon it. Gloria made him a cup of coffee and placed it on the table in front of him. She did not receive, or was even expecting, a thank you. She was busy frying the bacon in with the sausages, making sure that it did not get too crispy. God forbid what he would do to her if she made it too crispy. She cracked an egg into the pan as well.

'I'm going to take Cora to Torquay today,' she said, and got a grunt in return. 'We will be back on the train that will arrive at about five-thirty.' She placed all the ingredients onto a plate, carried it to the table and put it in front of him. 'Perhaps we could meet you from work and we could walk home together?'

'I'm going to the pub,' he growled.

'We could go with you,' she said, knowing that she was pushing her luck. She had to wait whilst he took a couple of mouthfuls although he responded without swallowing the food.

'Yeah. Perhaps we could,' he finally said. 'I finish at around six. You may have to bring some money. I don't think I'll have enough for all of us'.

His response surprised her, but she nodded her agreement. She did not know why she wanted to spend more time with her husband, but she just thought it would be good to have some family time together.

Cora always waited in bed until her father had left for work. She was a bit surprised as there was less verbal abuse that morning than usual. Her mother had obviously cooked breakfast to his satisfaction. She vowed there and then that she would never allow her husband to treat her like that.

At quarter past seven her father left for work. She knew that he had to be there at eight. She had walked it herself and had taken about half an hour to complete, but then, she did not have a flask of whiskey in her pocket to sip on the way.

She listened for a few more minutes in case he returned. When she felt that it was safe, she got out of bed and pulled her dressing gown off the door peg. She put it on and tied the belt. She looked out of her bedroom window; it looked like it was going to be a lovely summers day. She made her way downstairs.

Her mother was washing the dishes. Gloria did not need to turn around as she heard her daughter approaching. 'Good morning, love,' she said.

'Morning, mummy,' Cora replied.

'What would you like for breakfast?' Gloria asked.

'I'll just make myself some porridge,' Cora said. 'Would you like a cup of tea or coffee?'

'Cup of tea would be lovely, darling,' said Gloria. 'You may need to be careful, though. I was talking to a few people yesterday and rumour has it is that the *'government is looking at rationing food.*

'Can they do that, mummy?' Cora wondered.

'They can do anything they want, it appears,' said Mrs Culver.

Cora started to prepare her breakfast whilst her mother finished off the dishes. They did not speak much whilst they continued with their respective chores. Cora lifted the whistling kettle from the stove and made the drinks. She had boiled up some milk for her porridge. She poured that over her oats next. She handed her mum her drink before taking hers and the porridge over to the table and placed it there. She went back to the drawer and took out a spoon. She went back to sit at the table. She stirred in the milk. She could have put some sugar on it but decided against. She took a mouthful.

Her mum brought her cup of tea over and sat next to her. 'I've got a bit of a surprise for you today.' she said. Cora looked at her in anticipation but did not say anything because her mouth was full. 'We're going to Torquay on the train. How does that sound?'

Cora looked very happy indeed. She swallowed the food in her mouth. 'That sounds fantastic, mummy,'

'Can Marion come with us?' she beamed.

'I did check with Mrs Tucker, but they had visitors down so Marion will not be able to join us I'm afraid. So, I hope you don't mind, but it will just be you and me.'

'I don't mind that, mummy,' Cora replied. 'That will be very nice.'

'And we return to the train station later we are going to meet your father and walk home.'

Cora tried to keep the smile fixed to her face but was not sure if she was successful. 'Thats - great – I look forward to it.'

'It will be fine, Cora,' Gloria said sensing her daughter's anxiety. 'He will be fine.' Cora just nodded and ate another spoonful of porridge. 'So, what are we going to do in Torquay, mummy?'

'We will walk along the beach,' Mrs Culver said. 'Perhaps go searching in the rock pools. Maybe even have an ice-cream. Would you like that?' She tweaked her daughter's nose making Cora giggle.

'That sounds great, mummy,' said Cora.

'Let us finish our breakfast and chores, and go and get ready,' said Cora.

'Okay, mummy.'

Gloria had to warn her daughter not to rush her food but could tell that the young girl was excited. Although Richard kept most of the money from his promotion, every now and again, when she caught him in a good mood, he would give her extra cash so that she could treat their daughter.

Cora finished her breakfast and washed and put away her dishes. She had to sweep through whilst her mother dusted. After that they went upstairs to change. Cora was ready within minutes and had to wait for her mother downstairs. It was not too long before they were walking towards the railway station.

It was a sunny day and fairly warm. Cora held her mother's hand as they walked the path that took them besides the river Lemon and Bradley Manor. Mrs Culver was carrying a small basket in her other hand. She had made a small picnic for them to enjoy at the beach later. She hadn't packed much, just a couple of sandwiches, some crisps and two apples.

Cora kept her nose pressed against the window of the carriage virtually the entire journey. She remembered the last time she was on a train and where she had ended up. The hospital where she had learned so much from her early days. She had felt something was wrong as she looked nothing like her parents and her father seemed resentful that she was in their lives. Adoption explained so much to her, but

she had never broached the subject with her parents. What would she say them? Perhaps today would be the day to discuss it with her mother.

Cora looked up in amazement at the Grand Hotel that greeted them as they came out of the station. She could not believe how big it was. She stood there and looked at it. Although she knew that she would never stay there, she loved just looking at the building that had been standing there for about seventy years. She had never seen anything like it. They had passed the Queens Hotel, in Newton Abbot, on the way to the railway station, but that was nowhere near as large as this one.

Gloria also looked at the Grand Hotel. However, she was thinking what might have been. She had worked there before becoming pregnant with Daniel. She was just a chambermaid, but she could have worked her way up to become a manageress. The hotel manager had been speaking to her about it knowing that Mrs Byrd would be retiring soon. But family life got in the way, and, although it did not work out the way they had hoped, she was too proud to ask for her job back. Anyway, she would have missed the opportunity to become manageress and would have had to take orders from someone younger than herself. She took Cora's hand and gently pulled her away.

They crossed the road. Cora could smell the sea air the moment they had gotten off the train. Now she could hear the waves gently caressing the shore. All she could see was a red wall in front of her, but as they got closer, she caught her first glimpse of the sea. Her mother led her towards an opening which had steps that would take you down onto the sand.

Although Torquay was only about seven miles from Newton, Cora had never visited the beach. The sand was browner than she had imagined and the seaweed greener. She had been told that the sea was blue, but it did not look that that colour to her. In fact, it was very nondescript. She watched as her mother laid out a large towel and put the basket very close to it.

Mrs Culver let her daughter take off her shoes and socks. He blue dress was just above the knee so would not affect what she had planned next. She took off her sandals. Her dress was below the knee, but she knew that she would have to hitch it up.

'Come on, Cora,' Gloria laughed. 'We're going paddling.'

'Paddling?' Cora asked.

'You'll see,' Gloria laughed again. She grabbed her daughter by the hand and gently pulled her towards the water.

Cora was surprised at how cold the sea was. She was mesmerised watching the water wash away her footprints. Her mother helped her jump over the waves. She enjoyed it so much and she was glad to escape her father's strict regime.

They must have been paddling in the sea for a good hour, as well as splashing each other, although Cora got more wet than Gloria. The two laughed endlessly. They went back to the towel. Gloria took out the sandwiches and handed one to Cora. Cora thanked her mother.

After eating the picnic, Mrs Culver packed everything back into the basket and took Cora's hand. They walked towards the rocks. Cora was delighted to see the rockpools. Her mother pointed out a crab. She picked it up and handed it to Cora, telling her to be careful of its pincers. Cora looked in awe at the creature as it angrily tried to pinch her. Her mother *took it back and returned it to the pool. Gloria pointed out the barnacles clinging to the hard surface.*

They must have been searching the pools for a couple of hours. They lost track of time. Gloria brought her daughter an ice-cream. Cora loved to see the "shops" under the arches. She could also smell fish and chips. Soon it was time to get back to the train station. Their train was due at about twenty past five and they would get into Newton station at about ten to six.

They talked about their day. Gloria asked her daughter if she had enjoyed the day and Cora replied that she had thoroughly enjoyed the day. Gloria promised that next time they would go shopping.

On the train, Cora could not wait to talk to Laura about her day.

'Wow!' Laura exclaimed. 'You should live here. We only live about a twenty minutes' walk from the beach.'

'You're lucky,' said Cora. 'You must be down there every day.'

'Very rarely, actually,' Laura admitted. 'It gets very boring.'

'Oh, Laura. I cannot believe that,' said Cora.

'Mrs Miller takes us down there sometimes,' Laura said.

'How's it going with Mrs Miller now that everything has been sorted?' Cora asked.

'It's brilliant,' gushed Laura. 'She's still trying to refer me to a higher education, but because of the war it seems to be put on the back burner. You would love Mrs Miller. I don't know why she has never had any children'.

'If anything happens to my parents, then I'll move in with her then I'll get her to adopt me,' said Cora.

'Good idea,' Laura agreed. 'If anyone could pull that off, then it's you'.

'Hey, I'm used to being adopted,' Cora pointed out.

'Have you said anything to your parents yet?' Laura asked.

'I wouldn't say anything to my dad,' said Cora. 'I haven't asked my mummy either. I think it would upset her. I was going to discuss it with her today, but

we've had such a great time, I don't want to ruin it. Perhaps I'll be brave enough to talk about it with her tomorrow'.

'I haven't said anything to mine,' Laura also admitted. 'Daddy will hardly ever be home because he will be commuting to London. He will be carrying out surgery on our wounded soldiers. The government are still using our holiday home as a war office. I hope they leave in the state it was before it was passed over to them. I'll probably wait until the war is over – whenever that is'.

'It's been going on for nearly a year now,' said Cora.

'And, listening to and reading about the news, it does not look like it's going to be over any time soon,' said Laura. 'That Hitler is the evilest person in the world'.

'I can't see what all the fuss is about,' said Cora. 'I haven't seen any bombing raids in Newton Abbot'.

'Oh, don't say that, Cora,' Laura chastised. 'I live in fear that they may bomb the RAF site at the back of us. If they miss, then they could hit our house'.

"Of course, I do not want to see bombs dropped, silly," said Cora. 'Anyway, me and you have got some investigating to do when we're older. I take it you

'have that piece of paper somewhere safe?'

'Of course, I do,' said Laura. 'We will have to make arrangements to meet up. And I would like you to meet Billy and Danielle.'

'Can't wait,' said Cora. 'I'm going to have to go now as we are getting close to the station. We will talk later.'

'Okay,' said Laura.

The train pulled into the station. Cora and her mother alighted the platform. Cora looked up at the big round clock and saw that it was ten to six.

Mrs Culver met a woman she knew and started talking to her. Cora sat on the steps that led out of the station and waited. She got bored but stayed there like a good little girl for a little while. Her mother showed no sign of stopping her conversation, although they were now walking and talking at the same time. Gloria beckoned her daughter to follow them.

They were heading towards Forde Park. Cora glanced back at the clock which she could see from the pavement. It was now well after six o'clock. She heard this noise. It sounded like a buzzing noise. She wondered where it was coming from. She looked around but could not see anything. The noise got *louder and louder. She finally looked up and saw two aeroplanes flying towards the station. She then heard a voice that sounded familiar shouting to her.*

'FOR GOD'S SAKE, GET DOWN,' her father shouted.

Mrs Culver also heard the voice and was now looking at the plane. She heard the machine guns starting to fire. Her friend collapsed beside her, and she saw the blood seeping out of the bullet wounds in her body.

Cora laid down flat but looked up as more machine gun fire erupted. She then heard like a loud whistling noise. She looked up and saw her mother's body almost ripped in two by the bullets. She wanted to scream but a massive explosion almost deafened her. Debris fell on her. It hurt but she still turned her head and watched in horror as her father was thrown through the air because of a second explosion. Another bomb landed near her causing more wreckage to rain down on her. One of the last things she heard was the sound of shouting and screaming and the running footsteps of people getting near to her.

'Mrs Miller...Teacher...Portreath school. Mrs Miller...Teacher...Portreath School,' she mumbled oblivious if anyone could hear her. The pain became

intense, and she screamed in her own head before welcoming the darkness that engulfed her.

CHAPTER TWENTY-ONE

It took a couple of days before Laura could get out of bed. Everyone was worried about her as no one exactly knew what had happened, or why, to make Laura blackout. The local doctor called in to examine her but could not find anything physically wrong with her. His recommendation was to refer her back to the mental institution. It was agreed by Mr and Mrs Hadley that he should write with immediate effect to the Doctor who had seen her last year.

Mrs Miller popped in a couple of times to see how Laura was doing but could not wake her from her self-induced coma. Danielle also visited but, again, could not wake her.

Billy had been away for a few days before Laura collapsed. He called around his friend's house on the day he got back without the knowledge that Laura was poorly. He knocked on the door. Mr Hadley answered it.

'Hello, Mr Hadley. Is Laura here?' he asked.

'You'd better come in, Billy,' said Mr Hadley and he stood aside for the young boy to pass.

Billy could tell immediately from Laura's father's response that something was wrong. He was escorted into the lounge.

'Hello, Billy,' said Mrs Hadley.

Her withdrawn look confirmed to the young boy that something terrible was wrong. 'What's wrong with Laura?' he asked.

'She's not very well, Billy,' Mr Hadley explained. 'She collapsed a couple of days ago and has not woken up since.'

'The doctor has examined her,' said Mrs Hadley anticipating the youngster's next question. 'Physically there isn't anything wrong with her, but...'

George looked at his wife. He knew that she still suspected that their daughter had mental issues, even though she had gotten a clean bill of health. There was one thing that he had not told his wife and that was that he had received correspondence from the specialist in London, whom he had met with his daughter, requesting a meeting with him with another specialist, Doctor Paige. He was due in London in a couple of days and had arranged with Doctor Turner's

secretary a time to meet with the two specialists two weeks after he arrived.
'Do you mind if I go and try to wake her up?' Billy asked.
Mrs Hadley looked sympathetically at the young boy before moving out of the way so that he could climb the stairs.
Billy could feel the eyes of Laura's parents watching him as he ascended the stairs. When he reached the landing, he stopped and took a deep breath. He walked towards Laura's bedroom door. He stopped outside and took a second deep breath. He, tentatively, raised his hand and knocked on the wooden panelling. 'Laura? It's me. Can I come in?' Billy was not expecting and did not receive any response. Instead, he placed his hand on the doorknob and turned it, so the door opened. As expected from what Billy could see, the room was immaculate. Not a single thing was out of place. He walked into the bedroom and his eyes were drawn to the bed. He saw Laura lying there, looking very peaceful. He strode over to the bed and looked down at her.

''Alright, Laura. It's time to stop being so bloody melodramatic and get up,' he said harshly. Laura's eyes sprung open at the sound of Billy's voice. 'Oh good. You're not dead.'
'Who said I was dead?' asked Laura.
'No one,' Billy replied. 'It's just unlike you to try and be the centre of attention. As far as I'm aware, you only fainted and yet here you have laid for two days like you are lying in state. Now, sit up.'
Laura struggled to sit up, but Billy did nothing to help her. 'I've been out of it for two days?'
'Apparently,' Billy shrugged.
They could hear footsteps thudding up the stairs. It was obvious that Laura's parents had heard her speaking. They flew into her bedroom. Mrs Hadley threw her arms around her daughter and hugged her tightly. Mr Hadley grabbed Billy into a tight embrace. 'How on earth did you do it, Billy, when all the medical experts, and I include myself in that, have failed to wake her from her coma?'
'I just told her to stop being melodramatic and to get up, Mr Hadley,' said Billy. His voice was muffled as he was being clutched very tightly.

Mr Hadley let go of the young boy and swapped places with his wife. Mrs Hadley clutched Billy into a tight embrace. If anything, it was even tighter than Mr Hadley's. 'Thank you, Billy,' she cried. 'Thank you so much.'

'I think this requires a celebration,' said Mr Hadley. 'I'll go and get some cakes and some lemonade.'

'Saffron buns would be very nice, daddy,' Laura smiled.

'Okay, Sweetpea,' her father smiled back.

'Would you like a hot drink while we wait for your father to come back?' Mrs Hadley asked as her husband left the room.

'Cup of tea, please, mummy,' Laura replied. 'Billy?'

'Same, please, Mrs Hadley,' Billy replied.

'I'll let you two catch up and thank you again, Billy. I was getting very worried about Laura,' said Mrs Hadley and left the two children alone.

'What was the last thing you remember?' Billy asked.

'I was sat at the table – or was it on my father's knee – not really important,' Laura explained. 'I remember a piercing scream echoing around my head and then I fainted.'

'Cora?' Billy asked, intrigued. Laura nodded. 'Do you think she was hurt in some way?'

'Yes,' said Laura as the tears came to her eyes. 'I think she may have been badly hurt. I just do not know how.'

'Why don't you see if you can talk to her?' Billy prompted. 'If you can then you at least know that she is not seriously hurt.'

'That's brilliant, Billy. Why didn't I think of that?' said Laura.

'Probably because you've been in a coma for a couple of days,' Billy joked but he could already see that Laura was concentrating.

After a couple of minutes, Billy knew that it was not going well. 'I cannot reach her, Billy,' Laura cried. 'Why can't I get hold of her?'

'I don't know, Laura,' Billy answered reassuringly. 'But I will find out.'

Although Billy had promised this, he had no idea of how to find out. After he had helped Laura demolish the saffron buns and lemonade he left to walk home. Mr Hadley was going to accompany him, but Billy insisted that he would be okay by himself. He would be safe walking down the tram towards Portreath. Mr and Mrs Hadley thanked him once again for helping with their daughter before he set off back to his home.

Billy loved walking the tram in the summer. It was mainly dry, and he loved to see the canopy of green leaves. He enjoyed the heathers and the ferns on the banks. He loved the history of the tram, and sometimes imagined being one of the workers who would help push the carriage of tin from the mine all the way to Portreath harbour. On some days he would even pretend to be the one that controlled the horse that pulled the heavy load. He knew that the tramway had not been used in eighty years, but how he wished he had lived back in those days when it was in full working order.

The walkway brought Billy out by a park and behind the school which he knew so well. It was also close to Mrs Miller's house, and he noticed that Mr Miller's police car was parked outside. Although he was afraid of the policeman, who wasn't? He thought that this could be the way to find out if anything had happened to Cora. He decided to walk up the pathway and knock on the door.

Mr Miller was a very tall man, well he certainly looked like a giant to Billy, he was just over six foot, and young Billy felt very small indeed.

'Ah, Billy,' the policeman said in his gruff tone. 'What have you been up to?'

'Nothing,' said Billy casting his head down and shuffling his feet.

'So, what brings a guilty looking young boy to my doorstep?' said Mr Miller.

Billy thought carefully about his choice of words. 'I was wondering if you knew a way of finding out if something had happened in Newton Abbot recently?'

'In what way?' the policeman asked.

'A... friend of Laura Hadley's usually contacts her, but Laura has not heard anything from her,' said Billy.

'There is a war going on, young man,' said Mr Miller.
'I do know that, Sir,' said Billy. 'I'm eleven, not one.'
'Less of the cheek, young Billy,' said the policeman but had a smile on his face. 'As it happens, I've just been reading something in "The West Briton". Come in and have a look.'
Mr Miller stood aside for the boy to enter. He closed the door behind him before ushering Billy into the lounge.
'Would you like a glass of lemonade, young man?' Mr Miller asked.
'No, thank you, Sir,' replied Billy. 'I've been drinking some at Laura's and if I have any more it will make me want to pee.'
The policeman chuckled to himself. This boy was going to go far. He picked up the folded newspaper which was on the arm of the chair. It was the size of a broadsheet, so he unfolded it and handed it to the boy.

Billy looked up at the policeman as he took the paper from him. 'I believe you need to read a report on page five,' said Mr Miller.
'Thank you,' said Billy.
He had trouble holding the paper and trying to turn the pages until Mr Miller let him put it on sofa so that he could read it better. Billy opened to page five. He looked for the headline. It certainly was not the main headline. Nor was it the second or third. Right down the bottom, tucked away in the corner, was the report he was searching for. He read that Newton Abbot train station had been hit in a German bombing attack. There had been some casualties, but the actual number was not known. Rumours were spreading from between seven and twenty. Many were wounded and the death rate was liable to rise. It mentioned a girl of about ten but did not go into detail.
Billy reread the passage and again for the third time. He was trying to memorise it all. He had not realised that that the policeman had left and had returned with some scissors. 'Here, lad,' he said. 'You obviously want that so cut it out,'
'Thank you, Inspector Miller,' Billy said enthusiastically.

He cut it out and thanked Mr Miller again before leaving and returning to Laura's house. If the Hadley's were surprised to see him back so soon, then they didn't show it. He went straight back up to Laura's room.

'Billy? What are you doing back?' Laura asked.

'Newton Abbot suffered a German bombing on the twentieth of August,' Billy explained. 'The same day you fainted.'

Billy passed Laura the newspaper cutting which Laura read. 'It mentions a ten-year-old girl. I just know that is Cora. Oh, my poor friend. How can I find out what happened to her?'

'Now that I won't be able to help with,' said Billy. They both gave it some thought. 'Couldn't your dad help? I mean he is in the medical profession.' Laura chewed this over in her mind. 'You're right, Billy,' she said. 'Of course, he might be able to find out. I just have to come up with a plausible story. But I need to stash this somewhere safe. In my bottom drawer over there...' she pointed to a chest of drawers next to her wardrobe, '...you'll find a shoebox.'

Billy walked over to the furniture and opened the bottom drawer. He had to move a few items before he found the box. He took it out and walked it back over to Laura. He took off the lid so that Laura could place it inside. He saw the piece of paper that Laura had "stolen" from Kneecap Cottage.

'That's a funny name for a house,' he remarked.

'It is, isn't it?' Laura agreed but did not go into further detail. She put the clipping in the box and

Billy replaced the lid and secured it back in its secret location. 'You must help me come up with a credible story, Billy.'

'Come on, Laura. You know that you are far better than me at creating stories,' argued Billy. 'Anyway, I've got to go. I'll see you tomorrow.'

CHAPTER TWENTY-TWO

As it happened, Laura did not have time to come up with a credible story as Mr Hadley left for London a few days later. Laura was upset at her father leaving and begged him to be careful as she had heard that the Capital had been under constant bombardment; the Blitz they were calling it. Mr Hadley promised. She hugged him so tightly that Mrs Hadley had to prise her away from him. She waved him goodbye, crying.

School helped her get over it. Mrs Miller was setting her tasks that were getting harder and harder, but it was improving her English to an even higher level. The teacher, however, was a little confused on why her mathematics and science was going in the other direction. It was not like the young girl could not add up or subtract, but it was taking her a little longer than it used to take. Her division and multiplication, on the other hand, was in need of so much improvement. If only she knew the reason behind this. She tried to coax it out of Laura, but the young girl always clammed up and just did not want to talk about it.

And the reason why Laura did not want to discuss it was because no one had believed her about Cora, so she could not tell them about it. How she had not heard from her in days. How she did not know where she was or what had happened to her. All she had was the newspaper clipping that Billy had given her saying that a ten-year-old girl was badly injured in a bombing attack in Newton Abbot. She knew this was Cora but, apart from Billy, who else should she tell?

A couple of days later, Mrs Miller was in full flow with a lesson involving art. She wanted her pupils to paint something that they would find over the rainbow. As expected, the boys were drawing war pictures, so it was easy to surmise that the war was affecting them. When she came across Laura's she saw that the girl had drawn two young girls holding hands. Another thing Laura was good at was art. She could tell that it was two young girls, definitely looking like sisters, looking up at a big house. In the window was a face that did not appear to have any features.

For a fleeting moment, panic overcame the teacher. She thought that the imaginary friend was back. Mrs Miller had not heard Laura speak of her "friend" in quite a while. And now it looked like she was back. 'That's a lovely picture, Laura. Can you explain it to me?'

'It's about peace, Mrs Miller,' Laura responded.
'Peace?' said Mrs Miller completely taken aback.
'Yes,' Laura replied matter-of-factly. 'The two sisters are going home after being refugees.'
'Oh. Right,' said the teacher. 'But who is the figure in the window? Is it their mother waiting for them to come home?'
'No. It is the ghost of their dead father making sure that they got home safely,' Laura said. 'They realise that his death has helped bring peace.'
'Well, that's a very good picture, Laura,' Mrs Miller encouraged.

Laura was not stupid. She knew that Mrs Miller would think that the picture was showing Laura and her imaginary friend, and she would have been correct. This was a picture about her and Cora and Kneecap Cottage which, the more Laura thought about it, she knew was integral to the beginning of her life, and, most definitely, Cora's too. She had to admit, though, that she had no idea why she drew the face at the window. The last time she visited the house, she had heard someone, or something, in that room. She had listened to Laura explain that the other woman she could communicate with knew about the cottage as well.

The class was interrupted by Mr Davidson. Laura looked up as he heard the headmaster tell the teacher that her husband was in his office but wanted to see her in his official capacity as a police sergeant. Before she left, she asked Laura to organise the class to tidy things away. She was trembling a little as she entered the office. She nervously smiled at her husband. Mr Davidson followed her inside.

'Good morning, Sargeant,' she said. 'Mr Davidson said you were here in your official capacity.'

'I am, Mrs Miller,' he confirmed. 'I have been contacted by Newton Abbot police regarding a young girl who has been badly injured in a bombing raid.'

'Okay,' said Carly looking at both men. 'I do not know what that has to do with me.'

'They informed me that all the girl is saying is Mrs Miller, teacher and Portreath School,' said the Sargeant.

'I do not understand,' Carly said confused.

'They think she is asking for you,' said her husband.

'But I do not know anyone in Newton Abbot,' she insisted.

'Do you have a relative?' Mr Davidson asked.

'All my family are Cornish,' Carly explained. 'My parents live in Hayle; my sister in Truro and my brother in Redruth. Most of my ancestors are buried in Gwennap graveyard. You know all my living relatives, Sam, as they were at our wedding.'

Mr Miller nodded slowly, more to himself than to responding to Carly. 'But that does not explain why a young girl is asking for you in Newton Abbot hospital, does it?' he asked.

'I cannot explain it,' said Carly. 'Does she have a name?'

'They have not managed to coax it out of her yet,' the policeman answered. 'But she obviously knows you.'

'How?' said Carly. 'How can a young girl, injured in a bombing raid, possibly know me?'

By the look on her husband's face, something had clicked. 'Would you be able to bring Billy Penhale to me, please, Mr Davidson?'

Mr Davidson left straight away to collect the young boy. Mrs Miller looked shocked. 'What has young Billy got to do with this?'

Mr Miller held up his hand to stop his wife from enquiring any further. They waited in silence as Mr Davidson escorted the petrified looking young Billy into his office. The policeman smiled reassuringly at the boy.

'Now, Billy, can you explain to me why you were so interested in a newspaper report about an air raid in a small Devon town – Newton Abbot – and, in particular, about a ten-year-old girl?' Billy shook his head. 'Oh, I think you can, Billy,' Mr Miller persisted.

'I had heard a report about the air raid in Devon,' Billy said. 'The girl was irrelevant. Anyway, it never gave her name.'

'But I guess you have an idea of who it might be,' the policeman prompted. 'Or least, one of your friends is aware of who it might be?'

'I really don't know,' said Billy. 'I could hazard a guess, but then, we could all do that. There is nothing to confirm who this girl is and, yes, I did enquire about a bomb attack in Newton Abbot, but the report about the ten-year-old girl was, as I said, irrelevant. How many ten-year-olds are there in this school? How many in Truro? How many in Cornwall? So, there are probably quite a few in Newton Abbot. Adults always dismiss things that cannot be explained. We know, Miss Miller, that a certain girl was never very good at sums, don't we? Then she became very good, but now she's gone back to being terrible.'

'Laura?' Carly said almost inaudibly.
'You all dismissed her as being crazy,' said Billy. 'But what happened to her at the same time as this air raid in Newton Abbot?'
'Are you saying that Laura and this ten-year-old girl are linked, Billy?' Mr Davidson asked.
Billy shrugged. 'That I do not know, and neither does Laura.'

'So, why would she be asking for Mrs Miller, Billy?' Mr Miller questioned.
Billy shrugged again. 'Unless she does know you, Miss. Or she at least knows of you and that you are kind and considerate teacher.'
'Well, there's going to be only one way to find out,' Carly said taking control. 'It appears that I'm going to have to go to Newton Abbot and find out exactly who this girl is, who clearly knows me, somehow.'
Billy went back to the classroom. He immediately told Laura everything. Laura listened, mesmerised by what her friend was telling her.
'It has to be Cora, doesn't it?' Laura said sounding very excited.
'I have to agree with you,' said Billy. 'It cannot be anyone else. I'm pretty sure that most ten-year-olds from this town, Newton Abbot, would not have heard of Mrs Miller.'
'So, my friend, Cora, has managed to find a way to

communicate with Mrs Miller,' said Laura. 'She is ingenious that girl. If only I had thought of that.'
'Don't put yourself down like that, Laura,' Billy begged. 'It must have been you who told her about Mrs Miller in the first place.'

'That may be so, Billy, but she had the common-sense to remember the details,' Laura shot back. 'I hope she's not too badly injured. Do you think I'll get to see her soon?'
Laura was talking at speed and Billy had trouble keeping up with her. 'I guess so,' he said.

But Laura was going to have to wait. Mr Miller drove his wife to Newton Abbot. He had received permission from his superiors; Afterall, nothing much happens in Portreath. And they allowed him to take the police car.
Mr Miller had made notes from the road map that would get them to Newton Abbot. Mrs Miller had made a flask of coffee and cut some sandwiches; nothing too fancy, just cheese and pickle. It was going to take them a few hours to drive there.
Carly was a little bit nervous. Now that she was aware that a small town like Newton Abbot had been hit by German planes, anything could happen on the journey. Sam could sense her uneasiness and tried to reassure her.

They stopped in a layby just past Jamaica Inn. Now Carly Miller was fascinated by this. She had just finished reading the book of the same name by Daphne Du Maurier. She was intrigued about the smugglers plots from around the Coast. She knew that it had happened in Portreath as there was still evidence of the tunnels. Carly had lent the novel to Laura. She had brought another book with her. Agatha Christie's "Sad Cypress" which had only been published earlier in the year. She did not know why she brought it with her as she could not read in the car as it made her sick.

The weather was on their side. Although it was late in August now, it was still very warm, and the sun shone brightly in the blue sky. They had to drive with the windows open.

They stopped twice more before they got to Newton Abbot. Mr Miller drove along East Street before turning up to the hospital. The first building was the workhouse. A second building was added in eighteen seventy-one. It became the Public Assistance Institution in nineteen thirty.

Sam parked up and turned the engine off. His wife did not move but just kept staring straight ahead.

'What are we going to do?' she asked.

'Do? What do you mean? Do?' Sam replied.
'What if she wants to come back with us?'
'Would you want to take her back home with us?'
'I don't know,' Carly honestly said. 'I haven't given it much thought.' She heard her husband laughed.
'What was that for?'
'If I know you like I think I know you, then you have been thinking about nothing else,' Sam smiled. Carly turned and jokingly punched her husband on the arm. 'Okay,' she laughed. 'I admit that I have thought about it. But I don't know this girl from Adam.'
'Just listen to what she has to say,' said Sam. 'And to what the experts have to say. This young girl has survived a very traumatic experience. For some strange reason she's asking for you. How she has heard about you, I have no idea. But she must have been informed that you are a good teacher and very kind to children. Are you ready to go in yet?'

Carly stared straight ahead before taking a deep breath and slowly nodded. Sam Miller opened his car door and got out. He closed the door and walked around to the passenger side and opened the door for his wife to get out. He closed the door as she smoothed her dress. Sam walked back to his side, put the key in the lock and locked the car. He pulled the key out and stuck them in his jacket pocket. He accompanied his wife into the hospital.

They were met in reception and shown to a waiting room. There were some magazines in the room but neither felt like reading anything. About quarter of an hour after they arrived a man wearing a white coat entered the room.

'Hello,' he said shaking their hands. 'I'm Doctor Roberts. I take it you must be Mr and Mrs Miller?'

'We are,' Carly confirmed. 'How is the girl?'

'She was badly injured,' Doctor Roberts said. 'Although many of her injuries are superficial and will heal in time. It is the mental scars that will take much longer to heal.'

'Do you have a name for the child?' Sam asked.

Doctor Roberts shook his head. 'She's not actually saying a lot. Just your name, Mrs Miller, teacher and Portreath school which, I assume, is your job and where you teach?'

'It is,' Carly replied. 'But I don't understand why she is asking for me. I have no relatives in Devon and do not know anyone from Newton Abbot.'

'I cannot be much help with that one, I'm afraid,' Doctor Roberts sighed. 'She's just not saying anything else.'

'Nothing at all?' Carly asked incredulously.

'Nothing at all,' the doctor confirmed. 'As I said, her mental scars are going to take a long time to heal. Two bodies were found in close proximity to her. Both were adult females. Both were dead. One was found almost ripped in half by machine gun bullets.'

'I think that is enough information, Doctor,' said Sam.

'Right,' said the Doctor looking between the two faces. 'Anyway, we are pretty sure that one of those was the girl's mother.'

'And she witnessed such a terrifying thing?' Carly said, almost crying. 'No wonder the poor girl is in the state she is in.'

'All I can say is that someone she knows must have told her about you, and that is why she is saying your name; she feels safe with you,' said Doctor Roberts.

The teacher did not look convinced. Not only had she never heard of this girl or Newton Abbot, but she could also not recall anyone who had spoken to her or knew about this place. And then something just popped into her head.

'Laura,' she said in a whisper. She remembered Laura asking her about somewhere called Ogwell in Newton Abbot.

'What?' asked her husband.

'Is there a...er...town...or a district called Ogwell near here?' asked Carly.

'There's a village just a mile up the road,' Doctor Roberts answered. 'Why do you ask? Do you have any information that can assist us?'

'I don't know. It might be nothing,' Carly honestly

replied. 'But I think a girl in my class may know her. Can I see her?'

'There is some administration to go through first,' said Doctor Roberts. 'Then I'll take you through. Fifteen minutes later, the paperwork was completed, and Doctor Roberts led them through to the ward. Carly probably would have been impressed with the hospital architecture, but she was so focussed on the direction she was being taken, and with the person she knew was waiting for her.
Mr and Mrs Miller were shown into a ward that only had the one bed in it. Carly could clearly see the body of the girl lying in the bed, but her head was bandaged. Her heart immediately went out to the little girl and went straight over to her. She took the young girl in her arms as she sat on the bed.
'Mrs Miller. She's a teacher at Portreath School,' Cora moaned.
'I'm here,' Carly said. 'Laura sent me.'
The young girl turned her head at the sound of the soothing voice. 'Laura? How is she?'
'She's fine. Worried about you though,' said Carly reassuringly. 'She told me your name. It's Cora,

isn't it?' The girl hesitated before slowly nodding.

'May I ask you, Cora, what do you want me to do?' The girl seemed to think about it for a while. 'Can you take me home with you?' she whispered in the woman's ear.

'If that is what you want, Cora, then that will happen,' Carly responded.

'Laura always said you were a kind person and would make a wonderful mummy,' Cora said quietly. 'Would you be my mummy? I don't have one anymore.'

Carly hugged the girl closer until she felt the girl wince because of the pain and pulled back a bit, but the girl hugged her tighter instead, ignoring the pain she was obviously in.

'Will she be fit to travel, Doctor Roberts?' Sam asked the medical expert.

'There would be a lot of paperwork to sort out before she can be moved,' said Doctor Roberts. 'And provisions will need to be made at your nearest hospital, but, yes, she is fit to travel.'

'How long will it take to fill out all the forms?' Sam wondered out loud.

'You're a police officer,' Doctor Roberts joked. 'You know how long it takes to fill out all the correct documents and follow the correct protocols.'

'Weeks then,' Sam laughed.

'Maybe not that bad,' Doctor Roberts chuckled. 'But you'll certainly be looking at a week to ten days. The police here will need to be informed as well as the medical authorities.'

'I take it there is a hotel in Newton Abbot?' said Sam.

'You've got the Globe and the Queens,' the doctor replied. 'They are not cheap, but they do have a very good reputation.'

Sam booked his wife into the Globe Hotel. He had to get back to work in Cornwall. He trusted his wife to sort out all the paperwork. He also knew that when she had her mind set up something nothing anyone else could say or do, including himself, could change her mind. They were definitely going to be having this child to come and stay.

Carly loved the room at the Globe Hotel. She could see St. Leonards Tower in one direction and, if she looked up the road, she could see the library. A few cars would drive by, but it was mainly horses and carts and pedestrians. It looked a lot different than Redruth or Cambourne where she usually did her shopping. Truro, on the other hand, was a lot larger. It was quieter, that was for sure.

In the morning, she exited the hotel and turned left. She turned right onto Union Street which curved around to the right at the top and brought her out next to Ye Olde Cider House and just opposite the hospital.

The girl was sat up in bed waiting for her to arrive. She heard the teacher's footsteps as she entered the

room. 'Is that you, Mrs Miller?'
'It is, Cora,' said Carly. 'How are you feeling today?'
The girl turned her bandaged head in the direction of the teacher and just shrugged. 'Will I be going home with you later?'
'I'm not going home today, Cora,' Carly explained. 'I've booked into a hotel in Newton Abbot so I will be here with you. I believe the police will be talking to us both later.'

'The police?' Cora asked grief stricken. 'What have I done wrong?'
Carly rushed to her bed and hugged her. 'Nothing. You have done nothing wrong. They need to ask you a few things about that terrible day and about coming to stay with me. Would you like me to be here when they ask you the questions?' She felt the young girl relax a little and nod. 'Then I will be. Would you like me to read to you?'
'I prefer mathematical puzzles,' said Cora.
'Like multiplication and division?' the teacher asked.
'More like code breaking,' said Cora.
If Doctor Roberts and the nurses were surprised at how chatty Cora had become, then they did not show it. Carly had noticed the change in the girl and welcomed it. 'So, you like that sort of thing, do you? I was never much good at it when I was at

school, but I got to be quite good at them. But how are you going to solve them when you cannot see them?'

'If you read them out to me then I'll be able to see the patterns. I'm pretty good at seeing them,' Cora said becoming more confident.

They must have been playing at code breaking for more than two hours. Each time Cora got the answer, Carly was surprised. She started setting much harder ones where A would equal one minus six in the twenty-six letters of the alphabet. So, Cora worked out the twenty-one would be A. After the two hours Carly could see that the young girl was getting tired, so she made her rest. It was during this time that two senior policemen arrived. They were happy to speak to Carly first. They asked her a lot of questions. Mainly about how she knew the girl which she answered as honestly as she could. When they had finished with her, they decided to have a break. Carly told the policemen that Cora wanted her to be in the room with her and they did not have an issue with it.

They waited until after lunch to interview the young girl. They asked her about her upbringing and about her relationship with her mother and father. Cora explained that her relationship with her mother had been very good, but the opposite could be said of the one with her father. It was the first time Carly heard the names Richard and Gloria Culver mentioned.

And she would hear them often over the next few weeks. They asked her about that day. She found it difficult to talk about it. Carly sat on her bed with her arm around the young girl. She asked for a drink for Cora and a nurse fetched it. She held it as Cora took a few sips. She described the airplanes flying overhead and the machine gun fire that killed her mother. She recalled hearing her father shouting at them to lie flat before a bomb landed nearby and he was flying through the air. The asked her about how she knew Mrs Miller.
Cora's eyes were getting heavy. Carly could tell this and told the policemen that the young girl needed to rest.
'I think we're just about finished,' said the first policeman.
Carly laid Cora's head back on the pillow and she was soon asleep. She escorted the policemen out.
'She mentioned about her father there, on the day of the bombing,' said the second policeman. 'Most of the bodies have been accounted for and we can now add Mrs Culver and her friend. So, we now know that fifteen people died in the attack.'
'What are you saying, Officer?' Carly asked.

'No body has been found that could be identified as Mr Culver,' said the second policeman. Mrs Miller looked blank. 'It's possible that he suffered a direct hit from one of the bombs so his body may never be found.'

Carly put her hand up to her mouth in horror as she got the gist of what they were now implying. 'Oh, dear God,' she said. 'He didn't sound like a very nice man, but you would not wish that on anyone.'

'Well, I think we have everything we need,' said the first policeman. 'I think that girl needs a safe environment to live in so we will not oppose her going to live with you. The paperwork will be ready for you to pick up in three days. This will give you the right to care for the girl.'

'But not adopt?' Mrs Miller queried.

'Without her father's body, adoption cannot be sanctioned at present,' said the second policeman.

'Of course,' Carly sighed. 'I did know that.'

'Thank you for your time, Mrs Miller,' said the first policeman.

Carly went back to the ward where the girl was. Cora was still asleep. She took her book out of her bag

and started to read. Suddenly, she heard Cora start to moan and mumble. 'Where are you?' Silence. 'Restrained?' Silence. 'Jailer?' More silence.

'Kneecap?' Silence. Carly kept looking at the child, wondering if she should wake her up. 'Uncle?' Cora carried on. 'Mother? MOTHER?' And she woke with a start.

Carly quickly moved to cuddle the young girl. 'It's okay, Cora, I'm here. Hush now, dear,' she soothed. Doctor Roberts and a nurse came running in but quickly saw that the situation was under control.

'Has she ever done anything like this before?'

'Not that I'm aware of,' Doctor Roberts replied. 'What actually happened?'

'It sounded like she was speaking with someone, in her sleep,' Carly described what she had just witnessed.

The doctor and the nurse took the girl from Carly and laid her back down. She had drifted back off to sleep again. Doctor Roberts examined what was unbandaged on the head, which was just the eyes nose and mouth whilst the nurse checked her pulse.

'Could be something as simple as a nightmare,' he suggested. 'After what that poor girl has been through, it's hardly surprising.'

'Pulse is normal,' said the nurse.'

'She was saying things like restrained and kneecap and uncle,' said Carly. 'It sounded like sense but now it doesn't.'

'We heard her shout mother. Was that to you?' Doctor Roberts asked.

'No. I don't think it was,' Carly replied. 'Perhaps you are right. She has survived a very traumatic

experience. She clearly will have nightmares.'
'Well, she seems to be resting again now,' said Doctor Roberts. 'We will continue to monitor it. Perhaps you should get some rest, Mrs Miller.'
'I'm fine, thank you, Doctor Roberts,' said Carly. 'I have my book. I'll be here when Cora wakes up.'

CHAPTER TWENTY-THREE

The two become close over the next few days. Cora did not have a repeat of the nightmares and Carly did not pursue it with her. It was agreed that Cora would be discharged into Carly's care the following Friday. Carly had been in Newton Abbot for nearly two weeks. It was agreed with Truro hospital that Cora could be taken there for her check-ups. Doctor Roberts thought that the bandages could probably come off in a further two to three weeks. He made arrangements with Carly's own medical practitioner to also check upon the girl.
As promised, the documents were ready for Carly to collect on the day they said they would be ready.

A health official had countersigned the paperwork. Carly noted that it was not Doctor Roberts who had signed them but someone who she had never seen whilst she had been visiting Cora. She wondered how it was possible that someone could sign off on something so important who had never seen her. When she asked Doctor Roberts how this could be, he assured her that she was being observed during her time within

the hospital; how she conducted herself with the staff and how she interacted with Cora.
The day she had arranged for her husband to pick them up, she did a slight detour to look at the area where Cora had been found on that terrible day. She was horrified to see the rubble still there. Houses, which people had lived in, had been demolished. She could see bullet holes from the machine gun fire in the rail station main building. She saw a spot with dry blood and wondered if that was where Cora's mum had been killed. Her heart went out to the people who had lost their lives that day, and also to the people whose lives had been changed, like Cora. What had this small town ever done to deserve the bombing in Germany's eyes. Was it purely down to the rail station? She could see the sheds where locomotives were fixed. Looking around, it was going to take a long time to clear everything up and rebuild this part of the town.

When she got to the hospital, Cora was being rebandaged, so she had to wait outside. Her husband walked into the reception room about ten minutes after she did.

'How is she?' he asked after he had greeted Carly with a brief kiss.
'She is quite talkative now,' Carly smiled. 'We've seemed to have bonded. She is very clever. I still haven't worked out how she is connected to Laura.'
'You still think they are connected in some way then?' Sam asked.
'Oh, yes,' Carly said firmly. 'No normal person would make up a random place called Ogwell in Newton Abbot with a girl who happened to be called Cora.'
'You've got a point,' Sam agreed. They had been talking on the phone most evenings. One of the benefits about being a copper was that he could use the station phone to call his wife which saved the cost of using the home one. 'Have there been any further nightmares?'
'None,' Carly confirmed. 'She does become fidgety when she's asleep, but there have been no more murmurings. She does openly talk about that day.'
'Has she mentioned Laura?' Sam enquired.
'We've skirted around the subject, but Cora

does have this knack for changing the conversation. I think, deep down, she does not know why or how she can communicate with Laura.'

'No doubt one or both of them will tell us one day,' said Sam.

'That's if they even know,' Carly said absently. 'It just makes you think how two unrelated girls have found each other in this crazy world.'

'Maybe they are not "unrelated", Carly,' said Sam. Carly looked at her husband as though he had grown two heads. 'Of course, they are not related, Sam. I remember when Laura first mentioned Cora, she just said she was a friend of hers, nothing more. And Mr and Mrs Hadley have only had the one daughter.'

'That we know of. Cousins, perhaps?' Sam mused.

'Doubtful, but I concede, possible,' said Carly. She gave it some thought and then appeared to dismiss it. 'No. That's very unlikely. Laura is very meticulous and would have said cousin and not friend. Although she is very young and very quiet, she never seems to make grammatical mistakes.'

'I'll have to take your word for that,' said Sam.

'Mr and Mrs Miller?' a nurse had entered the room. 'Cora is ready for you.'

'Thank you, nurse,' Mr Miller responded.

They were led back to the ward where Cora was. They had managed to get her some clothes, but she looked pitiful sitting on her bed with just a small bag which held all the possessions she had. Although they had her name, she could not remember where she lived. It would have been easy for the authorities to find out, but the young girl became frantic when they started asking her questions about her house. Under no circumstances did she want to go back there. To be honest, she could hardly remember where she lived which was a concern to the doctors, but Carly got suspicious that Cora was being economical with the truth. But still, seeing her sat on the bed with just that small bag was heart-breaking. Carly vowed to buy her new things when they got back home.

Mr Miller picked up the young girl as there were no wheelchairs around. He had handed the keys to his wife. Carly picked up the small bag. Cora put her arms around the policeman's neck as he lifted her. She felt a little giddy at first, but the feeling soon passed.

'Cor! You're heavy,' Sam joked although he was concerned on how little she weighed. That would change with his wife's cooking.

'No, I'm not,' laughed Cora.

'You're like a sack of spuds, young lady,' Sam said.

'Cheeky,' Cora said, still laughing.

When they got outside, Carly unlocked the car and opened the door so that her husband could put the

young girl on the back seat.
The drive back to Portreath was a lot more joyous than the journey up. Cora would start a song and the others would join in. She would then have a snooze. They stopped off near Launceston to have a drink and a bite to eat. They played eye-spy and other games before Cora fell asleep again. She did not wake up until the car was pulling up outside of their home. Sam lifted her up, which was what actually woke her.
'Nice house,' she mumbled.
Carly locked the car doors behind them before running up the driveway to reach the front door. She knew that her husband would not be struggling carrying the young girl, but she wanted to make it easy for him. For all she knew, the bandages could be slippery even though they were beneath her clothing.
When she got inside, she was pleased to see that her husband had kept it tidy whilst she was away. She made a beeline for the spare bedroom. Again, she was relieved that Sam had gotten it ready for Cora. They were not expecting to have children in the house, so it was just decorated in a cream colour with a beige carpet. There was no wardrobe, that would have to be fixed, but there was a chest of drawers and a bed-side table. Sam entered and laid the young girl on the bed. She went straight back to sleep. Carly decided to leave the clothes on.

'Should I stay with her?'
'I don't know,' Sam replied. 'I'm guessing when she wakes up, she's going to be startled and disorientated. She'll probably need reassuring. I would probably stay with her.'
And that is what Carly did. Her husband was right. When Cora woke up, she did wonder where she was and became quite frantic until Carly quietened her down.

'Would you like something to eat, Cora? Or something to drink?' Carly asked.
'Yes, please,' Cora replied.
'SAM!' Carly called for her husband.
'It's okay,' said Cora. 'I can walk.'
Before Carly could react, Cora had gotten off the bed and immediately fell to the floor.
'SAM!' Carly yelled.
''Don't panic. I'm not hurt,' said Cora. 'Well, I got that wrong, didn't I? Obviously, I cannot walk at the moment.'
Carly started to laugh. 'You are a funny thing.'
Sam did not know what was going on when he rushed into the room. All he saw was the young girl lying on the floor with Carly kneeling over her and they were both laughing hysterically.
'Is everything alright?' he asked.
'I've just found out the hard way that I can't walk,' Cora laughed. 'And it was a long way down from that bed.'

'Riiiggghhht,' said Sam who was still unclear as to why they were laughing.
'You needed to be here, love,' Carly said. 'Cora would like something to eat and drink.'
'But I think you may need to give me a lift,' said Cora which triggered off the laughter once more. Sam lifted Cora up. 'Is this what it's going to be like with two females in the house?'
'I guess it is, Sam,' said Carly. 'I guess it is.'
He carried her into the kitchen and sat her on one of the wooden chairs. Carly followed them in. She filled up the kettle whilst Sam looked in the fridge.
'How would you fancy a Cornish pasty?' he asked.
'A what?' Cora responded.
'Now, you're not telling me, Ma'am, that you've never heard of a Cornish pasty?' Sam said in a mock disbelief tone.
'I've never even heard of a Devonshire Pasty,' said Cora.

'Tsk. The Devon folk don't know how to make a pasty. They don't know how to make a proper cream tea, me handsome,' said Sam.
'You say some pretty weird things, Mr Miller,' said Cora, but he could sense she was smiling.

'That I do, lass. That I do,' Sam agreed.
He took the pasty out of the fridge and placed it in front of the girl. She looked at it and then at him before reverting her eyes back to the pasty. It virtually filled the entire oval dinner plate. 'Wow! That's very big. I don't think I'll be able to eat all that,' she said.
'You're a growing girl,' said Sam.
'If I eat all that, then you won't be able to carry me back into the bedroom,' said Cora
'How about I give you a half of it?' asked Sam.
'How about a third?' Cora counted.
'Okay. A third it is,' smiled Sam and he went to get a knife.
'I must say, Cora, that his mum makes the best pasties ever,' said Carly.
'I don't think I've ever had a pasty before,' said Cora.

'Well, you try that, me handsome,' said Sam as he put the cut piece of pasty in front of her. He watched as Cora bit off a mouthful. She chewed and chewed it. 'Well?'
'Give her a chance, love,' Carly laughed.
'I don't think I've tasted anything so wonderful,' Cora responded. 'It's mouth-watering.' She went into devour another mouthful.
'They're even better when they've just come out of the oven,' said Sam. 'I'm sure that we will get her to

make you one in a couple of weeks.
'I think I'm going to like living here,' said Cora.
Carly smiled at her husband, and he smiled back.

Cora did wonder if she would see Laura. But she was disappointed for the whole week. Carly had managed to arrange for the time off work, so she was able to stay with the young girl. She helped the young girl to gain some strength, and she was walking before the week came to an end.

To be fair to Laura, though, she had no idea that Cora was staying at Mrs Miller's house. She had not communicated with Cora until just before the bomb landed on Newton Abbot. She had heard the rumours that Mrs Miller had been "arrested" by the police and taken to Devon. Instead of worrying about it, she threw herself into her schoolwork. Under Mr Davidson's tutorage, she became more proficient at mathematics.
She got so excited, and nervous, on the Friday when Mr Davidson called her into his office in the morning. She did not know what to expect. She could not remember doing anything naughty. She approached the headmaster's door.
'Come in, Laura,' said Mr Davidson. Laura took a deep breath before opening the door and entering. Mr Davidson stood up and gestured for her to sit on the chair opposite his desk. He sat down just after

she did. 'I need to ask you a favour, Laura. I have to go to an important meeting and Miss Cummings is not well to cover me. Mrs Miller has something she needs to attend to at home. You are an intelligent child, Laura, so I was hoping that you may stand in for me.'

'Me, Sir?' Laura squeaked. 'But I'm not even ten.'

'I don't think your age will be a disadvantage, Laura,' said Mr Davidson. 'You have a very wise head on your shoulders. I think you will cope.'

'But what will I teach?' she asked. She was still nervous, but the excitement was starting to take over.

'From what I've observed, you like reading and writing, so why don't you just do that?'

'And what if the rest of the class turn against me?' Laura asked in a small voice.

'Just do what I do,' Mr Davidson chuckled. 'Threaten them with lines if they misbehave. It will just be until lunchbreak.'

'Okay, Sir,' said Laura. 'I'll do my best.'

'Thank you, Laura,' said Mr Davidson. 'We will go back to class now and I will explain to the others what will happen.'

Laura was probably in a state of shock as she followed the headmaster back to class. 'Oh my God. What have I done?'

'I don't know. What have you done?' Cora's voice entered her head.

'Am I pleased to hear from you,' said Laura. 'I've just agreed to be a teacher.'
'A teacher? Wow! That's impressive,' said Cora.
'How will I survive this?' Laura moaned.
'I've just survived a German bombing raid,' said Cora. 'I'm pretty sure that you can survive standing up in front of a group of younger and older children for an hour or so.'
'Sorry. That was very insensitive,' Laura apologised. 'How are you feeling?'
'Better than I was,' said Cora. 'I'll tell you all about it when I see you.'
'Where are you?' Laura asked.
'At Mrs Miller's,' replied Cora.
'Mrs Miller's?' Laura clarified.
'Well, you recommended her,' said Cora. 'I just listened.'
'I'll come and visit you tomorrow then,' said Laura sounding very excited.
Laura closed her mind as they re-entered the classroom. She listened as the headmaster explained what was going to happen. She stood her ground as all the attention focussed on her. She did not really hear what Mr Davidson was saying, but she suddenly felt that he was bending down, talking

to her.

'Like I said, Laura, I will not be too long. Just do your best and I'll take over when I get back.'

And then he was gone. Laura walked over to the teacher's desk. 'Get out your books, class,' she said confidently.

The lesson went very quickly. Most of the children were well behaved and responded well to her teaching. She helped those who were struggling with the text and complimenting those who were doing well; encouraging them to progress further. She cringed with embarrassment when Billy kept on addressing her as Miss Hadley.

It only felt like five minutes before Mr Davidson appeared back in the classroom. He sent them out for their lunchbreak but kept Laura behind. 'How did you enjoy that, Laura?'

'I loved it,' she said, her eyes wide. 'I think I am going to be a teacher when I grow up.'

'That's good to hear,' Mr Davidson smiled. 'Thank you again for helping me out. I'll be sure to call on you again.'

'Make sure you do,' she laughed and ran from the class to find Billy. He was waiting for her by the main school door.

'Hello, Miss Hadley,' he joked as she almost ran by him.

'Shut up, Billy,' she smiled. 'You're coming with me tomorrow.'
'Where?' Billy asked.
'To see Cora,' Laura answered.
'Cora?' said Billy. 'Where is she?'
'At Mrs Miller's,' Laura replied.
'Okay. I'll go with you...Miss,' said Billy.
Laura playfully punched him in the arm.

Laura almost exhausted her mother with her enthusiastic retelling of her day of becoming a teacher. She may have slightly exaggerated certain areas, but it was virtually non-stop for two hours. Mrs Hadley had been aware that the headmaster was going to ask Laura as he had contacted her to get her permission. To say that she had been surprised was an understatement. She had never heard of a girl who was nearly ten being asked to deputise for a teacher. Mr Davidson did explain that it happened often in rural communities; usually with older children but he found Laura to be an exceptionally bright child and, after discussing it with Mrs Miller, decided that she would be the best option to cover the class whilst he was away.
Mrs Hadley listened intently as her daughter rambled on and on. She found it difficult to

interrupt when Laura was in full flow. She just nodded and laughed, hopefully in the right place. Although her little girl was not yet ten-years-old, she knew that Laura was going to be a teacher, and nothing was going to get in her way.

'I'm going to go and see Mrs Miller tomorrow and ask her advice,' Laura finally finished.

'That sounds like a very good idea,' said Mrs Hadley.
'I can meet the girl they have brought back home,'
'Girl?' Mrs Hadley enquired.
'The girl who survived the bombing in Newton Abbot,' Laura explained. 'Mr and Mrs Miller have let her come to stay with them. She'll probably be going to our school so I can practice being a teacher on her.' Mrs Hadley had a thousand questions but right at that moment that telephone rang. 'That'll be daddy. I can tell him my wonderful news.' She jumped down from the chair and ran to answer the phone.

The following day Laura called for Billy so that they could go and visit Cora together. Mrs Penhale invited her in and offered her a glass of lemonade which Laura politely declined. She mentioned to Billy's mother that she was thinking of becoming a teacher. Mrs Penhale asked her questions which

Laura answered.
'Well, Miss Hadley,' Mrs Penhale smiled. 'It

sounds to me like you are going to be a very good teacher.'
Billy bounded into the kitchen. 'Hope you're not here to give me lines, Miss.'
'One more wise crack like that, Billy Penhale, and I'll give you the stick,' joked Laura.
'I'll be good, Miss. I promise,' said Billy in mock horror and they both creased up laughing.
'Well, you two are in good spirits,' said Mrs Penhale. 'Where are you two off to?'
'Over to Mrs Miller's,' said Billy. 'She's got a visitor we want to meet.'
'Have you been invited to visit?' Mrs Penhale asked.
'Yes, we have,' said Laura. She thought strictly that was true as she did arrange it with Cora.
'Well, have a nice time. Would you like to come back for a sandwich and a drink, Laura?' Mrs Penhale asked.
'Thank you, Mrs Penhale. That would be very nice.'

Laura and Billy walked down the tramway which led to the road. This took them behind the school and brought them out by Mr and Mrs Miller's house. They walked up the driveway and Laura knocked on the door. Mrs Miller opened it.

'Hello, you two,' she smiled. 'I take it you've heard we've got a visitor?' Both the children nodded. 'No need to ask how you found out, is there, Laura?' The girl looked all innocent. 'Well, you'd better both come in.' She stood aside for the two children to come through. 'How did your first day of being a teacher go, Laura?'

'I thoroughly enjoyed it, Mrs Miller,' said Laura. 'I'm thinking of becoming one when I'm older.'

'After my job then?' Mrs Miller smiled.

'Maybe one day,' said Laura.

'She was pretty good, Mrs Miller. Possibly better than you,' said Billy.

'Well, thank you for that, Billy,' said Mrs Miller. 'I'm making a drink for Cora. Would you two like one? She's having a coffee.'

'Thank you. I'll have the same, please,' said Laura.

'Can I have a squash, please, Mrs Miller,' Billy asked.

'Of course, you can. I'll take you through to Cora now.'

They followed the teacher through the hallway, up the stairs and waited whilst Mrs Miller opened the door and went in to check on Cora. They heard her tell Cora that they were here, and it definitely sounded like she was excited and begged that they be let in. Mrs Miller came out and she held the door open for them. They took this as an indication that they were allowed to go in. The door was pulled to, but not closed, behind them.

Laura crept cautiously into the room. She gasped when she saw Cora who, for some strange reason, also gasped. Laura was not expecting her friend to be covered head to toe in bandages.

'Why aren't you still in hospital looking like that?' she asked.

'They've only wrapped me in these for protection,' Cora explained. 'My wounds are only superficial.'

'You could have warned me,' said Laura.

'And you could have warned me,' said Cora.

'About what?' asked Laura.

'That you look so...' Cora began.

'Look like what?' Laura interrupted. 'Pretty?'

'Of course. But you'll soon see,' Cora replied.

'When do you get the bandages taken off?' Billy asked.

Cora seemed to notice the boy for the first time. She was pleasantly surprised by the look of him. 'I'm guessing you're Billy?' Billy nodded. 'Laura has told me a lot, and I mean a lot, about you. You're a bit cuter than I imagined.'

'Cora!' Laura admonished but giggled when she saw Billy blushing. She had never seen her friend looking so embarrassed.

'In answer to your question, Billy, the bandages

should come off within the next couple of weeks,' said Cora.
'You look like one of those Egyptian mummies,' commented Billy.

'You say the nicest things, Billy,' said Cora.
'So, what happened on the evening of the twentieth August?' Laura asked. 'I knew something terrible happened to you because I blacked out.
'She was out for a good few days,' said Billy.
'We had just gotten off the train,' Cora began. 'Mummy and I had just had a wonderful day in Torquay. I heard the planes before I saw them. The bullets ricocheted off the walls but then they tore into mummy's friend who was walking with us. The second plane's machine gun fire hit my mother; almost ripping her body in two.' Both Laura and Billy pulled faces at this information. 'I had heard this voice shouting at me to get down. I threw myself to the ground. I turned my head just as one of the planes released a bomb. I didn't see where it landed but I saw my father flying through the air, so it must have hit near him.'
'Oh, you poor thing,' sobbed Laura.
'I got hit by shrapnel and rubble,' said Cora.
'Why aren't you still in hospital?' asked Billy.
'They said that my injuries are only superficial,' Cora answered. 'If Mrs Miller hadn't responded then, I

guess, they would have kept me in. Until, that is, I was fit enough to be moved to the orphanage.'

'How did you manage to get hold of Mrs Miller?' Billy asked.

'Apparently, I kept on mentioning her when I was delirious,' said Cora. 'I think I must have been listening to Laura too much and the way she described her.'

'How do you two communicate?' Billy wondered.

'We use our thoughts,' Laura replied. 'Sometimes we can guess what the other is going to say.'

'Sometimes we can even feel each other's pain,' said Cora.

'That goes without saying,' Billy said. 'Laura obviously felt what happened to you.'

'I think we're going to be great friends,' said Cora.

And Cora definitely got that right.

CHAPTER TWENTY-FOUR

Mr Hadley finally managed to arrange a meeting with Doctor Turner and Doctor Paige on the day that Cora was to get her bandages removed; not that he was to know this. He made his way to the hospital looking at the bomb craters and devastation the blitz was causing. It had only started on the seventh of September; just under two weeks ago. He had been fortunate a couple of times. The hospital had been hit, but he had just managed to get to the basement where the air-raid shelter was located. The soldier he was performing surgery on at the time had also, miraculously survived. He had even joked that it was safer in the trenches in France. The German's were certainly damaging the capital.

When he arrived at the other hospital, he was shown into the reception room. Doctor Turner came out to fetch him.

'George! It's good to see you,' he said. proffering his hand.

'Bernard,' George replied shaking his hand. 'I apologise that it's taken this long but...'

'No need to explain, George. We all know what's going on. I heard your hospital got hit.'

'A couple of times,' George confirmed.

'Thankfully, this one has not been touched,' said Bernard. 'But if these aerial bombardments keep happening, then I cannot see we will continue to be lucky.'

'It does appear to be the new German strategy to bomb the hell out of London,' said George. 'I think if they succeed in bringing down the capital then Britain will surrender. But they do not know about the British spirit.'

'They will never defeat us,' Bernard agreed. 'Come through, George. My colleague, Doctor Michael Paige, is waiting for us. We do have a lot to go through.'

'Okay,' said George who was now starting to feel slightly apprehensive.

He followed Doctor Turner into his office where he was introduced to Doctor Paige.

'I must say, Doctor, I am a great admirer of your work,' said Doctor Paige.

'Likewise, Doctor Paige,' George returned the compliment. 'I read your paper on Extrasensory perception. Exceptional, if you would allow me to say.'

'Thank you,' smiled Doctor Paige. 'But something you do not particularly agree with I would imagine.'

'The jury is out for me,' George admitted. 'I think more research is required, like what you are no doubt doing. I believe that the so called sixth sense could possibly be present in animals and humans are, after all, animals. So, I will not dismiss it out of hand just yet.'

'If only everyone was like you, Doctor,' said Doctor Paige.

'Please, call me George.'

'Michael,' Doctor Paige gave his Christian name.

'I hope you do not mind me asking what this is about?' said George.

'You probably remember when you brought your lovely daughter her to be assessed, George?' Bernard Turner asked.
'Of course,' confirmed George. 'It's not everyday someone reports your daughter as being crazy.'

'Right,' said Bernard. 'Obviously she was not found to be insane. You confirmed that she was your only child?'
'Correct,' George replied slowly not really sure where this conversation was heading but could probably have hazard a guess.
'My colleague here was dealing with another case similar to your daughter's,' said Bernard.
'In every detail it was almost exactly the same,' said Michael. 'The way she recounted a deck of cards was astonishing.'
'I cannot see what this has to do with my daughter,' said George trying to curtail his impatience.
Bernard pulled a sheet of paper from out of the file that was on his desk. He handed it to George. It had all the card names written on it. 'Do you recognise the handwriting?'
'It looks like Laura's,' he admitted.
'I did take it from her file,' said Doctor Turner. 'I never got her to memorise a deck of cards. Can you

remember what the name of her "imaginary" friend was?'

'I believe it was Cora,' George replied uneasily.

'And you can probably guess what the Christian name of my patient was,' said Michael. 'She had an imaginary friend, too. She called her Laura.'

George went as white as a sheet. He had to sit down. Bernard poured him a drink of water that had been placed on his desk. 'I saw a girl when you sent me out whilst you did your tests. I thought it was Laura. May I use your telephone? I need to call my wife.'

The two specialists may have been surprised but Doctor Turner allowed him to use the one in his office. George got put through to Gail. 'Hello?' he heard her voice. It sounded so good.

'Hello, darling,' said George.

'George? Is everything alright, dear?' asked Gail.

'We need to tell her,' he replied.

'Tell her what?' Gail questioned.

'Everything, Gail. Everything.'

It had been agreed for the local doctor to remove the bandages at Mr and Mrs Miller's home. It was considered unnecessary to cause her stress in moving her to Truro. Cora also wanted Laura and Billy to be there for moral support. A nursing assistant also attended in case there was anything medically urgent that needed to be sorted.

There were seven people in that room when the

doctor and nurse started to cut and undo the bandages. They took their time as they did not want to harm the girl in any way. They finally unwrapped the last piece of bandage around the head five minutes after they had started. Her hair was matted but fell around her shoulders.

Cora turned to look at the others. There were audible gasps. Mr and Mrs Miller and Billy looked from Cora to Laura and back again.

'It's like looking in a mirror,' Billy whispered.

'You can say that again,' Carly whispered back. There was silence. 'It's like looking in a mirror,' Billy repeated.

'You look like me,' said Laura.

'I know,' said Cora. 'When I first saw you, I knew. I tried to tell you...'

'I saw you when I visited the hospital. At least I thought it was you because you looked a lot like me. But how? Why are we so alike?' Laura said.

'I can answer that.' No one had heard Gail Hadley enter, but all heads turned to look at her. The front door had not been closed properly and Gail had found it necessary to barge right in. 'I should have told you years ago.'

'Told me what, mummy?' asked Laura.

Gail looked as though she was choosing her words carefully. 'You know that house we pass? The one with the gnomes?' Laura nodded. 'Well, that house is just a reception centre. I used to work there. In the woods behind there were...are...were a couple of very large buildings. I was a nun and a midwife. We used to deliver the babies of vulnerable girls; usually underage. The babies were immediately adopted by couples who were waiting in the reception house for them to be born. Looking back, it was harsh, I know. Tearing new-

born babies away from their mothers, but, at the time, we had to do what the girls' parents requested us to do. It was hard, you must believe me. No. That's a lie. It was hard for some of us, others found it quite easy. I guess they thought they were doing God's work.
Anyway, that is beside the point. I remember this one night a young girl was in labour. She was only fourteen years old. She had a speech impediment, but she was a lovely young thing. She was certainly giving my fellow sister a run for her money. However, she had problems delivering the poor baby. That was you, Cora.'
Everyone was engrossed with her story, even the local doctor and nurse, but everyone turned to look at Cora when Gail had said that.
'It got so bad that the doctor had to be called in,' Gail continued, and all attention was focussed her way. 'That was your father, Sweetpea. Cora was delivered and I took her straight away to her new parents. No. Again, that's not true. I stopped so

that the girl could have a look at you, Cora. That was against procedure, but the young girl was begging me. She had gone through a lot, so what harm could there be. Then I took you, Cora, to your new parents. I don't really know what happened next, but my fellow Sister noticed that

the poor child was wanting to push again but there was a lot of blood. Your father fought hard but knew it would be a struggle to keep either the baby or the young teenager alive. I came back in just as you were being born, Laura.' There was an audible gasp from both the young girls. 'Yes, that's right, Laura, Cora. You are twins. Your mother died just after giving birth to you, Laura. Your father managed to save you but could not save her. You were not expected, Laura, but you looked so perfect. Your daddy and I became close after that. I left the convent, mainly because I disagreed with what they were doing. I did not think that God would want what we were doing to really happen. Your daddy and I got married and we adopted you. I'm so sorry, Laura. I hope that you can forgive me...us.'
Laura went over to her mother, put her arms around her and hugged her tightly. 'There's nothing to forgive, mummy,' she said. 'You've looked after me all these years, you are my mummy and daddy.' This made Gail cry.
'You're wrong about one thing, Mrs Laura's

mummy,' said Cora. 'I know that my mummy died in the bombing raid but the mummy who gave birth to me and Laura is not dead.'

'I'm afraid she is, Cora,' said Gail. 'I was in the room when she died.'
'I'm just telling you that I know she is not dead,' Cora repeated. 'I don't know where she is; she could be still at the house for all I know, but she is very much alive.'
'How, do you know, dear?' Carly asked.
'I speak to her sometimes,' Cora shrugged as it was a normal thing to say.
'I now know that you and Laura can communicate,' said Gail, 'because you are twins and twins have that special bond. How you do it, I have no idea. But no one can talk to the dead, my dear child.'
'Like I said. She's not dead,' Cora said for a third time.
'But Mrs Hadley was in the room, Cora, love,' said Mr Miller. 'They saw what happened to the young lass.'
'I'm just telling you that I think she's still alive,' said Cora.
'Is there any way we can find out for sure, mummy?' Laura asked.

'I don't really know how we can,' said Gail hesitantly when a thought entered her head. 'Unless George could...maybe that could...you know, there just may be a way. You're going to have to get better first, Cora, before I even think about arranging it.'

As it was, Cora's injuries were healing quickly. The doctor at Newton Abbot hospital had been correct in his assessment that the wounds were superficial. They were temporarily dressed, but the medical experts reckoned that the bandages could be taken off within the week.

The newfound twin sisters became inseparable. If Laura was not to be found at the Miller's house, then Cora would be at the Hadley's. Billy was usually found at both. Danielle also became started to join up with the three. It did make Cora a little sad that she had left Marion behind, but she enjoyed playing with Laura's friends.

On one of the visits to Laura, Carly and Sam were left to tidy up after breakfast. Cora had offered to help, but they were happy for her to be with her sister. After they had washed up, Sam made a cup of coffee and put the two cups on the table as he sat down next to his wife.

'She's going to want to go and stay with the

Hadley's, isn't she?' Carly said.
Sam took a sip of coffee but wished he hadn't because it was still very hot. 'They are twin sisters, Carly,' he replied. 'It goes without saying that they will always want to be together. There not even ten yet, but they've got a few years to catch up on.'
'Have they, though, Samuel?' Carly pondered. 'I mean, they've been communicating with each other for a number of years.'
'I still don't understand how they did that,' said Sam. 'It just does not seem normal.'
'Nothing about those two is normal,' said Carly. 'Remember, I dismissed Laura's ramblings as just being a young girl with an imaginary friend.'
'You weren't to know,' Sam replied.
'I knew something was happening,' said Carly. 'Laura was never good at maths, probably languishing in the bottom quarter, but she soon became brilliant. I understand that Cora is very good at mathematics.'

'Can you believe what the Hadley's did, though?' asked Sam.
'They gave a young child a wonderful life, Sam,' Carly responded. 'That's what they done. They saved her life as a baby and raised her as their own. We would have done exactly the same thing. Do you think the mother is truly dead? Only Cora is adamant that she is still alive.'
'Mrs Hadley says that she saw the poor child die,' Sam replied. 'Without any other evidence, I'm

inclined to believe her. Like Mrs Hadley said, she has a way to find out the truth. If we can be of any help, then I'm sure that she will ask us.'
'I know,' Carly sighed. 'I'm not sure if I want her to be alive or dead. One thing is for sure, it would be nice to have closure for the children.'

Laura, Cora, Danielle and Billy were in Laura's bedroom discussing the same thing.
'Are you sure you've spoken to her?' Danielle asked in awe.
'Of course, I'm sure,' said Cora. 'At first, she was quite difficult to understand. But them she became clearer.'
'That's creepy,' said Danielle, but was absolutely fascinated.
'Have you shown Cora that piece of paper you stole from the house?' Billy asked.
'Oh, yes,' said Cora. 'I had forgotten all about that. Let me have a look.'
Laura got up and went to her chest of drawers. She opened the drawer that contained the piece of paper and rummaged through before she eventually found it. She closed the drawer and walked back over to Cora and handed it to her. 'It does not actually tell us much,' Laura said.
Cora took the piece of paper and unfolded it. She smoothed it out and started reading. She was a little

disappointed that it did not give much away.
'You're right. It doesn't give much information. It doesn't mention our mother's name. I mean, who is Mr and Mrs Wellington?'
'They're down as next of kin,' Billy pointed out.
'They must be your grandparents,' said Danielle.

Cora and Laura looked at each other and then back at the piece of paper. 'Our grandparents?' they said in unison. 'Wow!'
'You can tell that you two are twins just by listening to you,' Billy laughed.
'I wonder what you mum has got planned, Laura, and when she's going to carry it out,' Cora stated.
'I don't know,' said Laura. 'It was when you were supposed to be better.'
'My bandages are being removed tomorrow,' said Cora. 'I'm going to be starting school next week. Perhaps we should ask her.'
'Perhaps,' Laura shrugged.
'I'm surprised you still call her mum,' said Danielle.
'She saved my life, Danielle,' said Laura. 'She raised me as my own. I've never seen or spoken to my other mummy like Cora can. Although I'm pretty sure that I heard someone that may have been her when I got that bit of paper.'

Cora's interest was piqued. 'I cannot remember you telling me that,' said Cora.

'I'm pretty sure that I did,' said Laura thoughtfully.

'Tell me exactly what happened,' Cora demanded.

'I crept upstairs and there was this door that was locked,' Laura recalled. 'I heard this noise. It did not make any sense. It just sounded like someone going yahehiouoooooo.'

'That's what she sounded like when I first heard her,' said Cora excitedly. 'I think it was our mother.'

'Do you think so? Really?' Laura said equally as excited.

'Definitely,' said Cora.

'But why can't Laura hear her like you can?' Billy asked.

'I reckon it is because Mrs Hadley showed me to our mummy, so she saw me and heard me. She never got to see Laura, and Laura never got to see her,' Cora reasoned.

'So, when you first spoke with Laura, how did you do it?' Billy was intrigued. 'I mean, you had never seen her.'

'I just imagined a girl who looked like me,' Cora simply replied. 'I don't think I was expecting any reply. Come to think of it, you spoke to me first,

Laura. Wasn't it about that house?'

'It was,' Laura remembered. 'I caught sight of my reflection in the window. I think I said something about the house. Next thing your voice popped into my head. I was speaking with mummy about that house. Perhaps I just wanted to have a friend at that point. I did not imagine that I had a twin sister.'

'I hope we find out something about our mother soon,' said Cora.

CHAPTER TWENTY-FIVE

Cora got her wish the following weekend. Her bandages were removed and all that were remaining of the wounds were tiny scars. The medical practitioner even thought that they would not even mark her for life.

The two sisters sat next to each other in Miss Miller's class. They were the centre of attention on the Monday. This pleased Cora but Laura wished that the ground would just open and swallow her up. The other children kept on asking them questions which Cora loved to answer so Laura let her.

Mrs Miller also recognised straight away that Cora was brilliant at mathematics and science. She had already had an inkling about this when she had visited the girl in the hospital. Laura, on the other hand, was excelling even more at English, history and arts. The other good thing was that each helped the other with their weaker subjects, so Laura started to improve with sums. This was immediate and some of the other children noticed it by the end of the week.

'Looks like you are going to have to up your game, Danielle,' Billy teased their friend. 'It looks like Cora will be taking top spot from you in sums, and even Laura is catching you up.'

'Shut up, Billy,' said Laura, clearly embarrassed.

'Yes. Shut up, Billy,' Danielle echoed.

'Just saying,' Billy shrugged.

Cora smiled. She was settling in quite nicely with Laura's friends, but she was enjoying the company of her twin sister even more. And that feeling was being reciprocated. Laura loved having Cora with her. She wanted her to sleep over but had not plucked up the courage to ask Cora, Mrs Miller or her mother.

Mrs Miller could tell straight away that Cora was the more confident of the two, but she could see that Laura was gaining confidence day by day. She was still amazed how these two girls found each other.

She accepted their explanation of how they communicated with each other, although she never really understood the science behind it. Cora was exceptionally good at science; probably as good as Laura was at English. It just did not make any sense to her. There was no science that she knew of that could explain how two people could talk to each other, using their minds,

whilst being miles and miles apart. But if that's how they say it happened, then that's how it happened. She did get a surprise when she went home to lunch on the Wednesday and found Gail Hadley waiting for her. The two women were getting on a lot better now the girls were together. They had made up since that day Gail had stormed out of her office when Mrs Hadley had thought she was saying that Laura might be insane. Carly had actually thought Laura was genius, but war had put paid to anything further happening on that front.
'Mrs Hadley,' she welcomed.
'Please, call me Gail,' said Gail.
'I take it this is about the twins,' said Carly. She was worried that Gail was about to say that she thought it best if Cora came to stay with them.
'Please come in, Gail,' she said opening the door. 'Would you like a cup of tea or coffee? And, please, call me Carly.'
'I would not say no to a cup of tea, Carly, thank you very much,' Gail replied as she stepped over the

threshold. She closed the front door behind her and followed Carly into the kitchen. She watched as Carly started to make the drinks. 'I never apologised to you, did I?'

'About what?' said Carly, although she knew what this was related to.
'You only had Laura's best interests at heart,' Gail explained. 'You never thought she was insane.'
'No, I didn't,' said Carly. 'I thought Laura was a very gifted child who needed some better opportunity at education to take her to the next level.'
'I know,' said Gail. 'I even knew it then, but even I had doubts about her mentality at the point. I had heard her "talking" to Cora. Laura used to talk aloud. Apparently, she had not quite mastered the art of telepathy.' Gail chuckled at the recollection which made Carly smile. 'I didn't know what was going on. To be honest, I was relieved when she got referred to be assessed for her mental state. However, I was delighted to find out there was nothing wrong with her. And then I got the phone call from Richard – my husband.'
'To explain that Cora and Laura were related?' asked Carly.
Gail nodded. 'It appears that Cora and Laura were at the hospital at the same time. George even

remembers seeing Cora, but at the time, he thought it was Laura who was wandering the hospital corridors lost. He was having a meeting with the two specialists who dealt with the girls. Do you realise that the girls even communicated with each other during the tests they had to undertake. Cora got Laura to help her memorise a deck of cards by asking her to write them down in the sequence she gave her. She then got Laura to tell her the cards in order when the Doctor asked her to recall them.'
'That's clever,' Carly remarked.
'I have to agree there,' Gail smiled.
'Just out of curiosity, has Laura ever mentioned Cora's parents, Mr and Mrs Culver?'
'A few times,' Gail admitted. 'She told me that Cora got on well with Gloria Culver, her mother, but the relationship with her father, Richard Culver, was very poor.'
Carly finished making the cups of tea and placed them both on the table. Gail thanked her but declined when Carly asked if she wanted a biscuit.
'So, how can I help you?' she asked.

'George will be coming home from London tomorrow,' Gail began.
'I hope he's alright,' Carly said, concerned. 'I've heard that London has been getting it particular

bad with bombing raids.'

'He doesn't really talk about it,' Gail admitted. 'I can tell he finds it difficult. Not only is he getting soldiers from the frontline being sent back for surgery, but he's also getting civilians being brought in that have been caught up in the bombing. I don't think he's getting much rest. I think he's been told to take a break before he collapses.'

'You both must come over for a meal,' Carly invited.

'That would be nice,' said Gail. 'But the real reason for my visit is that we are planning to visit Kneecap Cottage on Saturday. I told you there may be a way to get actual answers about the girls' real mother. I was hoping that you and Cora could come along?'

Whatever she might have been expecting Gail to say, it certainly was not that. 'I'll have a chat with Sam, but I would like to be there. Thank you for asking. What is your plan?'

And Gail outlined her idea to Carly. Carly chipped in with a couple of points. But from that moment on, the two became very close friends.

Laura, Cora, Billy and Danielle walked through the back entrance at Laura's home on the Thursday after school.

'Hello, Sweetpea,' she heard the voice of her father. 'Daddy,' Laura squeaked excitedly and ran to find him. He was hiding in the kitchen pantry, his usual hiding place. She leapt into his arms and hugged him. Mrs Hadley, who was stood in the kitchen, laughed.
George hugged his daughter tightly. He had seen some horrific injuries over the past few weeks. He knew that it was right for him to be sent home for a rest, but the brave soldiers at the front were not getting any rest. He put her down. 'I'll give you five seconds to hide and then I'm going to find you and tickle you until you plead me to stop.'

'No, daddy,' Laura screamed playfully. 'Not the tickling.'
She squirmed in his arms as he playfully tickled her under the arm. He set her down. 'One,' he began counting.
'No,' squealed Laura as she ran off laughing.
'Two...three...four....five,' he finished. 'Coming ready or not. As he turned the corner to the back door, he instantly saw Laura crouched down behind the three children he was next expecting. 'Oh! Hello.'
'Hello,' they replied in unison.
His eyes were immediately drawn to Cora. She was, without doubt, the spitting image of Laura. His mind was cast back to the day he had helped

delivered them. Although, he had not had anything to do with Cora's birth, he was there for Laura's. That was the day he lost their mother. He remembered the blood. It was everywhere. 'Now, anyone who is protecting my daughter will also get a tickling.'

He had never seen three children scatter in different directions so quickly before. There were screams of delight as they disappeared. This left Laura unprotected. She was giggling. 'Don't tickle me, daddy. Please don't tickle me,' she said laughing her head off.

'Okay. I promise I will not tickle you if you help me find the others,' said George.

'Okay, daddy,' Laura said. 'I'll help you.'

It did not take them too long to find the others, although Mrs Hadley did help a bit. She had poured some lemonade and put some saffron buns on a plate so when George and Laura had finished tickling them, they sat at the table to eat and drink them.

'Wow! These are really tasty,' said Cora munching one of the saffron buns.

'I love 'em,' said Laura. 'The Portreath Bakery make the best ones in Cornwall.'

'You mean the world,' Billy said with a mouth full of bun.

'Billy? I'm sure your mother would say finish what is in your mouth before you speak,' Gail said.

'Sorry, Mrs Hadley,' he said, but still had a load of bun crammed in his mouth.

After they had finished, they went up to Laura's room to play. George helped Gail clear away and then helped her prepare for dinner. Gail waited and waited for her husband to say something, but in the end, it got too much for her. 'So, what do you think, George,' she asked.
'I cannot believe how much alike they look,' said George, knowing what his wife was implying. 'When those scars are gone, and they will disappear, it will be almost impossible to tell them apart.'
Gail nodded in agreement. 'Their personalities are different. Cora is confident, greatly confident. Laura is quieter.' She stared out of the kitchen window. 'I'm glad that they've found each other. I should have told Laura many years ago.'
'We should have told her, Gail,' her husband said quietly. 'We both thought it best to tell her when she was much older. She was already questioning things. She asked me once why she did not resemble either of us.'
'She asked me that one, too,' Gail smiled. 'Do you think I'm being stupid doing this for them at the weekend?'

'We both know that their birth mother died, Gail,' said George. 'We were both there. Whoever Cora thinks she's communicating with, it's not her.'

'She's so adamant,' Gail persisted. 'But you never answered my question, George. Am I being stupid?'

George took his wife in his arms. 'No, darling, I do not think you are being stupid. The girls' will see their birthplace and, hopefully, discover what happened nearly ten years ago. We can only tell them so much. The written information will confirm everything we have said. They'll be able to read it for themselves.'

'You're right. George...' Gail said.

'But?' George knew there was something else concerning her.

'Who is this person communicating with Cora?' Gail asked.

'That, I cannot answer,' admitted George. 'She says it's her mother. We know it's not. As far as we're aware, they are not communicating with Laura, are they?' Gail shook her head. 'Well, if it was their mother, don't you think she'd be trying to reach both of them?'

'Of course, she would,' said Gail. She had not considered this and started to feel relieved. 'You never really told me what prompted you to give me that telephone call to tell the girls.'

'When I took Laura to be – assessed – I saw a girl that I thought was Laura,' George explained. I went and looked but could not find her. Laura was still in the office doing some tests, so it could not have been her. I did not think any more about it until I met with Bernard and Michael – Doctor Turner and Doctor Paige – who told me a funny story about Laura and Cora. It seems that Laura helped Cora memorise a pack of cards. She wrote them down as Cora told her, telepathically, and when Cora was asked to recall them, Laura told her the order Cora had given her. It was then I realised that these were the two twins who were separated at birth with our help. Somehow, they had managed to find each in this vast world. And that was when I decided that we had to tell them the truth.'
'All we have to do now is tell the girls,' said Gail.

And when they told them, they got very excited indeed. But the Hadley's and the Miller's were still surprised that neither child asked to sleep at the others. Sam also thought it was a good idea for Carly to go. He was on duty that weekend as there was an event happening in Hayle which was coming through Bridge and Portreath.
Carly could not get anything out of the two girls on the Friday. They were giggly and excitable. Apart from Billy and Danielle, the other children did not

have a clue as to what was going on, but it became very infectious. Mrs Miller had to threaten the class with lines if they did not stop misbehaving. When that did not stop it, she threatened to call their parents in. That did work. By the time school finished for the day, it had felt like she had been working there for twenty-four hours. As soon as she rang the bell to indicate that class had finished, the room was empty. She sat at her desk with her head in her hands.
'Difficult day?' Mr Davidson asked.
'They've been in a funny mood all day long,' Carly said.

'My class could sense something going on in here,' said Geoff. 'But they just couldn't figure out what?'
'I think it was at its worse when they heard the chickens getting fed and they all started making clucking noises,' Carly laughed.
'Do you happen to know who started it?' Geoff asked.
'To be honest, I think Cora and Laura were behind it,' Carly replied.
'Cora has settled in well with the class,' said Geoff. 'They are like chalk and cheese, aren't they? Cora certainly comes across as being confident.'
'Possibly too confident,' Carly said. 'She's been through so much in her short life. It's probably a mask. I think deep down she's just a terrified

child.'

'You're probably right there, Mrs Miller,' Geoff nodded. 'Watching both your parents get murdered by the nazis must have been horrifying. Something you would probably never get over. Laura must have helped her settle in?'

'She certainly has,' Carly agreed. 'Although, I think they are helping each other. Laura is still quite a quiet type but is starting to come out of her shell. Actually, she likes helping me teach the class. That was ever since she stood in for me that time. Laura also does a pretty good chicken impersonation. Much better than Cora.'

'Do you think it wise what you're going to be doing over the weekend?' Geoff asked.

'Who knows?' Carly responded. 'It can't do any harm.'

'What if they actually find their actual mother?' Mr Davidson wondered.

'How can they? She died in childbirth,' Carly said.

CHAPTER TWENTY-SIX

The girls were awake long before the adults in their respective households. They woke up at exactly the same time, got dressed and were making cups of tea when the Hadley's and the Miller's came downstairs. They offered to make breakfast, but Gail took over from Laura in their house, and Carly took over at the Miller's. Both Cora and Laura did not feel like eating much but were told that they had to have something as they were in for a long day, possibly the entire weekend.
Carly kissed her husband goodbye and walked Cora up to the Hadley's. She was carrying a large bag which had treats in it for the journey. It was still fairly dark outside for an early October morning. Mr Hadley greeted them at the door.
Laura took Cora up to her room. She opened the drawer and took out the piece of paper.
'Should I show them this?' she asked her sister.
'Take it with you,' Cora advised. 'It could come in handy.'
Laura tucked it into her vest, and they went downstairs.

It was quite a tight fit in the car. Gail offered to sit in back with the children, but Carly would not hear of it. The two girls wanted to sit together so Cora sat in the middle. Carly squeezed into the free window seat. George put the small amount of luggage in the boot. They set off.

Carly played games with Laura and Cora; this was mainly I-spy and twenty questions, but she also included who am I? This was a game where they had to guess a person Carly was pretending to be. Even Gail enjoyed playing this game.

They stopped after a couple of hours after they made the moors in Devon. They loved the view, and they were fortunate it was dry and not misty. The next two hours took them past Bristol and from there it would take about another ninety minutes. Laura and Cora had still been very excited on the journey, but as they got nearer to the destination, they became quieter. Neither one not knowing what to expect. Cora had never seen Kneecap Cottage before so was not sure as what to expect. Laura knew it well and still remembered the inside from a year ago.

Laura squealed as she saw the house come into view. Cora looked out the window and gasped at how magnificent the house looked. It was a cottage she could imagine herself living in.

'Is she communicating with you yet?' Laura asked Cora.

'Not yet,' Cora admitted. 'But I can definitely feel

some presence.'

Mr Hadley parked the car and they all got out and stretched their legs. They had set off at half past six and had taken them six hours, which had included a couple of stops. Cora looked up at the house in awe. It looked even more grander close up than it did from the car window. She saw the gnomes.

'What are the gnomes for?' she asked.

'We used to place a gnome for every set of twins that were born,' Mrs Hadley explained. 'Whether they survived or not.'

'Can you remember which gnome was placed for us?' Laura asked.

'It was nearly ten years ago, Laura,' said Mrs Hadley. 'There must be, what? Nearly thirty gnomes here now. I think there may have been half that number when you were born.'

'I wonder if Sister Ida is still here,' mused Mr Hadley.

'She'll still be here,' said Gail. 'She'll be her to the day she dies.'

'How old would she be now?' George asked.

'She'll be in her seventies by now,' Gail replied.

'Any other profession and she would have been retired ages ago,' George said looking at the house.

'I cannot believe that you delivered babies in this house,' Carly said.

'We didn't,' Gail replied. 'There are two larger facilities in the woods over there. This house was

always a front. It helped the families relax more.'
'I'm guessing it was quite stressful for everyone involved,' said Carly.
'It certainly was,' said Gail.
'Whether you agree with what we were doing or not,' said George. 'It was always done with everyone's agreement and the best interest of the pregnant girl.

You needed something like this to remind them of home.'
'I shudder to think if those poor girls had to go to those unlicenced clinics,' said Gail vehemently. 'Or worse, they could get an abortion from those women who perform the – operation – at home, in dirty conditions, which mainly result in death for the poor young, pregnant girl.'
Cora was surprised to hear Laura's mother speaking that way. She had always found her to be jovial and kind-hearted. Laura, on the other hand, hoped her mother had not reverted back to how she used to be. Her mother changed since she had been assessed and they had been getting on very well.
'I can understand that,' Carly nodded.
Gail must have seen the look of concern on her daughter's face. She bent down and hugged her. 'When you become a mother, Laura, you'll understand the meaning of my words,' she whispered. She felt Laura nod.
'We really should be going inside,' George said. 'I

know we're a little early, but I'd rather that than be late. You do not know what strings I have had to pull to get back inside this place. I was fortunate that both

Bernard and Michael know Jeremy Irving. This establishment comes under his jurisdiction.'
'I just hope we get results,' said Gail who had now stood and was holding Laura's hand.
'Just what are you expecting to get from this?' asked Carly.
'Answers,' Gail responded simply.
'And the truth,' said George. 'Even if that confirms that we know their birth mother did die during childbirth.'
'But she's not,' said Cora, and they all turned to look at her.

The inside of the cottage was much larger than Laura remembered, so was surprised when Cora whispered 'it's exactly as you described it.' The furniture was in the same place. It was a bit dustier, so looked slightly older. The reception desk stood out like a sore thumb. It was new but a quite plain design. The

wood was a different type and colour. The only

good thing about it was that the receptionist kept it very tidy. Laura had the impression that the secretary probably measured everything to make sure that it was in the correct position.

The receptionist, herself, wore a white blouse with grey jacket and skirt. Her blond hair was tied up in a ball, and her face was plastered in make-up. Laura concluded that she was trying to appear younger than she was. She noticed that the woman gave her father a wonderful smile, but when her mother stood forward, it turned into more of a scowl.

'How may I help you?' she asked sounding as though she was not going to be helpful at all.

'We have an appointment with Sister Ida,' said Gail.

'Sister Ida is very unwell,' the receptionist replied sternly. 'I'm afraid that your appointment will have to be rearranged.'

'We have driven...' Gail was getting a bit fiery, but George raised his hand to stop her.

'In that case, I suggest you get on the telephone to Sir Jeremy Irving,' George responded with a smile.

'I'm sure you are aware of that name. Only he arranged this meeting on my behalf.'

Under the caked-on make-up, Laura and Cora both saw the receptionist visibly get paler when Mr Hadley mentioned that name.

'Please wait here, Sir, while I make the necessary

arrangements,' the receptionist said quickly. 'I will say though, Sir, that you and the children will not be permitted in the room.'

'I completely understand that,' George acknowledged.

The woman left the room. They could hear her going up the wooden stairs and clomping along the landing. George flicked through the visitors' book. It was still the same one as when he worked here. It looked like they were just adding pages to the book. He flicked back to try and find nineteen-thirty. He managed to find the close to the date but noticed that the page he wanted had been torn out. He huffed.

'What is it, George?' asked Gail.

'The page that would have given us more information has been ripped out of the book,' he replied.

'Damn!' Gail swore.

Laura looked at Cora. Nothing was needed to be said, but Cora just nodded. Laura reached in under her vest and pulled out the crumpled piece of paper. She unfolded it and walked up to her father. She handed him the page she had torn out previously.

'I'm sorry, daddy – mummy – I tore the page out when we travelled up last time to hand the house over to the military. You remember the time when I was not feeling well as we got near this house?'

'Don't tell me you were pretending to be ill, Laura

Hadley?' Gail scolded.

'No, mummy,' Laura said honestly. 'I really did feel poorly. But when you went off with that old nun woman, I looked through that book. I thought it could help Cora and me. It just gives the names of someone called next of kin. We have no idea who that is.'

George took the paper and read it. 'This, Laura and Cora, could very well be the names of you grandparents.' He folded the paper and put it in his inside jacket pocket because he could hear the receptionist returning. He winked at the two girls. 'Sister Ida is being made ready for the meeting. It will take half an hour to prepare her. I have been asked if you would like a meal and a drink?' the receptionist asked.

'Why don't you four have the meal and I'll go on to another meeting?' said George.

'George? A word outside?' ordered Gail. Mr Hadley followed his wife outside. 'You did not tell me anything about another meeting, George.'

'The next of kin only live about twenty minutes away from here,' said George. 'Seeing as I'm not allowed in with you to see Sister Ida, I thought I could visit them and see if they had any information.'

This made sense to Gail, so she nodded. 'We probably will not get much out of Sister Ida, so that is a good idea. Would it be better if you take the girls?'

George shrugged. 'We could ask them,' he said. 'I'm betting that they would prefer to stay and have something to eat and drink with you, though.'

And George was right. Both the girls wanted to have the meal. So, they all gathered outside to wave Mr Hadley off. They were then shown to the staff canteen where there was a buffet, so they could choose their own food. The receptionist promised to come back and collect them when Sister Ida was ready.

The food was exceptional. There were sausages, bacon, pie, chips, mash potato and salads; there were also beans, peas, sweetcorn and various other vegetables. Cora and Laura wanted to load everything on their plates but were warned by Mrs Hadley and Mrs Miller not to go too mad. They sat at one of the many empty tables to eat.

George had a map opened whilst he was driving. It was closer than he thought, and it had only taken him twelve minutes. The directions on the map were now sending him down narrow country lanes. He thought he had taken a wrong turn when he went down a lane with high hedges and grass growing down the middle. But soon he came across a quaint cottage. It was made of red brick and had a thatched roof. It had a wooden fence surrounding a large garden, which was very well maintained. It must have looked wonderful in the spring and summer as he could see that a wisteria was being trained to arch over the front windows and door. George parked his car by a gate and got out. The late autumn sun was still managing to give off a little heat, but the dark clouds were gathering ominously on

the horizon. He opened the wooden gate and walked up the pristine pathway. He could see no presence of a vehicle, but that did not mean anything. Some people did not welcome these monstrosities in the country. He walked up to the door and knocked on it.

True to her word, the receptionist returned just over half an hour later to take them back to see Sister Ida. Cora and Laura were stuffed by what they had eaten. They actually enjoyed dessert the best; it was jam roly-poly with custard. They were offered ice-cream, but both preferred the yellow, hot, creamy, smooth texture that surrounded the suet pudding.
Cora looked around as they walked back towards the house. She could just make out a high chain-link fence through the trees. She wondered what was behind it, but the heavy woodland obscured her view.

Laura and Cora were told to wait downstairs as the receptionist took Mrs Miller and Mrs Hadley up to visit Sister Ida. There were comics and toys left for

them by the chairs. Cora waited for the footsteps to quieten on the floorboards along the landing above.
'I'm not one for reading comics and playing with these stupid toys, are you, Laura?' she asked.
'Well, the cuddly toys look quite fun,' protested Laura.
'We could go on an adventure,' said Cora excitedly. 'Did you see that wire fence amongst all those trees?' Laura shook her head. 'Well, I did. And that got me thinking. What are they trying to keep out? Or, more importantly, what are they trying to keep in? Shall we go and have a look?'
'Shouldn't we stay here in case them come back?' Laura asked sounding just a little bit frightened.
'I reckon they'll be gone quite a while,' Cora responded matter-of-factly. 'We'll be back long before they return.'
'I'm surprised Mrs Miller did not stay with us,' said Laura trying to change the subject.
'Don't you remember in the car?' queried Cora. 'Your mum and dad asked her to go in with them to be a witness.'
'Oh. Yes,' said Laura vaguely.

Cora walked to the door. 'Now, are you coming to join me or not?'

Laura reluctantly got to her feet and followed Cora out of the door.

CHAPTER TWENTY-SEVEN

The room was lit by four candles, but it was still dim. They could see that the old woman was propped up by three, plumped, pillows. Her coif had been put on her and was framing her face, but even in this light she looked poorly. Two chairs had been placed next to bed and these were where Gail and Carly were to sit. Before she sat down, Gail took the nun's hand in hers and said a silent prayer.

'Do I look that bad, Sister Abigail?' the nun's voice surprised Carly as it was still very strong.

'I am not a nun any longer, Sister Ida,' Gail replied.

'Once married to God, always married to God,' Sister Ida retorted.

'You've got me there, Sister Ida,' said Gail.

'As you can see, it will not be long before I meet my maker,' said Sister Ida.

'Nonsense,' exclaimed Gail. 'You are as strong as an ox.'

'Not anymore, my dear. Not anymore,' she replied.

'And who is this young lady?'

'This is Mrs Carly Miller,' Gail introduced.

'And why is Mrs Carly Miller visiting me?' asked Sister Ida.

'I'm a teacher at the village school where Mrs Hadley lives,' Carly replied.

'Doesn't really explain why you are visiting me, though, does it?' said Sister Ida.

'I teach Laura,' Carly began.

'Not really helping,' said Sister Ida. 'I don't know anyone called Laura.'

'Do you remember that little girl I turned up with here a little while ago?' asked Gail.

Sister Ida appeared to be searching her memory bank. 'Oh, yes,' she recalled. 'Wasn't she feeling poorly?'

'Yes, she was,' Gail replied.

'So, Laura is your little girl then?' said Sister Ida.

'Yes, she is,' Gail responded proudly. 'Except I wonder if you remember how I got her?'
'I may be a nun, Sister Abigail, and taken the vow of celibacy, but I know a little about the birds and the bees,' smiled Sister Ida.
Both Gail and Carly laughed at this. 'That's not what I meant, Sister Ida, as well you know,' said Gail.
'We were both midwives,' said Sister Ida. 'We delivered hundreds of babies, but I don't recall you ever being pregnant. Well, you wouldn't, would you? You were a nun.'
'Do you remember one girl?' said Gail trying to jog the nun's recollection. 'I think she was about fourteen. She said that she was made pregnant by her uncle.'
'They all say something or another,' said Sister Ida. 'But if they were good catholic girls then they would never get into that mess.'
This made Carly and Gail bristle. They knew that sometimes it was not the fault of the young girls. It was obvious that males forced themselves upon them. Gail composed herself before continuing.
'She gave birth to her first child quite easily – a girl - and the parents who had adopted her were waiting outside and baby was given to them to take. But what we did not realise was that the teenager was pregnant with twins.

Complications set in and we are sure that the teenager died whilst giving birth to the second daughter.'

Sister Ida looked directly into Gail's eyes and Gail knew at once that the nun had remembered this young girl.

'Who are you? And what do you want?' asked the woman as she opened the door. A lit cigarette was fixed between her lips, but this did not affect her speaking. She was holding a packet of Players Navy and Swan Vesta matches. 'I don't buy anything from strangers.'

'My name is Dr George Hadley,' George tried to introduce himself.

'You're not my GP,' said the woman suspiciously. George reckoned that she was in her late forties but the cigarettes and, judging by the fumes coming from her. The alcohol made her look even older. 'So, what do you want?'

He pulled out the piece of paper from his inside jacket pocket and opened it. He read it but he already knew the names of the top of his head. 'Are you Mrs Edith Wellington?'

'I might be,' she said. George watched as a piece of ash fell from the tip of the cigarette to the floor.

'Ere. You're not the police, are you?'
'I've already explained that I'm a doctor, Mrs Wellington.'
'Oh, yes. Silly me,' she laughed. 'I suppose you can come in.'
'Thank you. That's very kind,' said George
Mrs Wellington put her cigarettes and matches on the little hallway table before she stood aside so that George could enter. She instructed him to go through on the left. The inside was not as well looked after as the exterior. There was a strong smell of stale tobacco and alcohol. Newspapers littered the floor and there were dirty plates with leftover scraps on them. She tidied up so that George could sit down. He looked at the stained sofa and decided it was safer to remain standing.
'Would you like a tea or coffee?' asked Mrs Wellington. 'Or perhaps something stronger?'
'I've got another meeting to attend,' George explained. 'I only came out her on the off chance. I didn't know if you were even going to be in.'

'So, how can I help you, Doctor Hadley?' Mrs Wellington asked.
'I believe a – relative – of yours was assisted by the staff at Kneecap?' he queried.
'My daughter, you mean,' replied Mrs Wellington. She stubbed the cigarette out in an overflowing ashtray causing more ash to spill onto the table and

carpet below.
'Your daughter? Was it about ten years ago?' asked George.
'Yes,' Mrs Wellington replied. 'She gave birth there, but my daughter made up some cock and bull story whilst she was there, about how she got in her condition. She was fourteen at the time.'
'What was her name?'
'Maxine.'
'And did they tell you what happened to Maxine?'
'They informed me that she had twins,' said Edith.

'Did they tell you anything else?'
She looked George in the eye. 'Oh, they told me plenty, Doctor Hadley. They told me plenty.'

The two girls ran towards the woods and soon came across the metal fencing that Cora had spied earlier. The followed it for a couple of hundred yards before they found a gate. Cora tried it but it was locked. There was a keypad visible.
'Oh, well,' said Laura sounding relieved. 'We'd better turn back.'
Cora examined the lock. 'The eight, seven and five are quite worn.' The first attempt she tried opened the gate. 'Well, that was handy, wasn't it?'
'Yes,' said Laura with a sigh.
She pushed the gate closed after they had gone

through. Laura didn't know if they needed to remember the code to get back through, and Cora only had her mind set on going forward. This was probably a good thing as she spotted a couple of members of staff

walking their way, on the pathway. They were fortunate that there were a couple of large trees nearby that they could hide behind. They moved around the trees as the staff approached. They watched as the two people walked towards the gate. Laura gasped as she now realised her mistake. They would know that the gate should be locked. She held her breath. Luckily, the two staff members were laughing and talking and were oblivious that the gate was unlocked, and they walked right through. They did not even check to make sure it had closed properly behind them.

Cora waited a few moments to be on the safe side before indicating to Laura that they should continue. They kept to the wooded area but followed the path. Cora soon spied a large construction. It looked modern. Both Cora and Laura had never seen this type of block. It was a lot larger than the house brick, and it was a completely different colour. The building was long but appeared to be only one story. There could have been two stories, but the windows indicated that there was only one floor. Neither Laura nor Cora could work out why there were secured bars to the

windows. They could not really see the roof.
'What is this place?' Laura whispered.

'No idea,' Cora whispered back. 'It must be connected to that cottage though.'
'Do you think this was where we were born?' Laura wondered aloud.
Cora seemed to think about this for a while. 'I think you could be on to something there, Laura. Except why would there be bars on the windows if it is just where babies are born? They can't be expecting the babies to try and escape, can they?'
Laura shook her head. 'I wouldn't have thought so,' she said.
'So, how do you think we can get in?' Cora asked.
'You want to go IN there?' Laura asked in disbelief.
'Of course, I do. Don't you?' Cora shot back.
'N-n-not really. I'm scared,' Laura replied.
'I think our birth mother could be inside,' Cora said matter-of-factly.
Now this got Laura's attention. 'Really? You really think she's inside?' Her eyes went back to sweep the building. 'Have you spoken to her?'
'No,' Cora admitted. 'I can just l feel she's there.'
'Are you here? You are, aren't you? I can feel you,' a voice shrieked.
'AIEghhh here? AIEghhh, aren't you? Aggebeee

feel you.' Cora could tell, by the look on Laura's face, that she had heard something too.
'You're right, Cora. You're right,' Laura said excitedly. 'I can hear her. She must be close. We must find her.'

Sister Ida started coughing and coughing quite badly. Gail's medical awareness kicked in as both she and Carly jumped to their feet. Gail shouted to Carly to go and get help. As she leant over the stricken nun. She told the patient to hold her breath, which Sister Ida struggled to do.
'Breathe through your nose,' Gail instructed. Again, the nun seemed to fight against this. 'Come on,

Sister Ida. As you ordered everyone when you gave them medical aid in matters like this.'
Her words appeared to sink in as Sister Ida held her breath and began breathing through her nose. This calmed her and the coughing got lighter and lighter until it stopped. Gail poured the old woman a drink as Carly returned with the receptionist in tow.
'Right. I think it's time that this meeting was stopped,' the receptionist ordered. 'Sister Ida is clearly distressed.'
'NO!' Sister Ida's voice was back to being strong after sipping the water. 'Leave us be, Muriel. There

is something I need to confess before I meet with God.'

'You're not going anywhere,' said Gail. 'As I said before, you are as strong as an...'

'...Ox. Yes, I know. Muriel! Please leave us,' the nun commanded, and the receptionist left. 'Please sit down both of you.' Gail and Carly returned to the seats and waited for the Sister to start. 'I remember that poor wee girl. She had a speech impediment if I recall correctly.' Gail nodded. 'I don't get too involved in how the girls' get into their condition. As a catholic, if a female behaves herself, then she will never get pregnant outside of marriage. But when I could

understand what she was saying, when she was coherent, she said that her uncle Richard abused her. I have heard this many times, but Maxine, I think that was her name?' she looked at Gail for confirmation.

'Yes, it was,' said Gail nodding.

'Maxine was unlike the others though,' Sister Ida continued. 'She was already institutionalised in the building next door to the maternity unit. She was believable. And only relatives were allowed to visit her. But it was not the Order's concern about how they became pregnant, we just had to deliver the babies. Maxine gave birth to a beautiful girl. Laura, was it?'

'No. The firstborn was Cora,' said Gail.

'Right,' said the nun but she was not really convinced. 'Anyway, Cora was taken to meet her new parents. Again, we do not get involved with that. Administration selected them. We just passed the baby over. Although, Sister Abigail, I know you did not follow correct procedure and allowed Maxine to see the baby.' Gail hung her head in apology, but Carly noticed that the Sister had a wicked smile on her face. 'If I also recall correctly, the Doctor was the man you went on to marry after you left the Sisterhood.'
'Doctor George Hadley,' Gail confirmed. 'He is a top-level surgeon now. He's helping out in London with the war causalities.'
'He's also here, isn't he?' Sister Ida asked.
'Dr Hadley did bring us here,' said Carly. 'And the two girls are also here. The receptionist would not allow them into this room.'
'Probably wise,' said Sister Ida. 'They wouldn't want to see an old woman like me lying in bed.' She coughed a couple of times and Gail jumped to give her some more water. 'Thank you, my dear.'
'I think you'll find that only members of the order and clergy would be permitted to enter this room at the moment, Sister Ida,' said Gail. 'Only you would have given outsiders the permission to visit you. If you were non-responsive, Mrs Miller and I would not be sitting here now.'
'True. Very true,' replied the nun, but Carly could

tell that her voice was getting weaker.
'So, what happened after Cora was taken away?' asked Carly.
'Oh, yes,' Sister Ida recalled. 'I think I was

waiting for the placenta to be delivered when I first noted the blood. It was only a trickle at first. But then Maxine said she wanted to start pushing. Initially I thought it was because of the placenta, but the poor girl seemed to be having proper contractions. How we never knew that the poor lass was expecting twins, I'll never know. Maxine seemed to be getting in a lot of pain. Now – did I send for help? Or did I fetch assistance myself? - I cannot remember, but Doctor Hadley came into the delivery room. By this time the poor girl was in and out of consciousness, and the blood was starting to flow more steadily. I prayed to God to help Maxine.
'We finally managed to deliver the second baby, which must have been Laura. She was very quiet, and we both thought she was dead. But I was good at my job and soon that wee baby had air in her lungs and, boy, did she let us know it. Maxine had delivered a second healthy baby. Doctor Hadley was working frantically to keep Maxine alive. She was losing a lot of blood. I could tell that it was going to be a fight to keep her alive. Doctor Hadley manged to stop the bleeding; he was a very skilful surgeon back then, but Maxine had stopped breathing. We both tried to resuscitate her; I think you may have

even been back in the room, Sister Abigail.

'I was,' Gail confirmed.' Maxine was declared dead. I think my husband even signed the death certificate.'

'Aye. I believe he did,' Sister Ida agreed. 'But then I noticed something when I was cleaning her up.'

Now she had Gail's and Carly's undivided attention.

'What did they tell you?' George Hadley asked. 'You know that Maxine was being held in the secured unit next door to the maternity unit, don't you?' Mrs Wellington asked.

This was news to George. He could have just nodded, but he felt that honesty was probably the best policy. 'No. I wasn't aware.'

'Yes. She was committed by the authorities with our agreement,' said Edith. 'Although they probably would have taken her without it anyway. She had this terrible speech imperfection from an early age. She was a backward child and to deal with it the authorities thought it best that she was committed. We were allowed to visit, and Maxine enjoyed it when we did –

so did we – you know, it's very difficult having your

daughter locked up like that.'

George could see the pain in her eyes and knew that she was being honest. 'I guess it must be,' he said. 'Do you have a daughter, Doctor Hadley?' Edith asked. George nodded. 'Then you know that you will do whatever is best for them.'

'That is true,' George agreed.

'The neighbours knew,' Mrs Wellington continued. 'We had to endure snarky comments from them about having a "crazy" child locked up. But we loved her. My husband died of a heart attack two years ago, but I think it was from sadness of what he had done to Maxine.'

George noted that Edith was using the past tense when speaking about her daughter. But he gathered early in the conversation that she was not a well-educated woman, but she seemed to be supporting the evidence that Maxine was dead. 'It must have been difficult for both of you,' he said. 'You were still allowed to visit her, though?'

'She was classified as a minor, so we had permission to visit,' she replied. 'Plus, she was our daughter. Close relatives could go and see her.' George tried to wrack his brains but, seeing as he only dealt with the patients when they needed medical aid, he could not remember visitors' coming into the secured unit. 'And then a couple of years later, they informed us that she was pregnant. Now, how did

that happen?'
'Did you find out?' asked George
'Maxine, who by this time was quite doolally, tried to blame it on a relative,' Edith answered. 'There was an investigation, and it was blamed on a fellow inmate. I think he was made a scapegoat.'
'Who did you think it was?'
'I reckoned it must have been a member of staff, and that's why they hushed it up,' Edith replied matter-of-factly.
'And then what happened?' George prompted.
'I was told she gave birth to twins,' Edith began and then stopped. George could see her eyes starting

to water. 'They said she died giving birth to the second. You know, I never got to meet my granddaughters. Those were the rules. That's where they are clever, you see. They mention all the gobbledegook when you are in no fit state to hear it, and then get you to sign a piece of paper which you do not understand what it's about.'
'You would have kept the babies?' George asked, reading between the lines.
'Of course, I would have,' Gail sobbed. 'They are my family. They are all I have.'
'Did you bury your daughter?'
'Bury my daughter? Don't make me laugh,' scoffed Edith. 'They would not let me see her body. I was told that in those circumstances, when a lunatic

died in the asylum, that the body is cremated in their facilities.'

This made George intrigued. As far as he was aware, any minor would have had to be relocated back to next of kin. This caused him a bit of concern. 'Did you ask for her body?'

'When people like us are told by the authorities that is what happens, then who are we to question them?' said Edith. 'But I've heard a couple of things since then which has made me wonder what really

happened. It might be people being cruel, but I just don't know how to find out.'

Stain or no stain, George sat down on the edge of the sofa, completely interested in what the woman was saying.

Cora looked at her twin sister in disbelief. She could tell that Laura had heard something, but she was startled by the sudden change in her.

'Are we going to stand around here all day? Or are we going to find our mother?' Laura demanded.

'You didn't want to follow me earlier,' Cora pointed out. 'If we are going to continue, then we must proceed with caution. There are bound to be people watching.'

'Perhaps we should look for another way in,' Laura

suggested.

Cora shrugged but started to walk down the side of building. Laura took this as an indication that they were going ahead. It was longer than they first thought.

It seemed to go on for miles. They did not need to crouch down as the windows were up quite high. There were a lot of brambles growing around the border. The woods were in close proximity, but some of the tree roots were growing towards the building like it was planning to tie the construction up in a large knot. Unfortunately, Cora did not see one of these stumps and tripped over, falling quite heavily. Laura reached her side and picked her up. There was a lot of dirt and a little bit of blood but nothing major.

'I've had worse,' said Cora.

'Can you still walk?' Laura asked.

Cora tentatively placed weight on her left leg. She was relieved to feel no pain. 'Looks like I can. Come on, Laura.'

They got round to the far end of the building. Cora had to pull Laura back because she saw two men. She put a finger to her mouth to stop Laura from protesting. She motioned for her to have a look around the corner. It was then that she saw the two men. They had blue overalls on and had a very tall stepladder. One was on the equipment, but she couldn't quite see what

he was doing. The other was not doing much. Except looking up at the man on the ladder.
'What do we do now?' Laura whispered to Cora.
'I guess we wait,' Cora said. 'And we'd better hide in the trees in case they come this way.'
They didn't have to wait too long, probably about five minutes, before the two men decided to go for a break. The two girls watched as the workmen made their way down the side of the building. They then ran towards the stepladder.
'What are we going to do?' Laura asked.
'We will be able to see through that window up there if we climb up to the top of those ladders,' said Cora.
'And what if we're seen?' asked Laura.
'We'd better not be,' said Cora. 'Or we can just say that we're lost.'
'That sounds like a good idea,' Laura nodded.
They put the step ladder by the window, and it was agreed that Cora should climb up first with Laura following. There were eleven rungs on the ladder. Cora

felt it wobble slightly as she got higher. She looked down at Laura who looked a little scared, and she was holding on tightly. She climbed to the second from last step and found that her head was just below the bars of the window. If she reached up, she could grab one of the bars and pull herself up to the top rung. Holding the bar would also steady her until Laura joined her at the top of the ladder. She could see that there would be enough room for them both. They could see clearly into the room. They imagined that it looked exactly like a prison cell except that the walls appeared to be to be padded.

Suddenly, a face appeared the other side of the window startling the two young girls. The ladder started to wobble frantically as the twin sisters grabbed the bars to try and steady it.

CHAPTER TWENTY-EIGHT

'What did you see?' Carly asked as both she and Gail stood and moved closer to the bed.

'I thought I was imagining it, at first,' said Sister Ida. The two women could tell that her voice was getting weaker. 'I noticed her thumb twitch. I thought it was just a spasmodic reaction but then it twitched again. I leant down and put my ear against her mouth, and I could hear a shallow breath. I started the resuscitation procedure again. Imagine my shock when she responded. She opened her eyes, but the poor girl was clinical dead for a while. I was sure that she would have brain damage.'

'Why didn't you shout for someone?' Gail demanded.

'You were busy with the second child,' Sister Ida replied. 'Doctor Hadley had already certified her as dead. But I did get help.'

'Who from?' Carly asked.

'That will be from me,' said a voice. Nobody had heard Muriel the receptionist enter.

'You were the novice,' Gail recalled. 'You've obviously come out of the sisterhood.'

'Very much like you,' said Muriel. 'I found love, too.'

'There is only one person to love,' said Sister Ida. Her voice had grown much weaker. 'And that is God Almighty.'

'The girl was in a bad way,' said Muriel, ignoring the old woman, 'but she was alive. She was very incoherent. We thought it safer to move her back to the top floor room in the house. Both Sister Ida and I took it in turns to keep her well. And she made a full recovery.'

'We thought it wise to keep her in for protection,' said Sister Ida. 'Her parents had abandoned her.

They were alcoholics. Not a very nice family. I heard the father died of a heart attack a few years ago.'

'Maxine, that was her name,' Muriel continued. 'We probably put her in the best place because she was a bit mental. I had to pretend to be her guardian angel on more than just a few occasions. Do you know that she claimed many times that she could communicate with her children? Well, one in particular.'

'I believe her,' said Carly. 'Cora told us that she could talk to her birth mother. She told us that she wasn't dead.'

'I take it that Maxine is still alive?' Gail asked.

'Yes, she is,' said Sister Ida. 'She's not a well young girl. She's only twenty-four, you know. But her mental age is still the same as when she gave birth.'

'She thought she saw one of the girls a few times,' said Muriel. 'We actually kept her in a locked room just along the landing.'

'My family have been past here quite a few times,' Gail admitted. 'It's on our way to our holiday home.'

'Your daughter, Laura, almost ruined it when you turned up unexpectedly not so long ago,' said Sister Ida, her voice sounding quite raspy now. 'I caught her upstairs. She was by the door where Maxine was being kept. And do want to know something?

Maxine knew she was there. I caught the young girl before she could cause any damage.'

'And you want to know something else?' said Muriel. 'It took me hours to comfort Maxine after her daughter had left.'
'But how could she know?' asked Carly. 'And how can she communicate with Cora? And Laura, to a lesser extent?'
'That's easy,' said Sister Ida. 'It's God's will.'
This caused everyone to reflect for a few minutes. Sister Ida's laboured breathing defeated the silence and the three standing women looked down on her.
'I think we should let Sister Ida rest in peace,' said Muriel.
'For once I agree with you,' said Gail.
'I'm not dead yet,' Sister Ida joked. 'Almost, but not quite.'
'Just one more thing, Sister Ida,' Carly asked. 'You mentioned that you believed that Maxine was made pregnant by her uncle. What was his name?'

George looked at Mrs Wellington. He was waiting for her to continue. Instead, she stood up and started looking for something. She knocked some more newspapers on the floor. She rummaged around on the table and the cheap looking wall unit.
'I think you put them on the hallway table when you let me in,' George had realised that she was looking for her cigarettes.
'Thank you,' she said, leaving the room. By the time she had come back in she had already lit another cigarette. She threw the two packets onto the wall unit and sat back down again.
'You were saying that there were rumours or stories,' he reminded her.
'Oh, yes,' Edith remembered. 'I think it was a member of staff. They put a note through my letterbox. It said something like not everything is as it seems and that someone was waiting to see me.'
'Do you still have the note?' he knew it was a long shot and was not surprised at the response.

'No,' she replied. 'We did not take it seriously. I think we burnt it. But then I ran into someone in town. They claimed to be an ex-patient from the Kneecap asylum. They told me that in the room next door a young woman was being held. She was called Maxine. How would she have come up with that name? She must have heard it.'
'But how would that person know that Maxine was

linked to you?' George posed the question.
Edith shrugged. 'Perhaps they saw me visiting her?'
George thought this was unlikely. In his experience visiting would have been carried out privately. 'Perhaps,' he conceded. 'Has there been anything else?'
'My brother always thought she was still alive,' she said. 'He had this sixth sense.' Not really evidence George thought to himself. 'He was adamant she was still alive as we had not been asked to identify the body.' Edith inhaled from her cigarette and blew the smoke out. 'Mind you, I guess he had a point. I just believed that when she died, the authorities knew who she was.'
'But they must have sent you any possessions she had?' George asked.

Edith gave this some thought. 'You know what? They didn't,' she said. 'Mind you, she would not have had a lot of stuff. I remember now that my brother said exactly the same thing. I think he may have tried to go and fetch them. I don't know if he had any luck.'
'Can't you find out? Does he live locally?'
'No, he moved down to Devon,' Edith explained. 'He went down there before all this happened. Him and his wife lost a child. They came back just at the time as all this started kicking off. He was a godsend. I think Maxine even liked his visits as it

settled her.

'I believe that Maxine stated that she was made pregnant by a relative,' George said.

'Yes,' Mrs Wellington spat. 'I think it was just the asylum trying to pin the blame on us.'

'Who was it that she blamed?' George asked curiously.

'My brother,' Edith replied angrily.

'What was his name?' George asked.

'What was the relative called, Sister Ida?' Carly asked again.

'Richard Culver.'

'What is his name, Mrs Wellington?' George repeated.

'Richard Culver,' she sobbed. 'But he died in a bombing attack in Newton Abbot recently.'

George felt sick. The room started spinning. He had to get out. 'I'm sorry for taking up so much of your time. I really need to get to my next meeting.'

'Thank you for coming to see me,' said Edith. 'It's been a long time since I've talked about Maxine.

George was out the door a minute later. By the time he got back to his car he was virtually hyperventilating.

Maxine had heard the disturbance outside of her window. She was lying on her bed at the time. She listened to the two young voices and knew at once that they had found her. She could hear the ladders being moved. At least it was not those horrible workmen who used to watch her as she was either dressed or undressed. She knew that they would climb the ladder. She had not communicated with them for a little while, even though she could hear their voices talking to each other. She was not going to get out of here, that was for sure. She thought it best to let them get on with their own lives. But Maxine was so delighted that they had come to find her.
The windows were not strong, and she could hear most things through them. A single pane of glass in a metal frame. It could easily be broken. In fact, she had lost count of the number of times it had cracked because of a large tree that used to be just outside. She had thought about escaping but knew that it was not the window that would impede her, but the metal bars on the exterior.
She could hear them starting to climb. One sounded quite fearful, the one she could barely communicate with. The other, the stronger one, was confident and was coaxing the other to climb. Maxine waited another few seconds until she thought they

were at the top of the step ladder, and she stood up and saw the two most wonderous, beautiful and, virtually, identical faces she had seen since the kind nun midwife allowed to have a quick glimpse of her baby. She immediately knew that they were both her children even though she only remembered giving birth to the one.
And then all havoc broke out. Maxine quickly realised that she had surprised the children by showing her face so quickly. She watched in horror as the step ladder fell away from them and they were left dangling by just gripping those bars. She ran to her door and started banging on it, trying to grab someone's attention.
'My girls,' she screamed. 'My girls are in danger.'

Gail had to sit down before she fell down. Carly put her hand too her mouth in horror. Muriel looked at them. She could not quite comprehend why the two women were reacting in this way. But she wanted Sister Ida to be able to rest.

'Can you both follow me, please?' she said.
They quietly left the room. Both women were still in a state of shock. They followed Muriel downstairs.
'I can't believe it,' Gail said shaking her head.

'Cora's adopted father was her actual father,' said Carly.
'Would you both like a coffee? Or a cup of tea?' Muriel asked.
'Something stronger would be more appropriate,' Gail replied. 'But a coffee would be fine.'
'Coffee, please,' Carly confirmed. Muriel left to go and make the drinks. 'I can't believe it. That bastard raped his niece and then took the child to be the adopted father.'
'It was obvious that he did not realise that that there were twins,' said Gail. 'Because he would have taken the two. Oh, poor Cora. Her young life must have been terrible. At least she's better off living with you now.'
Carly looked around the room. 'Wait a minute! Where are the two girls?'

Mrs Miller and Mrs Hadley frantically searched the room and called their names, but they were not there.

The face had startled them so much that the ladder was wobbling out of control. The twins managed to grab the bars to windows as the ladder toppled over and fell away from them, leaving them dangling. They were screaming and Laura was certainly crying. Cora seemed to be enjoying the adventure.

'I don't think I can hold on much longer,' Laura cried.
'If you fall now, you're going to break your legs,' Cora said. 'I'm sure someone will here you screaming soon and come to help.'
Cora was right. It wasn't long before the two workmen ran around the corner.
'Now, what's going on here?' said the taller of the two as he and his colleague picked up the step ladder and placed it under the feet of the two panicking schoolgirls.

Cora and Laura felt the ladder under their feet, and they became stable. The face was back at the window. She was smiling at them. The two girls looked at each other and then back at the face. She looked a lot like them.
'Okay, girls. Come down slowly, one at a time,' the second workman instructed.
Laura came down first. Cora took one last look at the woman, smiled at her and descended the steps.
'So, why are you two messing around here?' the tall worker asked.
'We got lost,' Cora replied.
'I don't know how you too managed to get in here, but you're trespassing,' said the workman.
'The gate was open,' Cora explained. 'We thought our mummies came this way.'
'And why would your "mummies" be coming this way?' asked the shorter workman.

Cora shrugged.

George Hadley arrived back at the facility just as his wife and Mrs Miller ran out of the cottage. He could see the look of panic etched on their faces. Muriel followed them out.
'What is it? He shouted. 'What's going on?'
'The girls have gone missing,' Mrs Hadley shouted back.
He ran after them. They went to the staff canteen first. They asked a couple of staff if they had seen two young girls, but both shook their heads. They all shouted for Cora and Laura but was met with silence.
'What about the mental patient block?' George asked.
'There is no way they could get in there,' said Muriel. 'Even you must remember how secure the perimeter is?'
'I still think we should go and check,' said Mr Hadley.
'Okay,' Muriel relented. 'Follow me.'
Just as they got to the keypad lock, the workmen and the two girls were walking in the other

direction. Cora and Laura ran towards the gate. Muriel tapped in the combination and opened the gate.

'Why did you two run off?' Gail shouted at them both out of relief more than anything.

'She's here,' said Cora who was hugging Carly.

'Who's here?' Carly asked.

'Our birth mother,' said Cora.

'Okay,' said Gail. 'I admit that we have discovered that your birth mother could still be alive, but she could be being held anywhere.'

'Cora is right, Gail,' said George. 'Maxine is still being held here isn't she, Muriel?'

They all turned to look at the receptionist. Muriel sighed. 'Yes, she is.'

'Maxine? Is that her name?' Laura asked.

'I suggest you take us to see her,' said George.

'I don't think that will do Maxine any good,' said Muriel. 'It could have a negative impact on her rehabilitation.'

'It could also have a positive effect,' Carly countered.

'I could just telephone Sir Jeremy,' said George. 'I'm sure that he would agree to it.'

Muriel looked at him furiously, but knew she had no other choice.

It took her thirty minutes for Muriel to make the necessary arrangements. The others went for another drink whilst they waited. Mr Hadley explained that the procedure included asking Maxine if she wanted to meet with them. If she said no, then that would be it. There would be nothing they could do to make it happen.

It was agreed between them that Mr and Mrs Hadley would go in first, as Maxine would have at least some knowledge of them; if she actually remembered them, that was. If Maxine agreed, then Mrs Miller would bring Cora and Laura.

CHAPTER TWENTY-NINE

Maxine sat in the locked visitor's room. She was rocking back and forth on her wooden chair, and she drummed her fingers on the side of it, showing that she was nervous. Her hands and feet were in chains. A nun sat to one side of her and what appeared to be an orderly stood behind. Another orderly sat next to the door.

'Are you sure you want to carry on with this, Miss Wellington?' the nun asked.

'Yes,' said Maxine. 'I need to do this.'

There was a knock on the door, the orderly next to the door stood up and opened it. Mr and Mrs

Hadley were led through by a further male orderly and yet another one was bringing up the rear. Maxine went to stand up but could not because of the chains.

'Does she need to be chained?' Gail asked.

'It is for her own safety and yours,' said the nun. 'You agreed to this, Mr and Mrs Hadley, so you were informed of the procedures.'

'It's okay, Sister Abigail,' said Maxine.

'You remember me?' said Gail almost crying. She went to give the young girl a hug.

'No touching,' said the orderly next to door. 'Please sit down.'

Mr and Mrs Hadley sat on the chairs that were provided, although they were a little way from the table.

'You were so kind to me, Sister Abigail,' smiled Maxine. 'You let me see my baby. And Doctor Hadley, you looked after me when I first came in. You kept me safe.'

'We owe you an apology, Miss Wellington, or can I call you Maxine?' George asked.

'No one has called me Maxine in a long, long time,' she replied. 'But I like the sound of it.'

'You told us that a relative made you pregnant, but we did not believe you,' said Mr Hadley. 'And when you gave birth to not one but two wonderful babies, you did die. I was there. I signed your death certificate.'

'But, as you can see, I'm clearly not dead,' smiled Maxine. They had to listen very carefully because her speech impediment was still quite profound.
'We're sorry we failed you, Maxine,' sobbed Gail.
'You did not fail me, Sister Abigail,' said Maxine. 'Far from it. As far as I'm aware, you left the sisterhood, married Doctor Hadley, and raised one of my babies as your own. I knew that she was in safe hands.'
'That's very kind of you to say, Maxine,' said George. 'Gail and I could never let the authorities take that lovely baby, so we decided to raise her ourselves.'
'Gail? You kept the name the convent gave you?' Maxine queried.
'I liked it,' Gail admitted. 'So, I kept it.'
'How has my youngest been?' Maxine asked.
'She's been so wonderful, Maxine,' said Gail. 'She is quiet but very clever. We hope you don't mind but we called her Laura.'

'Laura!' Maxine smiled. 'I like that name. I bet it suits her personality.'
'We think it does,' George laughed. 'She's brilliant at English. She even stood in for the teacher

recently. We think that's what she wants to be when she leaves school.'

'She's going to school?' said Maxine. 'I was never given that chance. As you are aware, I have this speech problem. Everyone thought I was a looney. Me mum and dad soon gave permission for the asylum to take me. They still came to visit. They did not abandon me completely.'

'And your uncle was also allowed to visit,' said George.

'Uncle Richard came to visit me quite regularly,' said Maxine. 'At first, people would stay in the room. He visited more times than my parents. Even though he lived in Devon. When they realised he was following the correct procedures less and less people stayed in the room. Then there was just the two of us. Uncle Richard became very affectionate. At first, he would just stroke me arm. Then he would peck me cheek. Next, we started cuddling. He would tell me stories about his son, and how his wife could not have any more children. And then...'

'We know what happened,' said Gail. 'You do not need to tell us.'

'What happened to my firstborn?' Maxine asked. George looked at Gail, she nodded to him. 'She's called Cora,' he explained. 'We have just discovered that your Uncle Richard officially adopted her. Richard and his wife, Gloria, were killed recently in a bombing raid on their town. Cora survived. She's staying with the teacher, Mrs Miller.

'I know she survived,' said Maxine.

'Is that because you've been able to communicate with her ever since she was small?' Gail asked.

'I was about to say because I saw her at the window a little while ago, but how did you know I could speak to them?'

This time Gail looked at her husband who nodded at her. 'Laura told us that she could talk to Cora in her mind,' Gail answered. 'At first, we thought it was just an imaginary friend. Then it got more in-depth. We got really concerned and we had to get her assessed.

She passed with flying colours. But when we met Cora, she told us that she communicated with you. She knew that you were not dead. We didn't believe her. We saw you die, but she was adamant. And she was right.'

'So, you know they are here. Would you like to meet them?' George asked.

'Do they want to meet me?' she asked excitedly.

Both George and Gail nodded. 'In that case, I would love to meet them.'

George went and had a word with the orderly who followed them in to the room. He left to fetch the children. It did not take him long to return with the two young girls and Mrs Miller who was holding their hands. The two girls were hiding slightly behind the teacher.

'Come and say hello, girls,' said George as he reached to take Laura's hand from Carly. 'This is Maxine Wellington, your birth mother.'

Cora strode confidently towards the table before an orderly stood in her way. Laura was more reluctant to move forward.

'I don't think it would hurt if the children could approach the lady,' said Gail.

'As stated previously, the procedures laid down say no one shall approach the inmate,' said the nun.

'Inmate?' George said, his voice rising slightly. 'I would prefer it if you referred to her as a patient.'

'These are her children,' Gail continued. 'For goodness sake what harm would it do to let them get close to Maxine?'

'If you don't want to obey the rules, then we will bring this meeting to an end,' said the nun.

If the looks from Gail and George could kill, then the nun would have been dead on the spot. 'It's okay, Sister Abigail,' said Maxine. 'I can say hello from here. I take it you must be Mrs Miller?'

'That's correct, Maxine,' said Carly.

'Thank you for taking Cora into your home,' said Maxine.

'The pleasure is all mine,' Carly smiled.

Maxine gave the children her warmest smile.

'Hello, you two,' she said.
'Hello,' said Cora.

'H-H-Hello,' said Laura hesitantly.
'I knew you weren't dead,' said Cora.
'I know,' Maxine replied. 'We've been talking to each other.'
'W-w-why can't we speak to each other?' Laura asked.
'I think, Laura, it was because I didn't get to see you,' Maxine answered honestly. 'I was given a glimpse of Cora, so I had a picture of her in my mind. I did feel your presence though. It felt to me that you passed this place quite a few times.'
'We did,' Gail confirmed. 'At least twice a year, sometimes more.'
'And you did not know about me,' Maxine said. 'But now you do. I'm sure we will be able to communicate to each other. Would you like that?' Laura nodded. 'I'm glad you came to see me though. You've both grown into beautiful young girls. I'm told that you both intelligent.'
'I'm good at maths,' Cora agreed. 'And Laura is exceptional at English and the arts. Her history knowledge is fantastic. She can name all the Monaches of England and when they reigned.'
'Wow! That's very clever, Laura,' said Maxine

clearly impressed.
'Cora can break any code that is set,' Laura responded becoming more confident.
'I am impressed,' laughed Maxine.
George could tell that the two young girls were having no problems understanding their mother where most people in the room had to listen carefully to what she was saying. 'I also know a young girl who can recite a deck of cards in order,' he said.
'That's not quite true. I had a little...' Cora began and then saw Mr Hadley laugh. 'Oh, you must have known that Laura helped me.'
'Yes,' said George. 'A little bird told me.'
'We have a strict routine here, and this meeting must now come to a close,' said the nun.
'Can we come and see you again?' asked Cora.
'I'd like that very much,' said Maxine.
Mrs Miller said goodbye to Maxine before escorting the two young girls out. Mr and Mrs Hadley stood up and looked at each other. It seemed they were having a telepathic conversation. 'What about if we put into the motion the idea of you coming to stay with us in Cornwall?' George asked.
Maxine looked at them in a state of shock. She was obviously processing what George had just said. 'I don't think this young lady will be going anywhere soon,' said the nun. 'One of her parents is still alive and they will need to consent to that.'

'But Mrs Wellington thinks Maxine is dead,' said George.
'Perhaps it is better for it to stay that way,' said Maxine quietly. The room went silent. You could hear a pin drop. 'It is very kind of you to think about me, but it's best for me and the girls if I stay here. I wouldn't be able to cope on the outside.'
'But we could show you,' Gail persisted.
'No,' Maxine said. 'I don't know how to be a mother. I look at my two children and I see that you two have raised Laura so wonderfully. I can see that she is very comfortable with you. It would be wrong of me to interfere. And Cora is very relaxed with Mrs Miller. She seems to have settled in with her. If she was still with her adoptive family, well, we wouldn't be having this conversation now because they would not have brought Cora in to see me. I think it would be best for them if I stay in here out of the way.'
'And you say you don't know how to be a mother?' said Gail. 'You're doing it now, honey. We're always looking out for our children. So, you see, you'll be a great mother.'
'It's still better for them if they don't have to worry about me being there,' said Maxine. 'I can tell they are going to have fantastic lives, but they don't need me for that. They're going to preoccupied with school, boys and careers. Don't let them make the same mistake I made. We will probably still talk to

each other, but Laura has you to look after her and Cora has Mrs Miller. They are still looking to you for guidance. Don't think I didn't see the sneak glances that Laura made to you two and Cora made to Mrs Miller. You three are where they get their confidence from. Not from me. I think they just look upon me as an older sister. Perhaps I am. I am only fourteen years older than them.'

'But you said you would let them see you again,' George pointed out.

'And I will,' smiled Maxine. 'They understand me. Everyone here has difficulty understanding me.'

'That's not true,' George protested.

'We all know it is,' said Maxine. 'I can see it in your faces that you're straining to hear what I'm saying. And that's another reason why I should stay in here. I'd be treated like a freak of nature if I was allowed out. Cora and Laura could understand me perfectly. In time, that will change, when they have their own families to be worried about. And I'm fine with that. I never thought I would ever get to see them. I will always be in your debt for that, but, no, I will not give permission to come and stay with you. And it's best that my mother keeps on thinking that I'm dead. She doesn't believe that her brother is the father of her grandchildren, so that means she doesn't believe me.'

'You're not wrong there,' said George.

'You've seen her?' Maxine asked in amazement.

'Yes,' George admitted. 'You're right. She does believe you to be dead. Although she has heard rumours stating that you are alive, but she tends to dismiss them. She also, as you said, does not think that Richard Culver is the father of the children. She thinks

that it was a member of staff. But I think she should be informed.'
'No. Please,' Maxine begged. 'I'm safer in here without her poking her nose in. It may not be the greatest of conditions, but I have a bed and I'm fed. They look after me here. And do you want to know something? Perhaps that makes me insane anyway.' She began to laugh. 'Okay. That's enough,' said the nun authoritatively. 'Please escort Mr and Mrs Hadley out whilst we get the inmate...' she saw the look that both George and Gail gave her and corrected herself, '...patient back to her room.

George and Gail were taken back to the reception room in Kneecap Cottage. Mrs Miller and the girls were already there waiting for them. Laura ran to her mother and hugged her tightly. Cora looked nonplussed although Gail was sure that she could see tear stains on her cheeks.
'I think it's time we made a start for home,' said George. 'It's going to be a long day.'

'I'll take Cora and Laura to the car,' said Carly.
'If you let me have the keys, George, I'll unlock it so that we can get it,' said Gail. He passed her the keys that were in his trouser pocket. 'Would you like me to drive?'
'We'll take it in turns,' George replied.
'Okay,' said Gail and she left with Carly, Cora and Laura.
George turned to Muriel. 'I know that you checked that I am an acquaintance of Sir Jeremy. And, no doubt, he has confirmed that I am.' Muriel nodded curtly. 'I ask you to contact me should anything happen to Maxine Wellington.' He took out his pen and pulled her notebook, which was by the typewriter, towards him. He wrote down his name, address and telephone number. 'Put this somewhere safe. You'll never know when you're going to need it.' 'He put his pen back in his inside pocket. 'You'll also never know when we will return, but I'm sure we will not have the same problems as this time?'
Muriel looked at him and shook her head. He smiled at her and left.

CHAPTER THIRTY

The journey home was uneventful. They stopped a couple of times for food, drinks and to go to the toilet. Everyone was fairly quiet. The two young girls dosed. Carly kept on looking at Cora and wondered just how hard a life she must have had. Richard Culver was, from listening to all the conversations, not a nice man. Only his sister, Edith Wellington, seemed to like him. Cora had not actually said much. Carly remembered Cora speaking about her mother and father when she was at the hospital.

'I cannot think of anything worse than that man having unlawful sex with his underaged niece,' Gail's voice impeded her thoughts. George had taken over the driving. 'How on earth can anyone defend him?'

'Some people believe only what they want to,' said George.

'But to believe him over her daughter?' Gail asked incredulously.

'They all thought Maxine was insane,' George explained. 'They probably thought she was making it up.'

'I'm with you on this one, Gail,' said Carly.

'Look, I'm not saying that Mrs Wellington is right,' George argued. 'Far from it. I'm just saying that there could be a reason for it.'

'Who would agree to have their daughter locked away in an asylum?' said Carly. Gail glanced uneasily at her husband who shifted uncomfortably in his seat behind the steering wheel. Carly saw this and immediately realised her mistake. 'I'm sorry. I was not implying that you...'

'That's okay, Carly,' Gail said. 'If the school had not alerted the authorities, then I would have. We had to get Laura assessed because we had never heard of anyone saying that they could speak to someone telepathically before. We were told that it was just an imaginary friend. To be honest, I'm really glad it was Cora. I think the two girls needed – sorry – need each other.'

'You're right there,' Carly agreed. 'It must be difficult to understand what someone else is thinking.'

'Hmmm!' George wondered. 'But could be very beneficial. Just imagine someone invading Hitler's thoughts. They could get hold of all his strategies and end this bloody war.'

They carried on in silence, contemplating what Mr Hadley had just said. They hit heavy rain at Okehampton which made Mr Hadley slow right down. It was getting dark, and the black clouds were only assisting this.

Back at the asylum, Maxine could hear the sound of distant aircraft. She smiled to herself. The air-raid siren was being rang. Maxine knew that it would only be the staff that would make their way to the air-raid shelter. What did it matter if the lunatics died? It was less for society to worry about. She started to laugh manically. Then she heard the rain starting to hit the roof, and this made her laugh even harder. Suddenly she stopped. 'I love you, girls,' she said. 'Please remember that I love you.' She closed her mind and started laughing uncontrollably again.

Laura woke with a start. 'Mother!' she whimpered.
'I heard her, too,' said Cora.

'What is it?' Carly asked, putting her arms around both girls and drawing them in close to her.
'She's in danger?' both girls said simultaneously.
'You can hear her now?' Cora asked. Laura nodded. 'Is she responding to you?'
'No,' Laura shook her head. 'I could sense that she was in danger, but I have no idea from what?'
'I'm sure that I could hear sirens,' said Cora.
'And I'm sure that I could hear the sound of distant airplanes,' said Laura.
Cora looked at her twin sister. 'Oh, not again. Please.'
George glanced briefly at his wife. From her reaction he could tell that she knew what was happening. They both knew that there was no way they could return. It would take them a good few hours. And, if it was a real air-raid, then there was

no way they would be permitted to enter the location.

'I can feel something else,' said Laura. 'Someone has found something. They seem quite happy with themselves.'

'I can't feel that,' said Cora. 'Why can't I feel that?'

They drove on until they reached the Portreath turn-off. The rain had now stopped, and the night sky was clear. They could see the stars clearly and the moon had just poked its head over the horizon and was starting its arched journey across the dark background.

Maxine could hear the bombs landing. Her laughter had not stopped. If anything, it had gotten worse. The raids had been going on for at least an hour. At first it had sounded like only two planes had deposited their cargo. Next it was five planes, and they were getting close. This time it was ten. The ground fire was not doing anything. The home guard had not been trained very well and were not proficient in their return fire. Every shot missed their target by quite a distance. However, the German bombers were getting closer and closer with theirs. Maxine could see a red glow in the near distance which made her laugh even harder. She could now hear the eerie whistle as the bombs began their descent. She knew that if there was another soiree of German planes, then the asylum would definitely be hit.

Maxine could hear the screams and tears of the other patients. She had already gathered that the staff had left to save themselves. It did not matter about the rest. Most could not even help themselves, so what chance did they have? She felt sorry for those that were on the maternity wing. Mostly young girls who would not have a clue what was going on. She was guessing that they would have been left to fend for themselves. Perhaps they would get lucky, and the bombs would miss them. But she was also clever enough to realise that the Germans had planned this raid and that meant taking out this asylum. Why? She had no idea. What was so special about this place? Nothing, as far as she could tell. Perhaps the Germans thought it was holding something more sinister. But what could be more sinister than a lunatic in an asylum? And this made her laugh even more.

The German planes were retreating away, but she could already hear the drone of the next batch that were to replace them.

The car journeyed down Penberthy Road and passed through the Village of Bridge. They turned right onto Sunnyvale Road. George slowed down when he passed Greenslade Park as Carly Miller lived a few houses up from it. The was a green Austin 7 car parked a bit further down the road.
'Hmmm,' Carly said. 'I've never seen that vehicle around here before.'
'Can't say I have either,' said George. He stopped the car outside of Carly's home. They waited to see if anyone got out of the other car.
'There doesn't seem to be anyone sitting in it,' Gail pointed out.
'They could be visiting someone else,' said Carly.
'True,' said George. 'Although I doubt Miss Trelawney will be entertaining visitors. And I believe that Mr and Mrs Nancarrow are visiting his sister in Falmouth for the next few days. Wait here a moment. I'll just go take a look.'
George got out of the car and walked towards the other one. He could tell that it was empty. There were a couple of cigarette butts on the floor by the driver's door. He looked around but could not see anything. Perhaps the owner of the vehicle was visiting Miss Trelawney. He walked back to his car.
'Anything?' Gail asked.
'Nothing,' said George. 'I'll see you to the front door, Mrs Miller.'

'Please come in for a cup of tea or coffee,' Carly offered.
Carly, Cora and Laura got out of the back of the car and started to walk up the path with George and Gail following them. They did not see or hear the person who was staggering down the road.

The planes were getting louder and louder so must be very close. Suddenly the door to cell swung open. Maxine saw the receptionist beckoning her out. The planes must have been right overhead.
The bombs were unloaded by the twenty planes

as they flew overhead. The whistle as they made their descent was loud, and they found their desired location; right smack in the middle of the maternity wing and the asylum. Kneecap Cottage was partially hit but was mainly unscathed.

Cora and Laura looked at each other. They had heard a scream in their minds. They wondered what it was, but they could have guessed. Their birth mother was in trouble.
'Hello, Cora,' a voice said behind them. 'Have you

forgotten your old man?'
Cora and Laura saw Richard Culver standing in the middle of the pathway. Both girls looked at each other before collapsing to the ground.

Copyright Graham Avery 2023

Printed in Poland
by Amazon Fulfillment
Poland Sp. z o.o., Wrocław
27 July 2023